Violet Hunt

The Human Interest

a study in incompatibilities

Violet Hunt

The Human Interest
a study in incompatibilities

ISBN/EAN: 9783337362645

Printed in Europe, USA, Canada, Australia, Japan

Cover: Foto ©Andreas Hilbeck / pixelio.de

More available books at **www.hansebooks.com**

THE
HUMAN INTEREST

A STUDY IN INCOMPATIBILITIES

BY

VIOLET HUNT

AUTHOR OF

"A HARD WOMAN," " UNKIST UNKIND," " THE MAIDEN'S PROGRESS."

FAIRE ET TAIRE

HERBERT S. STONE AND COMPANY
CHICAGO AND NEW YORK
MDCCCXCIX

THE HUMAN INTEREST

One dull afternoon — and it was in summer — a
London authoress of some repute, whose nom-de-
guerre was Egidia, was wandering along the pavement of a dull and imposing street in Newcastle.
Day was beginning to decline, but the approach of
evening was not alone responsible for the heartfelt
ejaculation of the South-country woman, "Oh, this
Northern gloom!" as she walked along under the
smoky pall that, summer and winter, shrouds the city.

She stood still presently, carefully scanning the
solemn, stately houses with pillared porticos all of
the self-same pattern, which run in an interminable
row to a vanishing point seemingly far beyond con-
jecture.

"Each of the houses is exactly like the other," she
murmured to herself. "In which, I wonder, does
the Muse of Newcastle hold her court? Like most
muses, she gave no number. I must judge by out-

sides.   Oh, here we are; green Liberty curtains in the windows—a more daring green on the door—a knocker of mediæval tendencies!   I will try."

She went up the steps of No. 59 Savile Street and rang the bell, and stood there pensive.

"I promised to call on this woman, and I am doing it, but I shall be bored.   She will talk of Ibsen, and Meredith, and tell me she had read Plato through before she was fifteen.   She will take herself seriously, and me too, and inundate me with questions about the people in London.   All these provincials do.   Still, she pressed me so prettily to call that I could not say No.   But I shall be bored!—Is Mrs. Mortimer Elles at home?" she enquired of the handsome, full-blown parlour maid who opened the door widely and invitingly.

"Oh, yes, ma'am—this is Mrs. Elles' day at home."

"Much too familiar!" thought Egidia, as she followed the swing of the maid's cap streamers through portièred doorways and past Syrian shawl-draped cornices, and other pathetically futile attempts to conceal the impossible architecture of a commonplace house, built in a bad period, and decorated originally on the worst principles.

"Muslin curtains are a mistake in an atmosphere like this of Newcastle!" she thought, "and a parlour-maid should not aim at looking like Madame Sans Géne."

She was shown into a drawing-room, "stamped with the evidences of culture," as the interviewer would say, and "redolent of a personality." Books were scattered about; the piano stood open, with the latest "mood" of the latest fashionable composer lying on it; there were magazines, with paper-knives negligently bisecting their leaves. There were, on the walls, some grim old pictures—family portraits, presumably—of ill-tempered, high-stocked old gentlemen and prim, dignified ladies, but they were interspersed with sundry scratchy and erratic modern etchings and photogravures; there were great bowls of flowers—whose apparent substance, the authoress could not help suspecting, was cleverly eked out with artificial imitations procurable at drapers' shops. The whole effect was rather pretty and French, and thoroughly out of keeping with the grim realities of Northern hardness and abnegation of art-feeling that reigned outside.

A young woman, beautifully dressed, who was sitting over the fire, though it was not cold, rose eagerly to receive her distinguished guest, exclaiming, with the most flattering and heart-felt emphasis,

"Oh, Miss Giles, how good of you to come! I was afraid you would have quite forgotten me and my day!"

She was a slight woman, not tall, but slender enough to look so. Her eyes were very large and bright, her cheeks, flushed, perhaps with the fire. She made wrinkles when she laughed, but she did not look more than twenty-eight. A little powder, carelessly and innocently cast there, showed on cheeks "hollowed a little mournfully," as the poet has it.

Her hair was arranged in hundreds of little waves and curls, and her dress—Egidia had been in the best houses in Newcastle, during the last few days, but had seen nothing to equal the style and taste of this little solicitor's wife. Thought and ingenuity had gone to the devising of that gown, but the wearer of it had forgotten to fasten the last two buttons of her sleeve.

"The artistic sense strongly developed — but very little power of co-ordination." So the authoress, taking all these points into consideration and exercising her own professional faculty of classification, mentally assessed her hostess.

"This is my day," Mrs. Elles was assuring her. "I partly hope people will come, and partly not. I would so much rather have you to myself—but then, some of my friends were so anxious to meet you when I said I knew you—so I had to give them a chance— you don't mind being lionized a little, do you? We can't help it!"

The "celebrity" had been a "celebrity" so long that she had left off objecting to the outward indications of her supremacy. Though she was a lion, and gave lectures, she was modest and easily pacified. She was fascinated by something curiously plaintive and beguiling about her hostess's voice and manner; a suggestion of childishness, of almost weakness as she thought, in its artificial cadences. For it was an affectation, Miss Giles, whose nom-de-guerre was Egidia, decided, though a pleasing one.

"I wonder if she scolds her servants in that tone?" she thought, while submitting to the charm, and, lying easily back in her chair, listened to her hostess's ecstasies about her books and her lectures, her prettily expressed enviousness of the presumably happier conditions of her guest's life in London.

"Oh, what it must be to be in the midst of life, really in it—of it—part of it! Here one sits, and yearns, and only catches the far-away echoes, the reverberations of the delightful things that are happening, away down there, where you are—in the very, very heart of it all!"

The peri left out of Paradise clasped her pretty, soft, pliant hands, and the novelist asked her, willing to be instructed,

"Is Newcastle, then, worse than other provincial towns?"

"I only know Newcastle, but I am sure it's worse. There are a few nice advanced people, but they go away all the time, or if they bring nice people down from London, they keep them to themselves. I never see any one worth talking to. Oh, it is hopeless— hopeless!" She shrugged her shoulders. "It is simply a form of Hades,—this life for me, for I have 'glimpses of what might make me less forlorn,' of a life to live, a world to move in. I feel I was not meant to merely stagnate—to vegetate—to wither gradually away, consumed by my own wasted energies. You laugh! coming straight, as you do, from that paradise of life and movement, that I am sure London is, you can have no idea of what Newcastle and my life is! Inertia kills people like me, one's soul is starved, don't you know?—one's mental life has nothing to feed on, no pabulum, except books—and they are not easy to get—new books. I am the trial and pest of the libraries here!"

"You read a great deal?"

"Oh, yes. I live on books. They are the greatest possible comfort to me. They are literally my saviours. I quite sympathize with the heroine of a novel I read lately, who was kept from suicide by the sight of her favourite poets on her book-shelf! I make myself up a dream-life, don't you know—the life I should like to live if I could choose. One dream-life, do I say?" Her eyes lightened and brightened: she was extraordinarily alert and vivid. "Two or three—a perfect orgy of dream-lives! They cost nothing. But I have always read a great deal. The classics I don't neglect. I read Plato before I was fifteen—in Jowett's translation, of course."

Egidia smiled.

"And your books?"

"Don't! don't!" Egidia held up her hands.

"But I love them—I go to them for comfort and help. I have them all—on a shelf near my bed—a whole row of my favourites—Browning, and Meredith —and Ibsen. I am a great Ibsenite—are not you?"

"It is very fashionable!"

"Oh! but really, don't you think—?" She was becoming quite incoherent in her excitement. "Now,

Nora in the 'Doll's House'?—It is the story of so
many of us. Only it is a mistake of Ibsen to make
the husband a cheat—that seems to put him too much
in the wrong, he is wrong enough, without that.
Oh, Nora was so right to leave him, I think. So
strong! Do you know the sound of the house door
banging in that play stirs me like the sound of a
trumpet?"

"You should write a book yourself!" suggested
Egidia, indulgently, knowing well the answer she
would receive.

"Ah! I haven't time. But if I did, I could put in
things—things that have happened to me—experience
—more of feeling than of incident, perhaps. I was
an only daughter; my father was in the army; I
travelled a good deal; but I have not had a life of
adventure; I married when I was seventeen. My
husband was a widower then, and his son, Charles,
lives with us—and his aunt, Mrs. Poynder." She
had an involuntary little shudder. "He is a solicitor; you know that. And he has a huge practice.
He is very much occupied, and takes no interest in
the things you and I care about. Of course, he
laughs at me for my—enthusiasms—but I should die
if I didn't."

There were tears in her eyes.

"Some day, if you will, you must come and stop
with me in town," said Egidia, in an access of
womanly compassion for this somewhat ungrammat-
ical but sincere tale of misfortune.

"Shall I? Shall I? Oh, how lovely that would be!" Her brilliant smile came out again. "To see —to have a glimpse of all those wonderful literary people in whose company your life is spent."

"Well, I happen to know more of artists than I do of literary people," said Egidia. "You see, my own 'shop' bores me. Do you collect—I am sure you do?" She had seen the unmistakable flame of the auto-graph-fever leap into Mrs. Elles' eyes. "I can send you some, if you like. I have one in my pocket now that I can give you, from Edmund Rivers, the land-scape painter."

"The R. A.?" Mrs. Elles, who always took care to have a Royal Academy Catalogue sent up to her every year, and learnt it by heart, enquired eagerly.

"Yes, the R. A. and my second cousin!" Egidia answered, carelessly pulling a crumpled note out of her pocket and handing it to Mrs. Elles. "Read it!"

"Dear Alice," (read Mrs. Elles), "I am so sorry that I cannot have the pleasure of dining with you on the 31st, but I hope to be in the North on the 26th, at latest, to begin my summer campaign. I see the spring buds in the parks, and the Inspector of Nuisances has invited me to clip my sprouting lilac bushes, and it all reminds me too painfully of the paradise of greenness that is growing up in the country, and calling me. I shall soon be 'a green thought in a green shade'—as Marvel says, and very much in my element. Yours ever, Edmund Rivers."

"The twenty-sixth," said Mrs. Elles, meditating.
"This is the thirtieth. Then he is gone."

"Oh, yes, no one will set eyes on him again till
November, when he comes back from what he calls
his summer campaign. He takes good care that none
of us shall even know where his happy hunting
ground is—somewhere in Yorkshire, I believe! Oh,
yes, you may keep the letter."

Mrs. Elles took the letter with her pretty, be-ringed
fingers, and scanned it again with the air of a con-
noisseur.

"Do you know," she said, "I take a double interest in these things; first of all, because they are autographs of distinguished people, but, in the second
place, because I can read their characters so well
from their handwritings."

"I wonder if you can tell me anything of this
man's character, then?" said the novelist, with a look
in her eyes which set Mrs. Elles thinking. Miss
Giles, in her way, was attractive. It was not Mrs.
Elles' way, but Mrs. Elles had sufficient discernment
to see merit in a style that was not her style at all.
Miss Giles had no pose, unless it was that of bonhomie. The charm of her face lay in its nobility,
touched with shrewdness; a certain modest mannish-
ness as of a woman who had to look after herself, and
who had cut out a way for herself, marked her appearance. Her dress was not in any way unfeminine, but
Mrs. Elles decided that she would have looked well,
dressed as a boy. She had beautiful eyes, and dark

hair that curled. She must always have looked thirty-six, and would probably never look any older than she looked now.

"It is a very odd, characteristic handwriting indeed," she began gravely, "he is complicated, tremendously complicated, I should say."

"He is an artist, a genius indeed, in my opinion," said the novelist, soberly.

"Ah! then, of course, he has a right to be eccentric. They all are, aren't they? Well, isn't he a little —how shall I say it?—fanciful, faddish, difficult to get on with?"

"You have, in the words of the song, 'got to know him first,'" quoted Egidia, laughing.

"And you do know him, well, of course! But still, I should say he is what is called a misogynist."

She was watching the effect of her words on the other. Even the strong-minded authoress of novels with a purpose has her weak spot, she was glad to see.

"Hating women! Well, I can't say he pays them much attention. I don't suppose he ever looked at a woman in his life!" There was certainly a touch of bitterness in this speech, and Mrs. Elles was delighted.

"Not married then!" she exclaimed. "And yet, I should say that he is not obtuse to the charm of material things—that he is even a great lover of beauty—in the abstract, then, I suppose. Nature— you said he was a landscape painter, didn't you? Does he never put people into his pictures—never put you, for instance?"

Egidia laughed.

"No? Well, I must say I don't care for pictures without any human interest at all."

"Then you wouldn't care for Edmund Rivers' work, unless you could get your romance out of the scarred, weather-beaten face of an old windmill or a ruined castle! He leaves the human interest entirely out of his pictures."

"And out of his life, too, it seems," said the other, "and both suffer in consequence. Don't tell me; there is something wrong about a man who doesn't care for women! Some day one will awaken him. But meantime I see a certain want of sympathy in the determined uprightness of these capital N's that refuse to merge properly into the letters that come after, and obstinacy in the blunt endings of those g's. And yet he must have great delicacy of touch—he seems to feel certain words as he writes them. Isn't his painting very refined and delicate?"

"It is all sorts, strong and delicate at once," Egidia asseverated with enthusiasm.

"And he is a great friend of yours!" Mrs. Elles remarked conclusively, folding up the letter and putting it in her pocket. She was now quite confirmed in her theory that the authoress had a secret passion for the painter. "Is he young?"

"Fifty!" said Egidia, bluntly; she was beginning to guess the drift of her companion's thoughts, and, though secretly amused at them, was minded to put her off a little, "and his hair is turning grey."

"But I adore grey hair," Mrs. Elles exclaimed hastily and enthusiastically, as the door opened and a Miss Drummond was announced.

"Oh dear!" ejaculated the hostess, almost in the new arrival's hearing, but made amends for her discourtesy by a very effusive greeting. She introduced "Miss Giles—Egidia, you know;" with a flourish as one with whom she was on deeply intimate terms, casting at the same time a pathetic, imploring look in the latter's direction, as much as to ask her not to discount her statement. Then more people came in. The room was filling.

"Don't go," she whispered to Egidia, more as an appeal than a civility, and the good-natured authoress stayed and watched her, and studied her.

She saw that dim notions of Madame Récamier to be emulated and a salon to be held prevailed in the mind of the lady whom she had dubbed the Muse of Newcastle. Such culture, such an atmosphere of literary gossip as is current in many a second-class literary centre in London, flourished here, and Mrs. Elles led the inferior revels with aplomb and discrimination. She manœuvred her guests very cleverly, on the whole, and talked much and well—with the slight tendency to exaggerate which Egidia had already noticed in her. Like many restless, excitable people, she did not seem able to both talk and look at a person at the same time, and her restless eyes were continually directed towards the door, as if expecting and dreading a fresh arrival.

About half-past five the mystery was solved; a tall, well set-up woman of fifty walked in, bonnetless, who seemed to know nearly everybody and shook hands with all the painful effect of a bone-crushing machine, as Egidia experienced when "my aunt, Mrs. Poynder," was introduced to her. The stout lady then took a tiny seat near Miss Drummond, and Egidia was much diverted by her loudly-spoken comments on her niece's guests. She was a woman to whom a whisper was obviously an impossible operation.

"And which is Fibby's grand London authoress she's so set up with?" she was heard to ask. "Fibby mumbles names so that I haven't a notion which it is! Oh, deary me, here's the Newcastle poet. I'm sure he has no call to stoop as he comes in; he needn't think he's tall enough to graze the lintel. . . . But I would dearly like to cut his hair for him. . . . Po-uttry! No! po-uttry I can't stand . . . why, if a man's got anything to say, can't he say it straight without so much ado?" The Newcastle poet, who wore his hair nearly as long as poets do in London, shook hands and presented a slim, green volume to Mrs. Elles.

"You must write 'Phœbe Elles' in it!" his hostess said, imperiously, and led him to a side table, where, with many a dedicatory flourish, he did as she required. Then she introduced him to Egidia, with the air of one introducing Theocritus and Sappho.

"And do you kill the lovers?" she asked, alluding, presumably, to characters in the volume she held.

"How relentless of you!"   She added to her guests, "I had the privilege of reading it in the proof, you know."

"Ah!   I had to kill them," he murmured, plaintively, "sooner than let them know the sad satiety of love."

"My goodness!" Mrs. Poynder muttered.

The conversation, appallingly immoral as it was, yet seemed to interest the good lady, for she drew nearer and formed a chorus to the very modern discussion that ensued between the poet and Egidia and her niece, of which London and London literary society was the theme.   The epigrams that were flying about she visibly and audibly pooh-poohed.   "Give me Newcastle!" she murmured at intervals, and "You, a mere lad, too!" was elicited from her by any world-weary extravagance of the poet's.   He was in self-defence; driven to incidentally mention his age— quite a respectable age, as it appeared.   Mrs. Elles was not to be outdone—

"I am twenty-six," he remarked, with an air of reluctant candour.

"And a very good age to stop at!" observed her aunt, with intention.

The novelist looked with compassion on this poor woman who, like Widrington, fought the battle of pose and society, at such frightful odds.   The poet presently drifted in her direction and they held a short but epoch-making—as regarded Mrs. Elles— conversation.

"Mrs. Poynder is to me just like an upas-tree," he confided to Egidia, wringing his hands together. "In her shadow, any poetical idea would wither and die!"

"There is, indeed, a good deal of shadow!" remarked Egidia, alluding to Mrs. Poynder's truly majestic proportions. "She is a handsome woman in her way!"

"Yes," he replied wearily, "plenty of presence, and all of it bad, as they said of George III. But seriously, you know, she leads our dear friend a sad life. She contradicts her in everything, and thwarts every instinct of culture. If Mrs. Elles had not plenty of pluck, she would have given in long ago. And her husband!"—he held up his hands.

The poet's indiscretions bore fruit in a hearty invitation from Egidia to Mrs. Elles, to visit her often at the house where she was staying in Newcastle.

"Brave little woman! I will try and cheer her up a bit!" she thought, as she left the house.

The little party broke up soon after, and Mrs. Elles was left alone with her aunt, who, as the door closed on the last guest, opened her lips and gave, uncalled for, her opinions of the guest.

"That's a real nice woman!" she said, "that littry friend of your; I approve of her. It's a good thing I didn't take your advice, Fibby, and go trapesing up to Jesmond, this afternoon, to call on Miss Drummond. Why, the girl was here. And such a crowd, too. You said there wouldn't be anybody here to-day!"

"Did I? One never knows," replied her niece negligently, sauntering up to the piano, and opening it.

"I'll be bound you knew well enough, Fibby. Wanted to be rid of the old woman, eh? Well, I'm glad I defeated your little plans, and saw your friend, who seemed a sensible sort of woman, not the flyabastic sort you generally get here. Pity but she'd seen Mortimer!"

"Do you think Mortimer would have impressed her?" asked his wife, bitterly.

"And why not? Are you ashamed of your husband, Fibby? It's my belief that you are ashamed of us all, and hankering after those London people and the ramshackle life they seem to lead. Gallant times they have, to be sure! Thinking only of themselves and their pleasures and making love to each other's wives! And you are just savage because you aren't there, too! Oh! I know you!"

Mrs. Elles had broken out into a stormy mazurka that nearly drowned Mrs. Poynder's words, as possibly she intended it to do. "Ay! ay!" the latter remarked, "work it off that way—I advise you!"

"Don't insult me, aunt!"

Mrs. Poynder laughed in her own harsh fashion, and, looking towards the door whose handles just then turned, called out, "Come in, Mortimer! Come and speak to this wife of yours!"

The clumsy, thick-necked man who entered stopped short and looked round stupidly; his wife sat with her

back turned, playing; his aunt stood there, smiling
her cruel, blighting smile, that showed a set of the
most perfectly formed teeth that money could buy.
He took his cue from her, and going across the room,
laid a heavy hand on his wife's shoulder, saying
kindly,

"What's the matter, old lady?"

"Oh, Mortimer, please don't call me that. I can't
bear it!"

She hid her face in the keyboard and sobbed violently.

"Well, really!" said he.

"Hysterical!" said the aunt, still smiling. "I
don't wonder, after the conversation we have been
having, and the things we have been hearing!
Fibby's had grand new London friends here—to put
her out of love with us all. We're all too plain and
common for Fibby now!"

Still smiling—was a smile ever so denuded of grace
and benevolence?—she gathered up her crochet and
left the room. Mrs. Elles then rose from the piano,
and, dabbing her handkerchief to her eyes, made a
step in the direction of the door. But she changed
her mind and stood still by the mantelpiece with the
figure half averted.

"I'm sure I beg all your pardons," she murmured,
almost inaudibly. "Oh, damn! where's the paper?"
said Mortimer Elles. Securing it, and sinking into
an arm-chair with a great, puffing breath, he hid his
face behind the broad white sheet. His coat tails

caught the Oriental cloth on a small table near him and dragged it nearly off. Mrs. Elles rushed forward and saved one of the many pieces of china that rested on it from destruction.

"Throw the beastly thing on the fire!" he growled out, without looking up. "This house is far too full."

A gong sounded.

"I am going up to dress for dinner," she said, aggressively, standing in front of him. "Shan't you, Mortimer?"

"There's nobody coming, is there?"

"No—unfortunately—but I like to dress."

"Dress if you like, but don't bother me!"

"Oh, I do wonder what you married me for, Mortimer?" she complained with plaintive savageness.

"I do wish you wouldn't talk nonsense!" he answered. "What has marriage to do with dressing for dinner?"

"Perhaps more than you think," she murmured still in a low key, as she walked past him and opened the door. She crossed the hall slowly, like a somnambulist. It was true the conversation of Egidia and of the poet, who was no fool, and who had been brought out by the tact of the London woman, had set her thinking, and her mind travelling in a new direction. She trod on her gown going upstairs, and picked it up with the tragically careless gesture of a Joan of Arc going to the stake. She made herself the effect of a prisoner in a strange land—an alien princess in the hands of the Saracens—the Lady of "Comus" among the rabble rout. She was a delicate piece of porcelain among rough earthenware pots—a harp played upon by unknowing boors. She muttered to herself phrases of philosophy and resignation that she did not feel—her whole soul was in revolt against the conditions of her life.

"Oh, it is all so ugly!" she murmured.

She paused on the landing and looked down. Charles, her step-son, had just come in and hung up his hat and clattered down every other hat in the hall.

"Hallo, Mater!" he shouted up, "don't commit suicide over the banisters and make a mess! Hurry up and get ready for dinner!"

'I am glad I did not have a child," she said to herself. "He might have been half like that!"

She dressed for dinner, in a very handsome, vaporous tea-gown, drank a little sal-volatile, read a couple of verses of Omar Khayam, and sailed into the dining-room, determined to be resigned, pathetic and amiable. Her husband's untidy, baggy shooting jacket, and Charles's abominable "blazer," gave her the usual jar, while Mrs. Poynder's cheap white lace tippet with pink ribbons was only another item in the general tale of the inappropriateness and disgust. She pouted, and dropped gracefully into her accustomed seat, looking like a piece of thistledown suddenly lighted on the dull leather-covered mahogany chair.

The mild, provincial dinner proceeded. "What's this?" asked Mortimer, when a dish came round to him. "Put it on the table, can't you?"

"Chicken croquettes. I like things handed!" she pleaded.

"Do you? I don't. I like to have what I am eating in front of me. You won't take any, Phœbe? Oh, very well. You want to get scraggier than you are. A lean wife is a standing reproach to a fellow."

"Fibby is afraid of spoiling her fashionable figure!" observed Mrs. Poynder, drawing herself up, to show her own to the best advantage. It was of a certain solid merit, not to be gainsaid.

With these, and other family amenities, was the time of dining enlivened. Mrs. Elles' attitude was one of faintly raised eyebrows, but she did not allow herself to say anything to-day, that a heroine might regret. She was not generally so circumspect. As soon as dinner was over, she rose and followed Mrs. Poynder out of the room. Mrs. Poynder liked to go first, and she was allowed to do so when no one was there. Mortimer Elles, who was by no means in a bad humour, moved his chair a little to make way for his wife.

"Do you call that a gown?" he said, fingering a fold of the shining satin. "And pray, what may that have cost me?"

"Don't!" she said, drawing it away.

"Surely I may touch it if I am to have the privilege of paying for it?"

"It is not very nice of you, Mortimer, to remind me that I haven't a penny of my own, and must depend on your bounty!"

"And a good job, too!" he said, laughing; he was certainly in a very good humour. "It's the only hold I've got on you—the only way I have of keeping you in order."

"Mortimer—I am not a child!"

"No, by Jove, not quite! Let me see, you were nineteen when I married you—we have been married ten years—that makes you out—?"

"You needn't trouble to go on," she replied haughtily, "I can't say that the subject interests me —one only counts birthdays when one is happy."

She escaped to her room, tore off the gauzy tea gown, and put on a black one which she reserved for occasions like this, when the mood of gloom preponderated. It was a little affectation of hers to dress as far as possible in character with her mood of the moment.

Yes, she was very wretched — had been for the last ten years. She wondered how she had borne it so long, and if she could go on bearing it. The time had surely come for her to do something—what? She would go, to-morrow, and call on Egidia in the big house where she was staying at Jesmond Dene, and talk it all over with her. Egidia, being a professed searcher into the secrets of the heart, would be able to understand, and perhaps offer some solution of her dreadful predicament. She might even take a professional interest in it. "She can put me in a novel if she likes," Phœbe Elles said to herself, wearily, "but I must speak or I shall die!"

Die of dullness, die of disappointment, die of inanition, or, what was worse, lose her looks. "They are the silent griefs that cut the heart-strings," she quoted, from Heaven knows what recondite Elizabethan play, "and dull the complexion," she added on her responsibility. She always read everything more or less with reference to herself, and twisted the most impassioned utterances of poetry and the drama into apt coincidence with her own affairs.

Up till now, she had sedulously preserved the one virtue of neglected wives—she had never "peached." She had scrupulously disdained the common vulgarity of confidences, the petty relief of expansion, and no one had ever heard her abuse her husband. She had learned to speak of him with an amused tolerance, whose undercurrent of contempt was not necessarily apparent to the merely superficial observer. It was a point of honour with her; but deep below her graceful reticence lay the point of vanity—she wanted people to think, if possible, that Mortimer, whom she had ceased to care for, was still desperately in love with her.

She had read many French novels, and she knew that, socially speaking, there was one modus vivendi to be adopted by a woman in her position. She might create for herself some outside interest—she might get up the harmless, necessary flirtation, by which women, circumstanced as she was, are apt to console themselves.

Without the remotest intention of actually pursuing it, she began to cast about in her mind for a possible coadjutor in such a course of action. She began to count heads, to consider all the eligible flirtations that Newcastle afforded, with a drear little smile at the paucity of attractions, at the inferiority of the subject material which presented itself to her mind.

The poet! He was handsome, clever, romantic; he admired her much, but only on condition that she returned his compliment and admired him more! That would not do. Besides, her present pose to him was that of a mother—a very young mother of course —and promoter of his incipient predilection for the handsome and "horsey" Miss Drummond, Atalanta-Diana as he was pleased to call her; the girl of strong physique and mannish tastes, who was the complement of his own nature. Then there was Dr. Moorsom, who lived next door—"The man whose business it would be to doctor me if I fell ill!" she sneered to herself. Everyone was supremely uninteresting—as uninteresting as Mortimer. That was the worst of it —Mortimer was odious, but then, so was everybody else.

No, better be "straight" and a martyr, than set herself, at the cost of her reputation, perhaps, to wrest from society a merely nominal happiness, and court a catastrophe that would have none of the elements of grandeur or romance about it. She would go back to her "dream-lives"—to the literary simulacra of existence which, till the epoch-making advent of the South-country novelist, had sufficed her, and had been as the mirror Perseus held up before Andromeda, affording her the harmless vision of the Gorgon's head with the snaky horror of its locks that may stand for life and the hideous complications thereof.

CHAPTER II

"But then, you know, I have never seen your husband," Egidia was saying to the pretty little woman who, sunk deep in the billowy mound of a very easy chair, her feet upheld to the glow of a North-country fire blazing away in the very height of summer, as usual, was expatiating in the sweetest of voices on her matrimonial unhappiness. She was telling Egidia all the truth, or thought she was, and the novelist, in her double capacity of friend and gatherer of welcome "copy," was listening sympathetically from her sofa.

It was a charming house in the suburbs of Newcastle, the abode of charming people, where Egidia was staying, and Mrs. Elles deeply appreciated the friendship with the fashionable lecturer, which had gained her the entry into this home of modernity and culture.

"Yes, if you once saw Mortimer," Mrs. Elles went on, "you would understand all!"

The way she uttered the last word would not have disgraced a tragic actress.

"I want you to come and dine—will you? What day shall it be? Tell me, and I'll fix it. Then you will see him, and judge for yourself."

25

"My dear," said the novelist, slowly, "I will come to your dinner with pleasure, but I shall not know any more than you have told me."

"Yes; I have been very, very frank," said Mrs. Elles. "And there is another thing"—she sighed vaguely. She was alluding to her husband's habit of tippling, to which as a loyal wife she forbore from a more direct allusion.

"As a general rule," Egidia went on, a little didactically, in her capacity of mentor, "no husband understands any wife. If he did, he wouldn't have cared to marry her. It is the mutual antagonism between the sexes which makes them interesting to each other in the beginning. But, afterwards—if they are unable to play the game—exciting enough, I should think—of observing, of adjusting, of utilizing their mutual divergences of character and getting amusement out of them—if she finds no pleasure in the exercise of tact, if he none in the further analysis of the feminine vagaries that he began by finding so charming—then, they begin to jar mutually on each other, and turn that into tragedy which should be the comedy of life for both of them."

"I understand," said Mrs. Elles, humbly; "but then —there is not, and could not be, any comedy of life with Mortimer, or tragedy either! There never was. I don't seem to care to appreciate his character, I know it—it is quite simple—I see it all spread out before me like a map—of a country I don't care to travel over."

"But perhaps he can say the same of you," hazarded Egidia.

"No, Mortimer has never understood me, never! I am a sealed book to him," said the wife, airily, although Miss Giles' suggestion had indeed given her a little shock.

"Don't flatter yourself, my dear, that you are a sealed book to anyone. It is the common delusion." (Another shock to Mrs. Elles!) "One is always so much less interesting, so much less complicated, so much less of a sphinx than one thinks."

"But I have always thought of mine as a very complicated nature," Mrs. Elles rejoined, pouting; "I am sure I can't tell you how many thoughts pass through my mind in a day, and I seem to have a perfectly new mood every minute."

"So we all have, but we don't take cognizance of them or act on them all. I should say that you are one of those people who begin with a radical mistake —that of expecting too much of life. You think you have a right to be happy. Good Heavens! You seek for midi à quatorze heures, you love change for its own sake; you positively enjoy hot water. You would rather have a painful emotion than none at all, you would like to cry, with Sophie Arnould, 'Oh, le bon temps, j'etais si malheureuse!' You have not mastered the great fact, that emotions are not to the emotional; to them is generally awarded the dreary crux of the commonplace, and that I think is hardest to bear of all, that one's cross should come in the way of material comfort and spiritual uneventfulness, and when it comes to the point, instead of action to be taken there is only temper—to be kept!"

"I always scorn to nag," said Mrs. Elles, "it seems so ungraceful."

"I am sure, my dear, that whatever you may feel, you always manage to look decorative!" said the other, smiling. "Still, you expect too much and give too little to be what I call easy to live with!"

"That is what I say," cried Mrs. Elles, triumphantly. "I call that being complicated."

"Do you?" said the authoress, drily. "I should be tempted to call it want of social tact—an almost culpable ignorance of the science of give and take, a—you must really forgive me for my brutal frankness"—she broke off suddenly and laughed confusedly—"but, you know, you asked me to speak freely."

"I love it," declared Phœbe Elles, adjusting a cushion behind her head. "I think I like to talk about myself, even if it is disagreeable," she added, with unusual frankness.

Egidia smiled irresistibly. It was impossible for her to help liking this unconscious egotist, who confessed to her failings with such a grace, and took plain speaking with such aplomb.

"I think," she said, trying to give a less serious turn to the conversation, "what you really wanted, in marriage, was a man who would have dominated you —have beaten you, perhaps."

"Yes, I do really believe I should," said Mrs. Elles; "that is, if I loved him desperately at the time and he loved me desperately—afterwards! But," she went on, seriously, "you have given me your views on marriage, and my marriage in particular, but, now you know all my life, what do you advise me to do?"

"Do? Do nothing! What can you do? What can any woman do?" asked Egidia, raising her well-marked eyebrows, and with an air of dismissing an impracticable subject.

Then, seeing the unmistakable look of disappointment in the eyes of her feminine Telemachus, she added kindly, "Ah, you see, when we outsiders come to the domain of practical politics, we are mere theorists—all at sea, and just as helpless and resourceless as any of you slaves of the ring can possibly be. I should advise you to make the best of it, and pray that you may never meet anybody you like better than the man you have got!"

Mrs. Elles rose to go, it was late. She had had a good time. She had enjoyed the personal discussion, but there was a wilful twist about her mouth, as of one which had swallowed much advice, but had swallowed it the wrong way.

"After this, I must not ask you to come and stop with me in London, I am afraid," added Egidia.

"Oh, please do, and I will promise to wear blinkers."

"Blue spectacles would be nearer the mark!" said the novelist. "Do that, and I will engage to introduce you to Edmund Rivers with impunity."

"Well, but you said just now he was incapable of falling in love with any woman."

"Yes, but I never implied that women found it impossible to fall in love with him!" answered Egidia, quite gravely. "He is handsome and indifferent, and I know of no combination more dangerous to the peace of our sex!"

.   .   .   .

Mrs. Elles' little dinner was arranged; the invitations, written on beautiful rough note paper with an artistic ragged edge, sent out. Mrs. Elles had conscientiously consulted her husband's list of engagements and saw that he was free, and put down a large cross for the eleventh. Mortimer would see that he was engaged, and would, as usual, be too lazy or careless to enquire further. On the evening in question, he would necessarily see "what was up," and would grumblingly admit that he was "let in for one of Phœbe's confounded dinners" instead of a happy gathering at the Continental Club with the "fellows."

His wife would, of course, have got on far better without him, as far as the success of her party was concerned, only society so far considers the husband, even if his social capacities are nil, as a necessary adjunct to the dinner table. He has not yet gone out with the épergne, and therefore must be tolerated. But with regard to Mrs. Poynder and Charles, the mistress of the house had put her foot down. She was famous for her little dinners, the entrain of which the presence of her husband did not seem, so

far, to have materially diminished. But that of the
other two would have been fatally destructive of
charm. The pair had been induced to see the matter
in somewhat of the same light—four members of a
family were a little overwhelming—and the question
of economy had weight with Mrs. Poynder. Aunt
and nephew were in the habit of considerately inviting
themselves out to high tea at the house of a relation
of Mortimer's in Newcastle on these occasions.
Mrs. Poynder, indeed, owned to a want of sympathy
with the "people Fibby contrived to get together," and
she was not informed that Miss Giles, for whom she
had developed an unaccountable fancy, was to be of
the party.

"My old woman of the sea," so Mrs. Elles sometimes spoke of her to her intimates, in whose eyes the
ways and speeches of the terrible old lady amply justified the want of reticence implied in her niece's indiscreet sobriquet. Why must she form part of the
Elles household? Everybody wondered, but Mrs.
Elles knew.

For on this point the husband was immutable. He
saw plainly that on Mrs. Poynder did his manly
bourgeois comfort depend. His wife only attended
to the show side of housekeeping; she saw that there
was always plenty of flowers in the drawing-room,
winter and summer—but Mrs. Poynder attended to
his shirts and their proper complement of buttons.
Mrs. Elles ordered dinner, but Mrs. Poynder kept
the books and interviewed the tradesmen. His wife

paid the smart calls, but Mrs. Poynder looked up his
dull and important relations, and, in her rough
undiplomatic way, advanced his affairs. She exer-
cised a certain modest supervision over the whisky
bottle, and without saying much, curbed Mortimer's
drunken tendencies a good deal.

Mrs. Elles herself was vaguely cognizant of the
advantages of this system, and realized that Mrs.
Poynder's presence in the ménage gave her leisure
to attend to the cultivation of the graces of her own
mind and person, and exonerated her from the thank-
less task of confronting Mortimer on the tedious matters of servants, wages, and housekeeping and partial
abstention.

"Aunt Poynder goes down into the arena for
me, and fights with wild beasts in the kitchen," the
ungrateful young woman used to say. "She likes it,
I verily believe.—But some of their roughness rubs
off on her," she would add, and nobody would gainsay
her. Mrs. Poynder was the professed Disagreeable
Woman of Newcastle, and people were apt to fly up
side alleys and into shops when they saw her come
sailing majestically down Granger Street.

"Oh, Mortimer, why did you go and have such
awful relations?" Mrs. Elles exclaimed casually to
her husband, one afternoon, when she came back
from a visit to Egidia at Jesmond. She was impelled
to say it. Mrs. Poynder's coarseness and Charles'
roughness seemed now-a-days more obtrusive by contrast with the pleasant manners of the people with

whom, by the accident of her friendship with Egidia, she had been almost daily thrown into contact. This had been her farewell visit. Egidia was going back to town; but, in the course of many and many a long talk, she had sown a plentiful crop of ideas in this wayward head—a seed whose harvest was to prove a very different one to that which she had expected.

Mortimer Elles was not seriously discomposed by his wife's remark. "That's a nice remark to make to a man!" was his not ungentle rejoinder. He had ceased to expect Phœbe to curb any expression of opinion out of respect to his feelings, and in return permitted himself his full measure of brutality towards her.

"Well, aren't they?" she repeated, yawning; "when is Charles going to pass his examination and relieve us of his presence? I did not bargain for Charles as a permanent lodger when I married you, nor Aunt Poynder indeed, for that matter, but I suppose all is for the worst, in this dreariest of all possible households!"

She expected no answer. These two always wrangled at cross purposes. There was very seldom a positive engagement between them. Mrs. Elles knew that Charles could not leave just yet, knew, too, that Mrs. Poynder would never go, was not positively sure that she wanted her to go, but just now, when her normal state of discontent was quadrupled by the new influences that had lately come into her life, she could not resist a repetition of an oft-repeated complaint.

She went on in a soft but irritating voice.

"I have no objection to Aunt Poynder's engaging all the servants and managing them, but I must say I wish she would let Jane alone. I have reserved the right of choosing my own parlour-maid, and when I have succeeded in getting one that suits me, I don't want her bullied and the place made impossible for her."

"Who bullies her? An idle, good-for-nothing trollop of a creature."

"There, you see, you don't like her."

"No, I don't," he replied brutally. "I don't like her style. She copies you, and you're not a particularly good model."

"Ah, how miserable I am!" she exclaimed, irrelevantly. "Mortimer, tell me, why can't we get on? It is not my fault, is it?"

"Oh! no," he replied ironically. "You are always in the right. There is nothing more tiresome in a woman."

"You are frank, Mortimer, and almost epigrammatic!"

"Shut up, can't you?" he exclaimed, in accents of annoyance. "I wonder why it is that you always contrive to rub me up the wrong way. Here you are abusing me—abusing my relations—why can't you let them alone? I don't abuse yours."

"Mine are all dead!" she said, pathetically. "Fair game for you!"

"And a nice lot they were!" said the man, now thoroughly roused to ill-temper. "That is, if you have told me the truth about them. You're pretty good at drawing the long bow, you know."

At this point in the discussion, Mrs. Elles withdrew. Her relations were—or had been—a weak point, and Mortimer had suffered—in his purse—from claims of a ne'er-do-well father-in-law, and a foolish, extravagant mother. Phœbe had been brought up badly as a child, had been neglected in her girlhood, and her marriage with Mortimer Elles had been the making of her—as her people said, and as she had agreed at the time—but it was a grievance with her that, try as she might, she could not give her history a romantic turn in her husband's eyes. He knew all about her, was full of preconceived notions about her, and she resented the impossibility of keeping up a consistent pose with him, being one of those who reverse the proverb and expect to be heroes to their valets de chambre and heroines to their husbands.

This weakness of hers entailed the other weakness to which her husband had alluded—her consistent ambiguity of phrase, her frequent lapses from truth. These lapses were for the most part unconscious, they were the good face she put on every matter, her artistic presentment of incidents relating to herself and other people, for, to do her justice, she applied the same method to her fellow-creatures, and was never known to retail a spiteful or unpicturesque version of another woman's affairs.

She considered herself the soul of honour, it is true; she literally would not have told a lie to save her life; but to save her pose and her dramatic presentment from discomfiture, she shrank from no form of embellishment or extenuation. So she "doctored" facts—served up the plain "roast and boiled" of everyday existence with a sauce piquante of her own devising, and thought of herself as one who, compassing under difficulties the whole duty of woman, makes herself as charming, as romantic, as mysterious as circumstances will allow.

.   .   .   .

Half an hour later she looked into the study, where Mortimer was sitting, a revolting picture of middle-class ease, with his legs on the table, drinking whisky and water.

"I thought I heard someone crying?"

"So you did. Jane. I have told her to go."

"What?" she screamed.

"Yes; we've had a row, Jane and I. I have sent her packing. I paid her her wages—told her to pack up and go—not later than to-morrow. She was cheeky to me—you teach them all to be damned cheeky to me—and I won't stand it." He filled his glass again, pouring with a want of precision that spoke of many previous attacks on the bottle.

"Jane cannot have meant"— his wife murmured humbly, cowed by the enormity of the misfortune that had befallen her. Jane was her ally, her confidante, her all.

"Oh, yes; Jane meant it fast enough. Don't talk to me about it. To-morrow she goes!"

He brought his fist heavily down upon the table. His wife started, a start partly real, partly affected.

"If Jane goes, I go."

"Nonsense, you are not a servant—I have not dismissed you!"

"Dismiss!" She tossed her head. Then the real, imminent need of propitiating Mortimer occurred to her. She must keep Jane at the cost of all humiliation. "Mortimer, listen—it puts me out very much. I have a dinner party of twelve next week!"

"The deuce you have! What a woman you are for kick-ups! And I don't suppose there is a soul coming that I shall care twopence for! Well, you must put it off, that's all!"

"One doesn't do these things!"

"Oh, I do. I'll write the excuses for you, if you like."

She stamped her foot. "Mortimer—I will not be put to shame before my friends! You have no right to do this to me! Oh, what shall I do, what shall I do, tied to a perfect beast like you for the rest of my life?"

'Grin and bear it, I suppose. You won't make me any better by swearing at me!"

"I don't swear at you! How you speak to me! To me! to me! Your wife! How dared you marry me, Mortimer?"

"I don't know about dare," he said, growing red.

"When all is said and done, I don't think you did much to prevent me!"

"That's enough!" she raised her hand with a theatrical gesture as if to stop him, and, sinking into an armchair, hid her face in her hands. "Insulting! No — I see now — you never loved me! Never! Never!"

He ostentatiously turned his back on her tragic pose.

"There you go! Always in extremes — always injured — always making the worst of it! You couldn't live without a grievance, I do believe! Of course I married you for love—if you must use the absurd word—and now you pay me back by plaguing my life out! And then begin to talk damned sentimental rot about my never having loved you, and so on! Now, really, don't you think we are both a bit too old for that sort of thing?"

"Oh, you are—impossible!" she moaned. It was what she felt. It was the one word which fitted the situation, which was no situation, except to herself. Mortimer kicked a coal out of the grate savagely with his carpet-slippered foot, and, her sense assaulted by the sickening smell of singed wool, she left the room.

.   .   .   .

Mortimer was drunk — he often was; it was the least heinous of his crimes. She went upstairs crying, and went to bed, but she knew she could not sleep that night, and yet she took no bromide or sulphonal. She wanted to think—she meant to think things out—so she lay, and thought, and thought, with extreme intensity and vigour, if with little coherence. So intent was she that she lay quite straight out and still, and did not toss, while the trains of thought succeeded each other with extraordinary rapidity. The tall clock on the stairs outside her door ticked loudly and monotonously, and the whole problem of her life arrayed itself and measured out its phases to the beat of the pendulum, which seemed to balance them, as it were.

Mortimer was impossible! He had always been impossible! His conduct this evening was of a piece with his whole conduct to her, ever since a few weeks after marriage. Halcyon weeks, which every woman has a right to expect, while they in no wise concern or affect the life that follows after. His taunt about the circumstances of her marriage to him she dismissed, she knew quite well that she had provoked him to it, he had not meant it, there was no foundation for it. He had wooed and won her in the usual, commonplace way, been timid and attentive, and had begged her for locks of her hair. And she had been complaisant and loving, and had treasured his photograph and made excuses for its ugliness, just like any other foolish girl with her first sweetheart.

Why had she done all this? Why had she bought that rose-coloured satin dress last Christmas, that she had taken such a dislike to, since, that she had only worn it twice? Her marriage was a very nearly parallel case, only she had been able to afford to throw aside the one bad bargain, and she had been obliged to abide by the other.

"Yes, I can't say I did not know my own mind, such as it was, when I took Mortimer, but, unfortunately, it isn't the same mind that I have now. It was a child's mind. The whole fabric of our bodies alters every seven years, they say—well, that means our minds, too—body and soul are one in my creed. It was not this me that was glad to marry Mortimer, as he so politely put it—" she laughed bitterly. "It was another me, who had not read Ibsen." She laughed again. "Books alter one—reading alters one —life alters one, after all! I married Mortimer like a blind puppy, not knowing, not seeing. I am nothing wonderful, but I do think I am too good for him! Why did I not see it then? Why is a girl such a fool? Why does nobody tell her? It is very hard. They say, as one has made one's bed, so one must lie on it. . . . But suppose I decline to lie on it?"

She almost leaped in her bed with the shock of this crude presentment of a new idea. Then she rose, lit a candle and walked out of her room, and across a landing, and straight into Mortimer's room. She softly approached the bed on which he lay, and, like Psyche over again, held the light up on high, and looked critically down upon her sleeping husband.

She felt an indefinable pleasure in thus surveying him helpless who was technically her master. This coarse, clumsy-fibred creature who had yet his full complement of the shrewdness and acuteness that gave him dominion over his fellow-men, and made him known as a "tough customer" in business, slept the sleep—well, if not precisely that of the just, at any rate that of the man whose balance at his bank is secure and his investment sound. He slept like a savage who has laid aside his clubs, and enjoys the dreamless, primitive sleep that he has earned by his feats of arms. His thick, broad eyelids rested peacefully on the cold, blue eyes whose empty glare his wife knew and detested. His lips were closed on his cruel little teeth in a firm, inexpressive line, pacific and meaningless, and his clumsy hands, with their short, square-nailed finger tips, lay palm outwards on the coverlet, as innocently as a child's.

She might stare at him as long as she pleased, with those burning, insistent eyes of hers, and not fear to break his sleep; his simple nervous system would surely withstand the hypnotism of her enquiring gaze.

But next morning, he would be "all there" as usual; the hectoring, bantering, exacerbating personality would re-assert itself, and make its hundred and one demands on her self-control all through the day, till sometimes it seemed as if she could not look at him or hear his voice without screaming.

"Why should I bear it? Why should I?" she asked herself, passionately, aloud; and the pettish exclamation was significant of the great revulsion that was taking place in her, a result of the passionate, elucidating fortnight she had passed.

She went back to her room and lay down again, but she closed her eyes no more that night, and by the time the pallid dawn of Newcastle had begun to filter through the window curtains, a whole plan of action had shaped itself in her mind. She came down punctually to the eight o'clock breakfast which was exacted by Mortimer and which he had never allowed her to forego, putting some constraint on herself to appear perfectly composed, for her heart was beating violently, and she felt the suspicious flush mounting to her cheek, which had so often given unkind friends occasion to say that she painted. But Mrs. Poynder, who was presiding over the tea and coffee, looked her over with some approval.

"Now, that's the first decent dress I have seen you in, Fibby, for many a long day!" she observed, contemplating the plain dress of blue serge—not very new, not very smart—in which Mrs. Elles had chosen to array herself.

"I am glad you are pleased, Aunt Poynder," replied her niece, demurely, gracefully accepting her cup of coffee from the stout, red fingers where the submerged wedding-ring, planted there by the late Mr. Poynder, glittered. Charles Elles, who could get more noise out of a cup of coffee than anybody, was drinking his and enjoying it thoroughly. Mrs. Poynder somehow contrived to knock her knife and fork together on the rim of her plate with vigour every time she took a morsel. Mortimer's carpet slippers, and the dish of bacon which his aunt had set down by the fire to keep warm for him, stood by the fire in grotesque proximity.

"I am going to put off my dinner on the thirty-first," Mrs. Elles announced, quietly. "Jane is going, and I couldn't attempt it with a new parlour-maid."

"I am glad, Fibby, to see you in such a peaceable frame of mind," Mrs. Poynder rejoined. "Mortimer says you were fairly put out at first about his sending Jane away."

"So I was, Aunt, but——"

"Ye're quite right, Fibby, to take it calm. Husbands must have their way. I never thought much of the girl myself; she's lazy and wears far too much fringe. Besides, a man must be master in his own house, and if he can't send away his own housemaid when it pleases him——"

"Yes, Aunt." Mrs. Elles was playing at meekness, and the sensation was so unusual that she found it rather amusing so far. Mrs. Poynder could not make it out at all.

"Are ye ill, my dear?" she enquired, with some show of solicitude. "To look at ye, I should say that your digestion was not in just apple-pie order."

'I am all right, Aunt," replied Mrs. Elles, with forced composure, stamping her foot, however, under the table. Her colour was high, as Mrs. Poynder had remarked, but very clear and bright, and she looked quite ten years younger. Her aunt continued to make little onslaughts of this kind on her through breakfast, but she did not retort. Her lips formed themselves every now and again into the words, "I am going—I am going—I am going!" as a kind of secret satisfaction. When her husband came down, she actually got up and fetched the terribly plebeian dish of bacon from the fender and put it down in front of him. He thanked her drily.

"If you will excuse me," she said to them all, "I will go and write some notes that have to be attended to at once."

She left the room, and the scratching of a feverish pen within the drawing-room was heard for the next twenty minutes through the open door, while Mortimer Elles, having eaten an enormous breakfast in the short time he had devoted to that purpose, went into the hall and began to rummage for his stick and hat and struggle into his coat. His wife knew the sound well.

"Good-bye, Mortimer!" she called out. There was a slight suspicion of mockery in her tone that he perceived and resented. He did not answer her, but went out, banging the door behind him loudly and aggressively.

"Helmer bangs the door; not Nora!" she smiled to herself. She felt extraordinarily gay. The more serious aspects of the step she was taking were not obvious to her at the present moment. She was for the time merely possessed by an irrepressible zeal for the assertion of self, and its disassociation from all trammelling human responsibilities.

Presently Mrs. Poynder went out too, to attend some Busybodies' committee meeting, and Mrs. Elles took three five-pound notes out of a drawer in her desk, locked it, and, going downstairs, ordered lunch and dinner very carefully. This duty accomplished, she went up to her room, and presented Jane, whom she found there, with a very handsome cloth dress she had hardly worn, and her blessing. The affectionate and devoted Jane wept, and it was with difficulty that her mistress prevented herself from crying too.

Then Jane went about her business, and Mrs. Elles locked herself in. She undid the complicated arrangement of her hair and with a comb parted it as severely as she could resign herself to do, and with a brush dipped in water smoothed out the little curls on her forehead, sighing deeply the while. Then she went to a cupboard, and from its most recondite recesses produced a box containing a pair of blue spectacles—her husband's. She put them on, and standing resolutely in front of a cheval glass, surveyed her appearance.

"Good God, can I bear it?" she said aloud, in tones of the very deepest anguish. Her face grew sombre for the first time since the conception of flight had become an established fact in her mind. She desperately tugged down a lock and disposed it becomingly on her forehead as usual, and then put it back again.——

"No! . . . Yes! . . . I must do it like this. . . .

It is the only way I can do it without blame. . . . It shows that my intentions are honourable. . . . I am going away to be free, not to flirt. . . . I must make all that an absolute impossibility!"

She flung a lace scarf over the glass and busied herself with a few necessary preparations. She got out a Gladstone bag—just the size she could manage to carry herself—and threw in a few clothes, including a fine white muslin dress she had worn at her "at home" that day, so fine that it would go through a ring almost and took up no room to speak of. A rather valuable sapphire ring she put on her finger, and on second thoughts added a diamond one. Then she opened the door of her room, and leaning over the banisters called out, "Jane!"

Jane replied.

"Jane, will you go and draw down those blinds in the drawing-room—all of them—half down. The sun is getting 'so strong. And then, will you take the heap of letters you will see lying on the bureau, and go and post them at once."

She put on a sailor hat and a white lace veil over her blue spectacles, and was downstairs and out in the street before Jane had got to the fourth blind of the drawing-room, which happened to look out on the back of the house. Nora was gone!

CHAPTER III

Mrs. Elles took a ticket for London. The train was due to leave in ten minutes. She was out of breath and felt the compromising colour mounting to her cheeks under her thick white veil. The young poet was on the platform, apparently seeing Miss Drummond off. Phœbe Elles smiled at the little love drama here developing. It would have been hers to further it if she had been staying at home, for she was a born matchmaker with a very kind heart and dearly loved helping people, from a variety of motives. But for the moment she had something else to do. She got quickly into her carriage. The poet had glanced at her, but had, of course, soon averted his gaze from such an uninteresting object as the pretty Mrs. Elles now presented.

Atalanta Drummond was probably only going as far as Darlington, where, as everybody knew, she had relations. But still her presence in the same train was a dangerous and delightful fact. Mrs. Elles felt all the exhilaration of a superior criminal evading the pursuit of justice and forthwith planned to play an exciting game of hide-and-seek with her unwitting fellow-traveller. She would manœuvre the most carefully-arranged, hair-breadth escapes from the unconscious pursuer. How nice it was to be running

47

away, so to speak, and how it at once removed everything from the region of the commonplace!

She got out of her carriage at Darlington, and
looked about the great station. She was one of those
persons in whom the mere sight of a telegraph office
immediately inspires a desire to send a message of
some sort, and she at once went into the bureau and
proceeded to compose a wire to Mortimer.

"Gone away for the present; do not be anxious
about me. Phœbe." Then she crossed out "for the
present" and substituted "for a change."

"I don't want him to be dragging the Tyne for
me!" she thought. "That is, if his affection for me
should prompt him to such an extreme course, which
I do not think it would."

When she got back to her carriage, a porter was
engaged in putting some effects into the rack, which
she at once recognized as belonging to Miss Drummond. In spite of her plans, terror then filled her
soul. Had that young lady recognized her? Was
she intending to join her for the pleasure of her company? Or was it only because this was a through
carriage to London?

The poor, hunted creature dared not stay to ascertain, but, seizing her bag, jumped out and searched
wildly for another compartment. She was bewildered
and uncertain. Nobody helped her or took any
interest in her, because she was unattractive, so she
thought, and the end of it was that the London train
moved on without her, as trains will.

She watched it steaming out of the station, but she was far too much excited to care. There happened to be another train, just like it, on the other side of the station, about to go westwards to Barnard Castle.

"Scott's Rokeby!" she said to herself. Scott was not one of her modern gods, but still the names—famous and familiar to everyone—"Brignal Banks" and Greta Bridge—had a certain old-world magic of their own. So, acting on the inspiration of the moment, she took a ticket for Barnard Castle, and at twelve o'clock found herself in the market-place of the sleepy little town on the Tees, in front of a char-à-banc full of tourists just starting for Rokeby, four miles off. She took a seat.

Once arrived there, she declined to make the tour of the famous Park with a guide and a noisy party of barbarians, with fern-leaves artlessly stuck behind their ears, but, leaving her bag in charge of the obliging porter at the gates, whom the more effectually to cajole she took off her spectacles for a second, started on a voyage of discovery in the opposite direction, across the bridge, following the course of the Greta, along a cart track in a wood, to the east. She did not in the least know where this path would lead her; she only knew that she was extremely happy. She felt just as she imagined the young journeyman heroes in the tales of Grimm must have felt when they walked, knapsack in hand, to seek their fortunes. She walked with an assured step, she sang to

herself, she listened to the jubilant song of the mounting larks that came from the fields on the other side
of the river, she enjoyed the country as only a town-
bred person can; she actually experienced the joy of
life she had read about so often. "I have not seen
enough of nature!" she said to herself, as one says of
a friend who lives a long way off, and whom one has
somehow neglected. Tags of poetry, scraps of philosophy, queer mythological ideas, born of her miscellaneous reading, about the Earth Mother and the
Earth Spirit, passed through her mind. What a
terribly artificial life it was that she had been leading!
Nature was the real thing after all!

And meantime, at home in smoky, sophisticated
Newcastle, Mortimer and Mrs. Poynder and Charles
would be sitting down to the substantial midday meal
that their souls loved, and that she had carefully
ordered for them before she left, as a valedictory
service. She pictured the complacent three, pent up
in the hideous, stuffy dining-room (Mortimer's taste
—she was only permitted jurisdiction over the drawing-room), with all the windows fast closed down in
accordance with that innate dislike of fresh air inherent in some persons, and a blazing fire for the crown
of discomfort.

She, whose spiritual needs were being so thoroughly
satisfied, for once, was not in the least materially
hungry, and, if she became so, would eat roots like
other heroines before her. There must be plenty of
things edible in this luxuriance of undergrowth in

which she was wandering, where all possible forms of vegetable life seemed literally crushing one another out in their mutual excess and exuberance. There were great, flame-coloured fungi glistering from the boles of enormous beech trees whose leaves grew so closely that, althougth he hot July sun, she knew, was beating outside on their thick panopoly, she yet was able to walk at ease in their cool penumbra. Beds of magnificent nettles, and the broad, green discs of what the children call "fairy tables" filled all the hollows of the dells. Here and there, tall-stemmed, pale lilac campanulas rose and lightened the gloom through which the sunbeams pierced in vivid streaks, like golden spears probing the dimness. The low bank of red sandstone that formed the background to the grove showed at intervals like a rosy wall, but on the opposite side the character of the country had changed; there were no more meadows; she was hemmed in; the granite cliff rose sheer, clothed with trees that found but a scanty purchase in the rocky clefts to which they seemed to cling frantically with hoary roots upturned, detached almost, the relative positions of roots and boughs nearly reversed. The call of the wood-pigeons that nested in these coverts —she sentimentally called them doves—came to her across the river that flowed along beside her, red like wine, over shiny stones and deep, rocky crevices that modified the sound of its ripples into a thousand musical varieties.

She was in an ecstasy. To herself she murmured,

softly, Rossetti's lines about the "Banks in Willow Wood":

"With woodspurge wan, with bloodwort burning
      red"—

and was in a mood to utter invocations to the "spotted snakes, with double tongue," that must be lurking in those dark beds of hoary nettles. She was a well-read woman, and had her poets at her fingers' ends, for use, not ornament, since she so frequently quoted them. She walked on, imagining that she heard the interesting rustle of wild animals that her footsteps affrighted, and presently, out of pure caprice, left the path and began to clamber up the bank, in the vague aspiration after blackberries in July.

The dell began to widen out, and the river, which up to that time had flowed in a more or less massive and self-contained flood, began to spread and lose itself in shallows. The noise of many counter-ripples, of the suction of large masses of water pouring into crevices and over many different levels, grew very loud. She stood, as it were, at the end of a funnel, looking towards a sunlit clearing where the trees grew more thinly and more interspersedly, and the cliffs stood away on either side.

She stopped and stood still, and pushed her spectacles, which she had been wearing very laxly, a little further up her forehead.

"This is like a glimpse of Paradise," she thought, looking towards the golden space in front of her, "coming as it does, just after this long, cool dark grove that I have been walking in for more than half an hour! That was a kind of Purgatorio. This is a painter's paradise, I might say, and there is the painter!"

For very nearly under her feet—she was half-way up the sloping bank that sheltered this little oasis on the south—was the white calico umbrella planted on its spiked stick, like a gigantic mushroom, which Mrs. Elles was well-informed enough to associate at once with the painter's craft.

The painter was, of course, seated on his campstool under it, and she looked down on the back of his sunburnt neck and noticed the way his hair curled a little on it. One rash step would bring her down on him in a helpless rush, for she was not an expert climber and her steps were rendered precarious by the crumbly nature of the soil on which she stood.

She settled her spectacles firmly on her nose—"I shall probably fall and break them into my eyes, but it can't be helped!" and began to skirt round to the left, intending to make a circuit of the umbrella and approach the artist from the front. She had a wild desire to speak to someone. She had actually not opened her lips since ten o'clock that morning, and she was a woman hardly cast by nature for the part of a Trappist! In this lonely place, the least a man could do would be to wish her good day! Then she might possibly go so far as to ask him to tell her the name of the place where she found herself, and a pleasant conversation would thereby be inaugurated.

She worked gradually round to him—how ugly the

world looked through the wall of cold blue in front of
her eyes!—and the continuous ripple of the water,
flowing over the many obstacles and narrow channels
of its bed, effectually drowned the noise of the snap-
ping of dry twigs and the breaking of pulpy burdock
stalks that attended her clumsy progress.

She was almost in front of him—a few yards off
only—but he had not raised his head. He did so
presently, in the natural course of things, and she
made a step forward.

"For God's sake, mind that foxglove!" he shouted,
but, even as he spoke, it was doomed and the splendid
column of pink bells fell prone to the ground. She
stood aghast.

"I beg your pardon!" he said, in a tone as civil as
was consistent with the most obvious and excessive
irritation, "but do you know you have completely
ruined my foreground?"

"I beg your pardon—oh, ten thousand times!" she
replied, ruefully surveying the snapped stem of the
injured flower. "But it will grow again, won't it?"

"Not that one—not this summer—and it came in
just right! Well, well; it can't be helped. . . .
Please don't apologise! . . . It is no matter."

But she continued to apologise, and he to beg her
not to do so. The voice in which she conveyed her
protestations, however, became more and more feeble.
The hot sun was beating down on her head as she
stood, and she was conscious of an overpowering
faintness and desire to sink down on the desecrated

bed of foxgloves and rest; but she felt also very strongly that she must resist and conquer the impulse until she could remove herself to a place beyond the artist's proximity.

"You seem faint," she heard him saying, and his voice, grown gentle now, seemed to come from miles away. "Sit down on this!" and he hastily emptied a bulgy canvas sketching bag and laid it down beside her. "Now shall I get you some water?"

She was so really ill that she could only nod in response to his offer.

"I have no glass," he said; "but this little thing will be quite clean when I have washed it out." He took the japanned tin attached to his water-colour paint box, and ran down to the river to fill it. She watched him.

"How nice of him!" she thought to herself; "and I was just thinking him such a bear; and I spoiled his poor foxglove; and I am so hungry!"

There were several crusts of dry bread lying about which he had thrown out of the canvas bag—how dry she dared not think, but she put out her hand and nibbled at one.

"Good Heavens, you must not eat that!" he said, when he came back, raising his eyebrows. His eyes were quite dark, though his hair was grey. "Mrs. Watson put some sandwiches into my bag this morning, but I regret to say I ate them all half-an-hour ago! I generally take them back with me untouched. How unlucky!"

He raised his voice and called, and after a time a lubberly boy came slouching up.

"Now, Billy Gale, where the devil have you been? What is the good of you?   Go up to the cottage and ask them for a glass of milk and a slice of bread-and-butter—on a plate, mind!"

The boy was off, and he turned to Mrs. Elles, who had drunk her cool, pure river water, and was looking less pale.

"You are very kind to me," she murmured, "and I know how you must hate being interrupted! Please do go on painting now as if I were not here. I won't say a single word, and, as soon as I am a little rested, I will go away and leave you in peace. . . . I am very fond of art!" she added, inconsequently. "I used to do a little myself."

But the artist seemed to have taken her at her word, and she did not think he could have heard her, as he sat complacently dabbling his brush in the little water-tin, now restored to its proper use, and then put it to his lips, and then touched his paper with it. There was no colour in the brush, and no particular effect upon the paper, so it seemed to the ignorant tyro at his side.   In spite of her promise of silence, she could not resist pointing this out to him.

"Don't be too sure," he said; "every touch counts."

"I do wish I might have a look at it!"

She was quite unprepared for the terrible frown that appeared on his mild countenance when she preferred this innocent-seeming request.

"You must excuse me, please. I cannot bear to
show my things before they are done. I could never
work at them again if I did. It is a peculiarity of
mine—dreadful, but—here is Billy! I am afraid he
will have spilt most of the milk by the time he gets
here."

"Mr. Rivers, sir," said the boy, as soon as he got
within earshot, "Farmer says as one o' they little
black pigs—you knows 'em, sir—?"

"Intimately, every one of them," replied the artist,
bitterly. "It's your business to keep them off me,
you young villain, and instead of that you go and let
them rout about in my colour box——"

"That's just it, sir," Billy answered, grinning joyfully; one of 'em has died suddent-like, and Farmer
says as how it died along of eating those little sticky
things o' yourn that squeedge in and out."

"One of my oil-colour tubes! What nonsense! Just
go and tell Mr. Ward—no, stop; I'll speak to him
myself, later." He turned and laughed at Mrs. Elles
very pleasantly. "What an absurd thing! But I
certainly have missed my Naples yellow, lately."

She laughed too. "Now I have heard your name,"
she said.

"Edmund Rivers."

"Yes, Edmund Rivers, the famous landscape-
painter—you see I know all about your fame—and I
have a letter of yours in my pocket."

As a matter of fact, she had not, she was thinking
of the muslin dress she had worn days ago, into whose

pocket she had thrust the autograph letter Egidia had
given her. The dress was in her bag, lying at the
Porter's lodge, a mile away. Still it sounded better.
The artist luckily did not ask to see the letter, but
looked puzzled, and a little displeased.

"I collect autographs!" she went on hastily, "and
Miss Giles—Egidia, you know, the famous novelist—
gave it to me. She said she was a relation of yours.
She is a great friend of mine, too. I am on my way
to stay with her."

"Oh, indeed!" he said, stiffly.

"But I must ask you," she went on, clasping her
hands together, "not to mention my name to her
when you write, or even to say that you have seen
me. Please promise?"

"But, my dear madam, I don't know your name,
and am never likely to."

"Oh, yes; but indeed you must know my name,"
she said simply, "Miss Frick."

It was a pseudonym adopted on the spur of the
moment; she had known a German governess of the
name. Once fairly launched in fiction she went on
easily.

"I am the daughter of a country clergyman, and
he's very poor—we are seven—and we all earn our
bread. It is a very strange story. My father married
again, an odious woman none of us could live with.
I did type-writing—that is how I weakened my eyes
—and then I broke down, and I had to go into the
country for my health."

"I am very sorry to hear all this," said the artist, languidly.

"Oh, not at all. And then—there was a further complication—there was a man, and he pestered me —annoyed me—molested me, in fact, till I got ill. It was not all the fault of the type-writing, you see" —she had a wan, well-executed smile under her veil. "My life was a torment to me. He followed me about; he even threatened to shoot me! You may have read about it in the papers."

"No, I never have." His voice betrayed no interest.

"People do such dreadful things, sometimes!" she observed, vaguely, to Nature at large, for the artist had become quite absorbed in his work and seemed to be paying no attention to what she was saying. "He is all the time wishing me at the devil!" she thought to herself, but she did not go. She was perforce silent awhile, but took the opportunity to look closely at and focus this personage who had so completely filled up her field of vision.

"He looks rather like a foreign sailor, such as one sees on the quays at Newcastle," she thought. " He only wants earrings to complete the effect. I suppose it is because he is so sunburnt, and his eyes are so dark. They are like brown pools—like the river here, as if they grew like what they looked on. There are all sorts of little wrinkles round them—not money wrinkles, as I always call Mortimer's—but wrinkles that come of screwing up his eyes to see effects, and shutting one of them altogether now and then, as he is doing. He talks languidly, like a society man, as if everything was a bore, but then his eager eyes are all over the place. I like that greyish hair in so young a man—it is 'a sable silvered,' as Hamlet said of his father. What a beautiful mouth! It is like a woman's, and yet it is strong. His moustache hides it a good deal. Well, a mouth like that should not be too obvious to the vulgar eye. It tells too much. He is very thin. I wonder if he is delicate? No, not with a figure like that—he must be strong, and his instep is beautifully arched—that comes of springing about these rocks—people grow flat-footed in Newcastle. . . ."

She started suddenly.

"Why am I sitting here beside a strange man of whose existence I did not even know an hour ago? It is as if I had been here all my life! I ought to go, of course, but where?"

She looked round her distractedly. The sun had declined; the day had changed from morning to afternoon. She had been in this man's company for nearly two hours, without any excuse beyond her temporary faintness. She got up nervously; though he did not seem to notice her, and wandered a little way off across the meadow trying to collect her thoughts and make a plan. A curious brown ball lying at the foot of a wild rose tree attracted her attention. She picked it up and, with childish inconsequence, carried it back to the artist to ask him to tell her what it was. Suddenly it uncurled in her hand, and a tiny snout appeared in front of the bristles! She dropped it with a modish scream, and the artist perforce raised his head. He saw the situation at once, and smiled a little. There was a cynical twist in his mouth that delighted her.

"Did you say you had been bred in the country?" he asked.

"Why, what is it?"

"Only a hedgehog—a 'hodgeon,'" as they call them here. "Poor thing: it trusted you, you see, and uncurled itself!"

"The darling; I must take it home."

"I would," he said dryly, and looked at his watch. "Four o'clock! I must go to my afternoon subject."

Trembling with apprehension, she watched him as he took the sketching bag, and rammed his sketching things into it. He then summoned Billy to take down the umbrella and follow with it, and shouldering the bag himself, raised his cap civilly, bade her good morning, and was gone.

She sat there stupidly staring at the little yellow patch of trodden grass where his feet had rested, and his camp had been set.

She was alone in the world again, a runaway wife, with all the problem of her life before her!

The obvious course was to get up and go; but where? To London? What did she care for London now? And anyhow, it was far too late to go on there that night!

The smoke was rising from the chimneys of the cottage up there on the brow, whence Billy Gale had brought the milk. Was the artist staying there? She cast her eyes vaguely round her as if to ask the mild heavens for help, and saw the boy in the distance, sitting kicking his heels about on a dry rock, in mid-stream, not far from his master, presumably!

Then she rose, having conceived a reckless plan of action which she felt the necessity of putting into execution at once; for if she were to allow herself to think it over, she would never be able to bring herself to do it at all. She beckoned to Billy Gale, and asked him to be so good as to direct her to Mr. Rivers' "afternoon subject" as she had heard him call it.

The lad stared, but obediently led her to a place about a quarter of a mile further down the river, opposite a ruined church, and a church garth full of antique, wooden headstones, smothered in burdock leaves; a scene of beautiful desolation.

Mr. Rivers was standing, sketch book in hand, on a little beach of pebbles under the shelving, undercut bank, executing with incredible dexterity what looked like meaningless parabolic curves, with a hard lead pencil. His back was turned to her. She jumped down the bank, and, though the crunching of the pebbles under her feet, and the sound of her own voice, affrighted her, managed to pluck up courage to address him.

"I must apologise for troubling you again—but you

were so very kind to me before—perhaps you would not mind telling me if there is any—if I could find any accommodation here?"

"No, none!" he replied hastily, without even turning round.

After an appreciable pause he added, unwillingly, "At least—there's an inn a mile off—about a mile——"

"But that is what I mean!" she cried, joyfully. "And is that where you stop?"

He turned on her a gaze of acute distress.

"Oh, yes, I suppose so, but I warn you—I, of course, can put up with anything—it is very rough, very rough indeed. They are not good hands at cooking—I have had a chop a day for the last fortnight. And the beds are very hard!"

Here he shuddered somewhat elaborately.

"I don't happen to mind that sort of thing at all."

"I chose it for quiet," he went on, pathetically. "The landlady is a good soul, who understands my little ways, but——"

"That quite decides me——"

"They may have a room—I am sure I don't know —but I should advise you not——"

"I should not be in your way at all," she went on, barefacedly assuming her acquaintance with the remoter causes of his feeble degree of encouragement, and smiling sweetly into his blank face, "in fact, I should be a comfort to you—I mean, I am very quiet, and if I occupy the room, no one else can, don't you see? I should at any rate serve to keep noisier people out."

"There is something in that!" he observed, as if to himself.

"So I will go along and see," she went on, pursuing her advantage.

"My lad can show you a short cut over the river," was the painter's unexpected rejoinder. She was not deceived by his mildness. He only wanted to get rid of her, and the moment he had spoken he turned round and resumed his drawing again.

"Delightful, but not quite human," she thought to herself.

His "lad," with frank confidence in her power of accommodation to somewhat unusual methods of pro-gression, piloted her across the river by way of a rough bridge of stepping stones, apparently half natural, half artificial, and then led her by many a varied and devious track, through a succession of brambly coppices, and over many stiles of many patterns, tantalizing enough to a town-bred woman. She enjoyed it, however, and was proud of her newly-discovered powers, as she surmounted one unusual impediment after another, and was as quick about it as the long-legged country lad who guided her. Then they crossed a couple of upland pastures where the great, mild-eyed cows were grazing, and half-turning their heads to look at her and Billy Gale, who left her no time to be afraid of them, and at last the slender smoke spirals from the chimneys of a little homestead rose in sight.

"The Heather Bell" was an old-fashioned coaching inn on the outskirts of the great park of Rokeby, and opposite one of its gates. The enormous beech trees leaned over the high Park wall and shadowed the inn that was only separated from it by the width of the road, and whose windows were darkened at noonday by their shade. The inn itself was a large, straggling building, with a low-pitched, tiled roof covered with houseleek. A bushy, garish-coloured garden on the south side, full of flowers, reached to where the fields ended. A woman was standing under the rose-hung porch, shading her eyes with her hand.

"Yon's the Mistress!" said Billy Gale, suddenly, "and she owes me a skelping, so I think I'll just mak' myself skarse!" He bolted, and just in time, for the landlady came striding up the garden path with obviously less zeal for the welcoming of the guest than for Billy Gale's discomfiture.

"Little, idle good-for-nought!" exclaimed she, shaking her fist in the direction of his recalcitrant back. "Is this the proper way for to bring fowk in? What's the front entrance for? Good morning, Mem. Coom in this way, since ye are here!"

Mrs. Elles asked for a bedroom, and was told that she could have one.

"It's a bit smarl, but ye're no very big yersel'," said the landlady, tenderly patronizing her already. People always did. "Coom, an' I'se show ye! . . ."

Ye'll be a penter, too, will ye?" she enquired, on the way upstairs. "Lord love ye, there's heaps on 'em cooms here! It's a fine place for such as them! There's the Joonction—the Greta and the Tees, ye know, and the Dairy Bridge and Mortham Tower, they're all bonnie—ye'se find plenty for to ockipy ye here. We've got a grand artiss here now. . . . That's his room, see ye, next yours—ye'll mebbies have seen his pectewers in Lunnon, Mem?"

"Miss," corrected Mrs. Elles.

"He's a permanent lodger like. It's a matter o' ten year since he first coomed here, seeking rooms. I seed he was a painter lad at onst, and I says to my man—I had a man then—'Tak' him, George, and ye'll ne'er repent it! He'll be out a' the day long a dirtying o' bits of nice clean paper, and amusing hisself, and no trouble at all!' . . . Well, he'll be in soon to his bit denner. Ye'll be having a chop to yer tea, along of he?"

"Oh, but can't I have a sitting-room of my own?"

"Nay, we haven't another setting-room, honey. There's only the big meetin'-room, ye know—'tis only fit for picnic parties, and sich like—but Mr. Rivers is a nice quiet body; he'll not be in your way, I promise ye."

But Mrs. Elles, whatever her private wishes might have been, was resolved not to have any appearance of intruding on the hermit painter; and six o'clock—for she was ridiculously, unromantically hungry—found her established at a corner of a long-rudimentary, wooden table, built on trestles, that ran the whole length of a bare, barn-like room, evidently a recent addition to the comfortable old coaching inn, for it was high-pitched, with three tall sash windows, and the walls distempered in French grey. The floor was sanded, and its raftered ceiling was not free from spiders, that ever and anon made terrifying voyages of discovery down their shadowy webs to the end of the long table that was spread with a coarse, white cloth for her benefit.

She was struck, amid all this roughness and rusticity, with the white, well-tended hands that served her. It was not a servant who stood behind her chair, and who was continually addressed from afar by the land-lady as "Jane Anne!" Jane Anne was a short, thick-set young woman in a well-made black dress, and an opulent watch-chain. Mrs. Elles did not like her face, with its heavy chin and sullen eyes and masses of crisped black hair parted carefully on a low fore-head, or the mincing Cockney pronunciation, grafted on a native Yorkshire accent, with which the girl answered the trifling questions she asked her. She wore no cap or apron, and performed her service with a silent concentration which showed that it was not her usual vocation. To all Mrs. Elles' remarks she replied civilly, but with a suggestion of closure in each answer. Mrs. Elles took a strong dislike to her at once.

The three windows of the room opened on to the garden, the main path of which led by a slight

upward gradient to the wicket gate and the series of
upland pastures which she had traversed a few hours
before on her way back from Brignal.   That, she had
ascertained, was the name of the place where she had
first met Mr. Rivers.   He must surely be even now
crossing them on his way home from his work.   She
went across to the window and leaned out, and gazed
disconsolately towards the empty sunset sky.

Two pretty brown cows were leaning over and rub-
bing their noses against the stumps of the gate, lowing
gently for human sympathy.   Suddenly their heads
were persuasively pushed aside, and the painter appeared, silhouetted against the saffron background.
He stroked them, and then coming through, closed
the gate carefully against their obtrusive noses.   Mrs.
Elles watched him as he walked down the path,
pebbly and uneven with the washing down of previous
heavy rains, between the low espalier pear trees, and
disappeared under the porch a few yards to the left.
Then, with a little suppressed sigh, she withdrew her
gaze from the gleaming sky and turned sharply, to
find the body of the girl who had waited on her at
dinner in close proximity to her own.

The girl had evidently been watching the painter's
entry, too, over her unsuspecting shoulders.   Mrs.
Elles conceived a violent dislike to her, which, in her
wilful way, she was at no pains to hide.

Everybody here seemed to be attached to Mr.
Rivers.   Through the open door of the room, she
heard the landlady's ecstatic welcome to him as he

passed under the rose-hung porch of the "Heather Bell." "Well, and here ye coom, sir!" as of one receiving a cherished lamb back into the fold. Presently, the listening woman heard him walk wearily into his sitting-room—it happened to be next door to the kind of annex in which she was—and close the door.

She now felt strangely and unutterably lonely. What had she come here for? During the rest of the evening, she sat in a hard cane chair by the window, and leaned her elbow on the equally hard stone sill. The light slowly faded out of the sky and the scent of the nightstocks came to her in sweet, overpowering wafts, and the evening primroses opened wider and wider till they seemed to shine like yellow moons in the dusky garden beds. Then the real moon came out, and still she could smell nothing but the sweet smells of the garden and she wondered whether Mr. Rivers would begin to smoke enormous strong cigars or a horrid pipe, like Mortimer, and thus kill all the poetry of the evening. His window was next to the one out of which she was now leaning, and it was wide open. Her window was raw and square, his was smothered in the leaves of an immense pear which she had noticed as she came in, growing, in stiffly arranged branches like a genealogical tree, all over the southern side of the house.

No, he was not smoking! What was he doing? She suddenly conceived the notion of going out of doors—of taking a walk in the Park, that is, if the porter would allow her to pass at this hour. She would see the famous yew grove she had read of, dark at noonday, and positively sepulchral at night, where the White Lady of Mortham walked and bewailed her unnamed woes. She would listen to the mysterious "hum" beetles, which served for "tuck of drum" to marshal the gallant outlaws of the ballad:—

> "Oh, Brignal Banks are fresh and fair,
>   And Greta woods are green;
>   I'd rather rove with Edmund there
>   Than reign our English Queen!"

"How strange his name should be Edmund, too!"

So musing, she went out. She did not trouble to put on a hat, and she took off her tiresome spectacles and put them in her pocket, for it had grown so dark that, even if anyone were to meet her going out of the inn door, he would not be able to see her face with any degree of clearness.

But when she got into the hall, she changed her mind capriciously and went into the garden instead of the Park.

As she passed the window of his room, she noticed that the white linen blind was not drawn down, and the lighted lamp inside showed the table with its queer, old-fashioned, rose-embroidered cloth, all littered with the paraphernalia of an artist's work, and the artist himself intently bending over a sepia sketch lying in front of him.

He had evidently forgotten her very existence!

No wonder! A plain woman with smoked spectacles and a bald forehead. So she characterized herself. That was all she had allowed him to see of her. She stood there for a very long time, watching him, her hand raised to her face ready to veil it in case he should look up. She had no scruples, for if he had objected to being looked at, he would have pulled down the blind.

Every now and then, a ripe pear, ruined by the insidious wasp that preyed on it secretly, fell heavily down on the sodden earth under the window, and startled her, but he never raised his head. She ceased to expect him to do so, and stood at ease, listening to the various puzzling night sounds and quite unconscious of the flight of time. Queer noises came from the great, mysterious demesne on the other side of the house—that excess of rank foliage in which it seemed that every known variety of animal might find a home; it was so "whick," in local parlance, so full of all the forms of sylvan life, crawling, creeping, rustling in among the long grasses and twisted boughs all through the summer night. Presently, the short, sharp bark of a fox, that came from the covert, did penetrate to his ears through the thickness of the pane; he looked up, seemed to stare at her, and she fled.

CHAPTER IV

A maid deposited a can of hot water, and knocked at Mrs. Elles' door next morning, as the latter had desired her to do over night. Thinking, perhaps, of her faithful Jane, she sleepily called out "Come in!" from force of habit.

The servant stared at the new inmate of the "Heather Bell," unrestrainedly, as she lay there, in bed, her pretty hair ruffled over her forehead, and the disfiguring spectacles lying on the dressing-table beside her. Mrs. Elles did not know what hour it was; she had left her watch behind her in Newcastle, but she was sure she had been lying awake for hours and hours, listening to the bewildering chorus of birds from the pear tree all round her window, and the rub-a-dub of the churning in the yard below.

"Nine o'clock, you say? Why did you not call me earlier? Has Mr. Rivers gone out sketching already?" was her first thoughtless question.

"Yes, ma'am!"

"Does he go every day?" Mrs. Elles further enquired, forgetting, too, to correct the title.

"Every day, unless it rains."

"And what does he do then?"

"Bides at home and pents."

72

Mrs. Elles was recalled to a sense of the impropriety of all these questions on her part, and she dismissed the girl haughtily. She dressed, put back her hair, and resumed her spectacles with a sigh, but without hesitation. She had no full length mirror here to show her the oddish, but not ungraceful appearance that she presented, for, although her facial beauties were temporarily obscured, her slight figure in its boyish trim had a certain attractiveness of its own. The average glance would cursorily set her down for a well-grown school girl, labouring under a temporary affection of the eyes, which was, however, not serious enough to interfere with her health and spirits.

After she had breakfasted, in pursuance of a plan that she had conceived, she got one of the landlady's sons to drive her over to Barnard Castle, where she purchased an outfit of drawing materials and a cheap Student's Manual of Art. In the afternoon—Mr. Rivers, she ascertained, never came back to the inn for luncheon, but took out some sandwiches, which he ate, if he remembered to do so—she selected a point of view, just by the bridge over the Greta, a stone's throw from the inn. She there began a study of the Student's Manual, and her own capabilities in the way of handling a pencil.

She had had no previous training, but she was just clever enough to produce a not utterly despicable result, and that was all she had dared to hope. She did not expect to see the artist that day, nor did she; but she was not bored, although she had no one to speak to, and, to a woman of her temperament, that fact alone would, in the ordinary course of things, have engendered complete despair. But then, things were not by any means in their ordinary course; the very air was full of adventure and excitement of the vaguest and most blameless nature. Mrs. Elles had no precise idea of what it was that she hoped and desired, and with the unconscious diplomacy of the dual mind, took very good care not even to formulate it.

But next day, as she sat on her camp stool, with a half finished sketch of the picturesque stone bridge across her knee, she felt, rather than heard, Mr. Rivers coming down the road behind her. Hastily she pushed her spectacles back into position over her eyes, and turned a very little in his direction.

"Good morning," he said, pleasantly enough.

"Good morning," she said, half rising. "I have been wanting to thank you so much all these days."

"For what?"

"For recommending this delightful inn to me, of course."

The spectacles interfered somewhat with the arch play of her eyebrows as she said this, very demurely.

He looked, if possible, a little abashed.

"Well, I can hardly say that I recommended it. In fact, I rather tried to warn you off it. I thought it would be too rough for a lady. I am glad you find it pretty comfortable."

"I only wanted quiet, like you," she said. "I have been very much overwrought, lately, and this is the very thing for me. You see, I am trying to occupy myself a little!" she pointed to her sketch.

"But you have not got the best point of view—not by any means," he exclaimed. "I am not venturing to look at your drawing, of course, but I know——"

"Oh, please!" she said, holding up the sketch. "If only you would, I should be so grateful."

He looked at her drawing carefully and critically.

"You really have not at all a bad idea; but I should sacrifice that sketch if I were you—you have not got very far on with it, and the abutment of the bridge comes so badly in it—and begin a new one, here, further down . . . I will show you."

Without any exhibition of the amateur's stubbornness, she rose cheerfully, and allowed him to move her camp-stool for her to a place where the abutment presented a more graceful aspect. Little did she care for abutments, but she was delighted that he should take an interest in her work. He stood looking at the view he had chosen for her with professionally half-closed eyes.

"It comes better from here, don't you think!" he said.

"Oh, I don't think—I know nothing about it!" she cried. "I am only a beginner, and have never had any instruction at all!"

"Yes, I can see that," he replied drily, "but let me tell you, you haven't at all a bad notion of per-

spective! Plenty of people learn perspective painfully and never get as near it as that. I have always
held that perspective came by nature—I never learned
it, at any rate!"

He looked down at her then with considerable
benignity, as supporting a beloved theory, adding,
however, sharply, "I cannot understand how you
manage to see through those. Well, persevere! You
will find it come very nicely like that—And now, I
must be off—!"

"Are you going to that place where I saw you the
other day?" she enquired, with eager simplicity.
Since he spoke to her as if he considered her a schoolgirl, she would use the privileges appertaining to that
inchoate and irresponsible age towards him. At the
same time she shot a glance—not precisely of the
schoolgirl—in his direction, that was only rendered
void and vain by the smoky barrier interposed between
it and its object. In another minute she would have
summoned up courage to ask him if she might go to
Brignal with him, but he nonplussed her by raising
his cap, in token of farewell, and making a quick,
decisive movement across the bridge, as if he had not
heard her question.

She sat down resignedly in the new place he had
chosen for her, and made a few ineffectual strokes
with her pencil. To herself she muttered, "I wonder
how old?—a forward sixteen?—or a stunted eighteen,
perhaps?" words which had obviously no reference to
her drawing. She knitted her brows with all the

petty rage of the amateur; she aggressively sharpened her pencil and broke it, five times over; and at last, in a fit of temper consistent with the extreme juvenility of Rivers' presumed conception of her, tossed both the sketches into the Greta and watched them float easily away on the changing ripples.

"They will go down to where he is," she thought, full of a sense of the continuity of this stream flowing down that long dark glen leading to the light, where the master sat in his earthly paradise and recked not of his hopeless and despairing pupil.

"And why should he?" was her next reflection. "What a fool I am! But, indeed, a man like that is wasted on Nature, and Nature is evidently the only thing in the world that he cares for!"

Signs of unusual activity, and the smell of piping hot pie-crust greeted her when she went rather drearily back to the inn for her luncheon.

The bare, barn-like room was swept and garnished unusually. Great bunches of pink phlox, tied up with blue ribbons, were nailed into the corners and clashed with the lavender-coloured plaster; festoons of miscellaneous verdure were disposed across and all round the severe texts on the walls, and the terrors of "Prepare to meet thy God!" were veiled in purple fuchias and yellow marigolds. Her humble little lunch of cold British beef was laid for her, as usual, on a corner of the tressel table. The landlady of the "Heather Bell" came up to her as she was eating it, and her buxom arms were floured to the elbow, where a couple of currants were sticking in token of her recent occupation.

"We're that busy," she began, breathlessly. "We've got a cheap trip comin' fra' Barney Cassel this afternoon—near a hundred of 'em. I've baked thirty pies this very morning, and I was a-goin' to ask ye, Miss, if ye would mind gettin' yer dinner along o' the gentleman, for we shall na have seen the last on 'em till fair on to neet, and a tarrible mess they'se leave behind, I'se warrant 'em!"

Mrs. Elles' heart leaped, but she controlled her emotions and recalled the busy landlady, who had turned away as if the point was settled.

'Stop, Mrs. Watson—I am not sure that Mr. Rivers will like that!"

"Hout, lassie, then he'll just hae to put up wi' it! Leave him alone; I'll settle it wi' him."

"No, no!" dubiously.

"But I tell ye, ye must! We canna let ye have the room to-day, and that's flat!" repeated Mrs. Watson, sturdily, but without acrimony.

"Then I won't dine at all!" Mrs. Elles said, vehemently, but without decision.

She took up her hat, however, and walked slowly down the road to the Park Gates, rang the porter's bell, and was admitted. She went along the Broad Walk and through the yew grove, till she came to the right bank of the Greta, which flows through the Park of Rokeby on its way to join the Tees, just outside its limits.

She sat there for the whole of the afternoon, watching the owner of the Park and the Hall, whose smoke she could just see curling through the trees, as he waded about in his own river, in his loose india-rubber leggings, and caught his own trout in calm and contentment.

She was surprised to find how little bored she was. She did not intend to be. She made a point of being amused by the varied aspects of nature—free untrammelled exuberant nature—that were being presented to her. It was the very quintessence of wild life that surrounded her now. The ceaseless ripple of the river was relieved by the frequent splash and flicker of the enormous trout that tenanted it, as they rose flippantly to the surface or were dragged there by the imperious rod. Queer cries, that came out of the brake behind her, betokened the sad little dramas of animal life that were going on behind the leafy screen. The squeak of the rabbit at its last stand before the murderous weasel; the scuffle of the little birds upon whom the sparrow-hawk dashed, leaving those sad heaps of grey, white-rooted feathers to tell the tale of rapine, came to her ears, as did the more peaceful coo of the wood-pigeons from the coverts of thorn and hazel on the other and steeper side of the river. "Milk the coo, Katie!" such was Mrs. Watson's homely interpretation of their cry, and she found herself repeating it over and over again to herself.

Everything pleased her and responded to the mood she was in. There was a "distant dearness" in the hills that bowered in this happy valley, "a secret sweetness in the stream" that flowed to a place two miles off, where, indeed, she would fain have been, but that would come in time. She was full of a great peace. She thought she could almost feel the wrinkles of ennui and harassment slowly fading out of her forehead, and the tangle of rebellious nerves that had driven her away from her home smoothing themselves out, as she sat there, and, like Words-worth's Lucy, allowed "beauty born of murmuring sound to pass into her face." True to herself, she immediately forced a personal application, and reduced Nature into subserviency to the Human Interest. With a well pointed tag of verse she pointed and emphasized the sensations of Phœbe Elles now become the motive and main pivot of the most beauti-ful landscape in the world.

For the moment with her the health motive reigned supreme. She was no longer a runaway wife, she was an invalid profiting by change of air. Nothing was going to happen; let the world stand still while she was happy for the first time in her life. Surely she had a right to a little happiness!

She stayed there until the one red-trunked fir tree, up there on the heights by Mortham Peel, caught and glowed in the sunset light, and the damp mists began to rise in their proportion from this enormous area of rank foliage that engendered them. The fisherman put up his rod and went home. The doves cooed in a continuous monotone. Mrs. Elles

knew well enough by all these signs that it was getting late. As she loitered slowly home, she could
hear on the other side of the high Park wall the
noisy passage of char-à-bancs, and vans full of jovial
people, whose hoarsely shouted refrain of "She's a
jolly good fellow!" testified to their appreciation of
Mrs. Watson's thirty pies and cheerful welcome.
Peace was evidently restored, and Mr. Rivers would
have had his dinner quietly and be done by the time
she got back. She was not at all hungry; she would
have a glass of milk and a sandwich in her room.
She was a woman who habitually took strong coffee
twice a day.

"How changed I am!" she thought.

The party of trippers had gone, silence reigned,
but the open door of the meeting room, as she crossed
the hall on her way in, showed a wild and hideous
scene of tea-stained table-cloths and broken meats.

"An awful sight, isn't it?" asked Mr. Rivers, who
was standing—a dark shape filling up the space, at
the door of his own room. Then he hesitated a
little. . . .

"Mrs. Watson tells me that I am to have the
pleasure of your company to-night?"

His tone was absolutely courteous, but she failed to
detect any very strong cordiality in it, as was of
course natural.

"He thinks me an awful bore!" she thought, but
what she said was "I thought you would have dined
by this time."

"Of course I have not," he replied, raising his eyebrows, "but I believe dinner is just ready."

He held the door of the sitting-room wide open for her with just the right gesture and the right attitude of courtly invitation.

"I must go and take off my hat," she said, quite humbly, and ran upstairs.

Indeed, she had given fate every chance of depriving her of this pleasure. Fate was against her—or for her! She conscientiously rubbed her hair flat with a wet brush, disposed her spectacles squarely over her eyes and walked demurely downstairs to join Mr. Rivers.

"Yes, it is fate!" she said to herself again, as she sat down opposite him. The slatternly maid removed the dull pewter cover from three sad and starved looking chops and the shapeless ghosts of three potatoes, and then shuffled out of the room like an escaped convict. It was not luxury, but it was Paradise.

Still, in order to lead up to a question she wished to ask him about the black-browed girl who had waited on her a day or two before, Mrs. Elles remarked, carelessly, "I don't think much of the service at this inn; do you?"

He shrugged his shoulders. "I think I warned you not to expect much, did I not? But it is clean, at any rate, and that's all I care for."

"Oh, yes, it is quite charming. But still that clumsy servant must be rather a trial to you?"

"I am not fidgety," he said. "And I have taught

her not to touch my painting things. That is the
main point, for me. I had to be very strict about
that, for she completely ruined a drawing of mine,
once."

"How?" asked Mrs. Elles, interested.

"Oh, with the enquiring thumb of her class. It
lighted on the sky, unfortunately. She was dreadfully sorry about it, and actually brought me five
shillings and asked me if that would cover the
damage? You know it takes an expert to handle a
drawing as the painter of it would like to see it
handled. I am quite beside myself sometimes, when
I have to stand by and see intending purchasers take
hold of them, and run their thumbs into the corners,
and make creases in the paper! But one can say
nothing, of course."

She looked at the artist's own hands, and noticed
the way he took hold of things. His long, thin,
eminently prehensile fingers had a way of deliberately grasping an object in exactly the place where
the eye had previously decreed that it should be
grasped, without false shots or clumsy bungling of
any kind. It was a hand skilled in all mechanical
exercises, and apt at all delicate manoeuvres. It was
firm and strong, too—the hand of an artist and a
craftsman.

He did not seem to notice that she was looking at
his hands and neglecting to carry on the conversation; he had a trick of becoming absorbed in his own
thoughts at a moment's notice, so she had observed;

but he could be recalled just as easily and quickly.
She went on presently—

"That other girl's hands wouldn't make a mark,
would they? She seems rather superior."

"Who? The landlady's niece. Oh, she has been
at school in London, and is quite a personage—
plays this piano in the winter, and reads 'George
Eliot.'"

"I don't like her," said Mrs. Elles, "and she
doesn't like me."

"Nonsense!" he said, as if he were speaking to a
child; "Jane Ann is a very good girl indeed."

"Her head is too big for her body," Mrs. Elles
added, irrelevantly; "and I can't bear people who
are what is called above their station. A little education is a dangerous thing, I think, if it makes
people priggish and stunts their growth. I notice
she never looks one straight in the face."

"Why should she?" said the painter, unexpectedly,
and that rather put an end to the conversation.

"I think of going and taking a little walk in the
Park, if I can, after dinner," Mrs. Elles presently
remarked, wishing to show that she did not intend to
be a nuisance. "I have spent the whole afternoon
there, already, and I think it must be most mysterious
and wonderful at night."

"Are you not afraid to meet the ghost?"

"I should perfectly love to meet it!" cried she,
clasping her hands together.

"Then, of course, you won't. 'The White Lady

of Mortham'—I believe here she is called by the less
poetical name of the 'Dobie!'—won't show unless she
is to produce her effect and frighten you."

"I might frighten her," said Mrs. Elles, still harping on her own grotesque personal metamorphosis,
which was ever present to her mind.

But he did not take her up and she went on—

"The Park reminds me of the Forest in Undine.
Do you remember Küheleborn and the mysterious
faces that used to come out of the Forest and peer in
at the window of the fisherman's cottage?"

She glanced as she said this at the window of the
room they were sitting in, the blind of which was not
drawn down, as usual. She could only suppose that
it was a fad of his, and that he had given the maid
orders to leave it so. She had not been in his company a couple of hours without realizing that he was
full of fads.

'The black night comes straight against the
pane," she went on dreamily. "All the ghosts in
the forest may come and look in on us if they choose!
I rather like it, I have a weakness for ghosts. I feel
as if the White Lady of Mortham—I prefer to call
her the spirit of the Greta—might be looking in on
us now!"

She gave a little shudder, part real, part affected.

"I did see a woman's face at the window—not now,
but last night!" mused the painter with a touch of
unexpected seriousness that finished the subjugation
of his sentimental listener. "I saw it quite clearly,

as I see you now. It was wild and distraught looking, as a spirit's face should be———"

"Oh, you believe in ghosts, then? I am so glad."

"A landscape painter must personify Nature a
little, don't you think? He should raise altars to
propitiate the divinities of rivers and groves, so
important for him. The Greta especially has a very
wicked tutelary spirit, who needs keeping in a good
humour, only I have not time."

"What do you mean?"

"It has its bore, like the Severn, or the Seine its
Mascaret, and comes down occasionally without the
slightest warning, like a brown wall, and sweeps
everything, including landscape painters, before it."

"You have seen it?"

"No, I have only heard of it, as yet. And I hope,
when it comes, it will not take me unawares—sitting
in the bed of the river as I so often do! I should
have to run—or rather leap for it!"

"It is a danger!" she said, quite seriously.

"Oh, one of the very few that beset the artistic field
of battle," he said, laughing; "there are not many.
It teaches us painters to 'look alive' and cultivate
some of the qualities of a sailor. I do have to get
into such funny places to paint from sometimes—
places where I literally must hang on by my eyelids!
. . . Now shall I ring for Dorothy to bring in some
other luxuries?"

Dorothy, summoned by a handbell, shambled in,
bringing a bleached and tremulous cornflour pudding

and three doddering baked apples, and set them down solemnly before Mr. Rivers and Mrs. Elles. The infatuated woman did not mind—

"A jug of wine, a loaf of bread—and thou
    Beside me, singing in the Wilderness,
Oh, Wilderness were Paradise enow!"

But when the maid had cleared the table, in her own primitive, knock-me-down fashion, and replaced the white cloth by the hideous tapestry one, covered with its pattern of pink roses, faded and dulled, more-over, by the constant splashing of the painter's brush in the tumbler full of water which she, as regularly as clockwork, placed on the middle patch of flowers every evening, Mrs. Elles was suddenly overcome by an unusual sense of shyness. This man made her shy as no man before had ever done. He was so polite and yet so distant. His want of self-consciousness seemed a reproof to her imperious and pampered personality.

To cover it, she rose and shyly looked round the room that the artist had occupied year after year, and on which he had presumably impressed himself, his tastes, his prevailing habit of mind.

That habit, to judge by its chosen surroundings, was a very ascetic one; as different from her own as possibly could be imagined. This was a workroom pure and simple. Not an attempt had been made, it would seem, to redeem its humble, commonplace ugliness. Abraham, in coloured worsteds, complacently sacrificed Isaac, over the mantelpiece; Mrs. Elles would have covered the pair with an art rug of some sort. The frosted-sugar top of Mrs. Watson's wedding cake stood on the console; Mrs. Elles would, regardless of offence to the poor old lady, have requested her to remove it. Every other available table and cornice was heaped and piled with sketch books; easels and bulging umbrellas filled up all the four corners. There was a little stack of books on the mantelshelf, but not a single work of fiction was to be discerned among them. There was Shelley—just the watery, bloodless, spiritually intense poet that she would expect Rivers to appreciate. There were some flowers in a little china dog on the side table, garden flowers, phloxes and stocks, but these Mrs. Elles rightly attributed to the solicitude of the landlady's niece. The whole room was intensely significant to her of those qualities, which, with her trick of hasty generalization, she now chose to attribute to this man,—modesty, endurance, and self-abnegation, and a whole-souled devotion to his art and the purposes of his art.

There was the old-fashioned, silk-fluted piano on one side of the room, to which he had alluded, and she paused, with her hand on the curved lid.

"Oh, that has stood there ever since I first came here," the artist said; "I have never dared to open it. Jane Anne plays on it in the winter, I believe. This house, from its neighbourhood to the park, is so damp that I am sure that no piano could endure it

and live.   That is the worst of all embowering trees!
Have you noticed that one's notepaper becomes like
blotting paper?''

How should she notice, who had no notepaper of
her own, and wrote no letters?   She opened the
instrument and played a bar or two.

"Quite tolerable!" she pronounced.

He quietly put a chair in front of it, without saying anything, and she sat down and played a bit of
her favourite Chopin.

He thanked her, not very warmly.

"Don't you like Chopin?"

"He does me no good.   Too restless!   What is
the use of setting all one's nerves in an uproar, as he
does, and giving one no solution?   I confess that I
like music that resolves me.   Beethoven, for instance."

"Oh, Beethoven resolves you, does he?"   She
hardly knew what Rivers meant, but she knew that
she did not care for Beethoven.   "What a pity I don't
know any of him!   Is he—" she hesitated; she was
becoming shy of airing her tentative little theories to
this man whose culture, as she apprehended, had its
roots in tradition, in a knowledge far deeper than she
could claim for her own, mere "self-made" woman
that she was—"is he the landscape painter's musi-
cian, as Shelley is his poet?"

"I should say that Wordsworth was that, more
properly."

"I hate Wordsworth!" she answered, with vigour

and truth, "and as for Shelley, I should call him the
poet of physical geography!"

He laughed. "You don't care for atmospheric
effects in poetry, I see. You prefer Keats."

"Yes, I do. And as for putting on his tombstone
that his name was to be writ in water, I think that
would have suited Shelley far better. Keats' name
should have been written in blood—he was passionate.
. . . . Shall I try to sing something to you." Her
singing was nothing wonderful, but sweet and sympathetic and never out of tune. All her gifts were
natural, she had always been too restless to apply
herself to any but that of pose, which she had
brought to so high a pitch of perfection.

But the songs which she sang were the kind of songs
that Rivers seemed to like, for his brown eyes grew
soft and limpid and his face looked less set and more
open as he listened.

For this parity in their likings she had to thank
her husband, who, in the days when she had cared to
please him, had insisted on her cultivating an
acquaintance with the simple national airs of all
countries that he could join in. She felt, somehow,
that a little French repertory she had would not be
appropriate just now and refrained from producing it.

She sang on until the sound of shutters closing and
the tramp of heavy-booted men—the landlady's two
stalwart sons—trooping up to their beds in the attics,
warned them of the lateness of the hour according to
country canons,

"If you do care at all for my songs," she asked, deprecatingly, as he lit her candle for her at the foot of the stairs, "may I come and play for you again another evening?"

Her glance—both their glances, as she spoke, were irresistibly directed to that scene of havoc and disaster, the meeting-room, whose open door confronted them. It was swept and cleared now of the litter of the tea, and freshly sanded, but still as dreary and comfortless an abiding place as could well be imagined.

"You had better use my sitting-room in future—that is, if you will. That barrack of a room is not fit for anyone to inhabit. But you will not mind my working as usual, and then, I am afraid I get so absorbed that I cannot talk, or even be ordinarily civil!"

"Oh, may I really?" she cried. "I assure you I shall be quite happy sitting—beside you," she was going to say, but corrected it into "with my book!" Though where the literature was to come from that was to keep her quiet was more than she knew. Excepting the Shelley, Taine's "Historie de l'Esthétique Anglaise" was quite the lightest work on Rivers' mantelpiece, and she had had, of course, no books among her luggage.

"Very well, then, we will look upon that as settled," he said, shortly, and held out his hand again to say good-night.

"I will come in in the evenings, if you will let me,

when it really is melancholy in that big meeting-room, but during the day——"

"During the day I am generally out, so you will be able to have the room entirely to yourself," he rejoined, in his own disconcerting manner, and the candle he was holding seemed to her to light up a little flicker of something like amusement in his eyes.

"Yes, I know," she said, desperately, "at that place in the woods where I first met you. Has the foxglove grown again? I wanted to ask you. I shall come and see for myself some day."

She spoke with an assumed archness, with all the while a fearful stricture about the heart, lest she was alienating him by her boldness as of the schoolgirl she believed him to believe her to be. Her candle-stick, which she had now taken from his hand, trembled in her own.

"Do!" he replied, civilly, in a tone absolutely devoid of all enthusiasm. Jane Anne crossed the hall as they loosed their hands. "And now, good-night!"

Mrs. Elles waited a whole day before she profited by the artist's invitation to visit him at the place where he worked. She was rewarded for her discretion, for, at dinner that very evening, he asked her coolly why she had not been? So, the day after, she walked over to Brignal and stayed full fifteen min-utes at his side. She managed to be so little of a nuisance that, next day, she was emboldened to take over her drawing materials at the artist's own suggestion, and began a series of minute and painstaking sketches of the vegetation of the immediate foreground, to be used by him afterwards as memoranda. He had admitted that it would be useful to him.

Then it became a settled thing that she should walk over every day after twelve o'clock, and take him his letters and the papers which were left at the "Heather Bell" by the postman from Barnard Castle quite an hour after his departure. Thus the compromising fact of her own total dearth of correspondence escaped his attention, if, indeed, he should take cognizance of such a detail.

She marvelled at his extraordinary power of detachment. Did matters merely mundane ever impress him? Did anything, humanly speaking, ever put him out, except in so far as it interfered with his work? Was he literally, as he used to say himself, only a registering machine of effects and views, pledged to render an actual transcript of Nature, seen, as is the condition of all art, through a temperament, but a temperament merely receptive, limpid, clear, and untroubled by the waves of passionate human yearnings and desires? There was actually something of what Browning calls the "terrible composure" of Nature about him, she thought, a patient, broad-minded, magnificent way of regarding things entailed by a continual contemplation of her vastness, her implacabilities, her unconscious cruelties and brutalities. She never could forget Rivers' behaviour in a thunderstorm that overtook them one

Sunday afternoon by Scargill Tower. Out came the sketch book, quick as the lightning that seemed to flicker in its horribly malicious way down by the stone wall that edged the road they were walking along.

"I must have that!" he murmured. "By Jove!"

He actually stopped, and stood still on the white road among the falling thunderbolts, as it seemed to her. She stopped too and opened her puny umbrella, trying to ward off some of the heavy rain-drops from the leaves of the sketch book. It never even seemed to occur to the artist that she might be afraid, or wet. She was not afraid, such was the contagion of his courage, but she was wet through. The rain splashed on his paper in spite of her efforts, and blended together colours that the artist hastily cast on, into shapes unexpected by him, but still a memorandum of the breathing light and steam of mist over there by Cotherstone, where the storm that oppressed them now was passing off, had been secured. It was quite worth her while; she had the satisfaction of knowing that Rivers could not think her a coward. He did not tell her so, but took her pluck and superiority to feminine weakness as a matter of course.

She was driven to try and please him by the achievement of new virtues, entirely foreign to her nature. She laughed, sometimes, when she thought of herself, the leader of what there was of advanced literary thought in Newcastle—the lady who could discuss the higher ethics, and expound the morbidities of Amiel and Meredith to a select cultured circle, —being forced to recommend herself to the man she loved by a display of mere physical courage, and even manual dexterity. Yes, she found she could really please Rivers best by attending to his bridge for him.

This was a rough arrangement of stepping stones, which the painter had made for himself before he came there, by manipulating the loose boulders of the river bed a little. It constituted a short cut from the inn to his sketching place, and saved him a mile's walk at least. He had taken good care to give the stream play between the rough piers of his bridge as it were, leaving enormous gaps and chasms, but still the river resented being interfered with, and altered the position of the stones and washed them away sometimes in the night, of malice prepense, as Mrs. Elles declared. She found plenty to do every day in replacing the stones that had been dislodged and adding new ones, and worked away merrily, thinking of Cincinnatus and his plough, and of the picture Dante began to paint for Beatrice, in this connection.

"The very first time the river comes down," Rivers prophesied, "all our work will have to be done over again. There will be no bridge left!"

She could, of course, have shown herself a great deal more agile without her spectacles, which hampered her continually, but she had made a point of never removing them in sight of her fellow creatures, and only ventured to push them up over her brows when she was alone with only cows and squirrels for witnesses. She clung to them, as a saint might hug his cross or an anchorite his hair-shirt. They symbolized the purity of her intentions, they were her armour of honourable woman and loyal wife to Mortimer; her ticket-of-leave indeed, when she thought of him and all that he implied. She put the odious and tiresome things on every morning, as a knight endures his panoply or buckles on his shield of proof, and honourably continued to wander about in a cold, blue, local atmosphere of her own, aware only through her other senses of the glow of yellow light and hope that lay outside, besieging the frigid unreceptive discs of her self-imposed barrier in vain.

'It is hateful, but it just saves the situation," she would say to herself. "And it makes me free. I can say what I like and do what I like, so long as I don't look what I like!" But, indeed, there were times when that last item of forbearance seemed the hardest item of all.

Yes, the odd and distressing thing was that, in consequence of her wearing them, she had never really seen Rivers' face, and, worse than that even, he had never seen hers. He betrayed no curiosity, no desire at all to see it, and his indifference affronted her vanity not a little. There must be something left out of a man, she argued, who could take pleasure in the society of such an example of unsexed, negative womanhood as she presented. For she was sure that he did take pleasure in her society, now, in an odd, misogynistical way—that he was glad when he saw her come stumbling and tottering across the bridge of slippery stones to him of a morning, sometimes even staying herself by one hand on the moist slabs of moss-grown rock that lay in her passage, the other holding high and dry her budget of letters and news. His voice, as he bade her good morning, sometimes even without looking up—he was so occupied—testified to a certain pleasurable anticipation of her company, or at least she thought so.

'Oh, only your bridge-maker!" she used to say to him as she came up, frankly accepting the position. "I have put three new stones in to-day."

"He doesn't treat me as if I were a woman at all!" she said to herself bitterly, "and I believe I am less of a woman than I was. I am more manly; I think less of my looks and more of my muscles. I never even knew I had any, till I came here!" She sighed. "Yes, I see I must cultivate this aspect of me, and keep the eternal feminine relentlessly down. It would frighten him, or at any rate disturb him. Would it? Ah, I dare not try. I must stay as I am, absolutely non-committal!"

She sighed again.

CHAPTER V

Mrs. Elles had arrived at Rokeby on a Monday. When Sunday came round, she had been prepared for the usual flying in the face of Philistine custom and observance that prevailed in her own circle and imagined that the artist would go out to paint as usual or perhaps as a concession to popular prejudice stay and work indoors. But to her intense surprise and amusement, eleven o'clock on Sunday morning found her murmuring the Litany by the side of the artist in the parish church, among the placid farmers and their complacent, Sunday-bedizened wives. Mr. Rivers, it seemed, was in the habit of going to church every Sunday, and, when she discovered this, it had seemed quite natural to go with him, though it was the first time she had been inside the walls of a church since her marriage. The service, to her mind unblunted by custom, seemed very picturesque; so was the church, a beautiful specimen of pure early Gothic, and the figure of this grave, handsome man, standing by her side, with his dark head relieved against the white plaster background, most natural of all.

"If anyone had told me, a month ago," she

thought, "that I should be doing this, I believe I should have laughed in his face."

She felt happy, but a little out of place, and looked it, perhaps, for the vicar, a stolid, white-bearded, dignified man, stared at her over the pulpit cushion, discreetly, while a thin, little, sharp-nosed lady, presumably of some authority in the congregation, did so, too, indiscreetly. Jane Anne, who played the harmonium, was discretion itself and never even glanced her way, but Mrs. Elles thought she read excommunication and condemnation in every turn of her not too supple wrist.

"So you go to church every Sunday?" Mrs. Elles said to Rivers, as they walked down the path and away together. "Somehow I thought artists——"

"Never went to church?" He finished her sentence for her. "Well, I don't know. I don't do it as a religious observance, exactly, I am afraid. I do it because I like it, here in the country. Besides," he added, "it is a beautiful church!"

Mrs. Elles, who considered herself an agnostic, was satisfied, by this speech, that Rivers' church-going was the result of his indulgence of æsthetic needs rather than spiritual ones; though, indeed, she would have been quite ready to embrace any faith to which he should pronounce his adhesion.

"How picturesque the Vicar's white hair is!" she remarked, aloud. "Do you know him?"

"Oh, yes; Mr. Popham. He will come now to call on you, since you have been to call on him."

"Good heavens! Does he go to see you?" she cried, with what would appear to be uncalled-for emphasis.

"Yes; he comes now and again, but I am always out. We generally meet somewhere about the place, and then we get on very well. He had a tiresome habit of coming and looking over my shoulder at Brignal, but I have trained him not to stay very long."

"Is he married?" she enquired, eagerly.

"Yes; that was his wife in the pew to the right."

"Does she come and look over your shoulder, too?"

"She takes a tender interest in my work," Rivers said, laughing. "She is by way of being an artist herself, you see."

"That little, starved, angular, high-cheek-boned woman, without a touch of artistic feeling about her, and bonnet strings of the wrong colour!"

"You must not go by bonnet strings entirely. They are a matter of convention. Mrs. Popham has a very good eye for colour, let me tell you, only she is dreadfully shy of publicity, and would think it quite improper to exhibit. One never knows into what vessels the spirit will be poured. I go in in the evening sometimes and look over her sketches; she is very good to me. She walked all the way to Brignal once, with a cork mat for me to put my feet on!"

"And did you use it? I never see you!"

"It bores me—that sort of thing bores me. You will find it in my sketching bag, though."

"What is the good of carrying it there and back every day, if you don't use it?"

"Ah, but in case she were to come, I would hastily adjust it under my feet, so as not to hurt her feelings. But she is not likely to walk so far."

"I suppose she is perfectly devoted to you, like everybody else?"

He did not take any notice of her remark.

"So is Jane Anne!" she next observed.

"Jane Anne is a very clever girl," replied Rivers, too single-minded and too busy to see the construction that might be put on the turn of his phrase.

"She may be a mute inglorious Milton!" remarked Mrs. Elles, "but I am sure she is not a nice nature. She looks a potential murderess with those lowering brows. As for Mrs. Popham, I don't know her."

"Ah, but you will!"

"I hope sincerely I shall not," Mrs. Elles muttered, under her breath. Mrs. Popham might be a noble soul, and a very fair water-colour artist, but still a woman with surely an enquiring mind and a scent for irregular situations.

She began to dread the Pophams and Jane Anne, and to regard them as natural enemies. Jane Anne she could not avoid meeting about the house, and the girl was so antipathetic to her that she made a point of not encountering her eyes, and did this so obviously as to provoke an enmity which, possibly, had so far only existed in her own imagination.

The vicar and his wife, whether by accident or

design, never crossed her path.   One day, when she
made her accustomed pilgrimage to Brignal, she saw
that Rivers was not alone, and, at first, thought it
was the sacerdotal back that blotted the fair landscape.   But it was not Mr. Popham's; it was that of
the opulent farmer on whose land Rivers had taken
up his position, and with whom the dispute of the
pig's unlawful consumption of Naples yellow had long
been arranged amicably.   Farmer Ward was standing
by the side of the artist, passing his felt wide-awake
from one hand to the other and staring up into the sky
as if he expected the first rain-drop of the autumn to
fall on his expectant features from moment to moment.

"No, it won't rain to-day," Rivers was saying,
decidedly, "but you had better make the most of the
opportunity, for I won't vouch for this spell of
weather lasting."

"Aal reet, Measter, I'll take yer word for't. . . .
Ye see, Miss," he turned to the young woman who
now approached, "artisses and sech like, they seem
to know the meanin' of it all!—" he waved his hand
comprehensively round the horizon,—"a deal better
nor we do."

"We are bound to notice it," said Rivers, indulgently.   "You see, the weather affects our crops,
too!"   He pointed to his canvas.

"Ha! Ha! Measter, I takes ye!   And if I might be
so bold as to ask, what might ye happen to get for that
little pectewer there?   A matter o' fifteen shillin'—
or saxteen, maybe."

"My good man, how do you think I could possibly live at that rate? I have been at this thing a month already!"

"Ay, ay, Measter, but then, some folks is pertickler slow!"

"There's a snub for me!" whispered Rivers to Mrs. Elles.

"But it's a grand pectewer, all the same," continued the honest farmer, "though I'd like it better a deal, I must say, if there was a bit o' life in it, just a hen and chicken preening about maybe, or a bit doggie, ye knaw, or even the young leddie here! . . . Well, I'll just be going now, I'm thinkin'!"

He touched his cap and withdrew, tactfully, conscious that the "gentry" might perhaps be getting a little tired of him.

"Why do you never put people into your pictures?" Mrs. Elles enquired. "I confess I am like Farmer Ward; I should like it better, too!"

"Somehow, I never care much for the human interest in landscape."

"Or in life either?" Mrs. Elles hazarded. It was the same remark she had made to Egidia.

"I don't know anything about that," he replied, distantly, "but I think the introduction of figures is always somewhat of an insult to landscape. One ought to be able to make a transcript of nature interesting without the adventitious aid of figures, it seems to me, though certainly Turner had no such theory. There is generally a boy and a kite, or a man and a dog in the foreground of his pictures. There is often a suggestion of cruelty, of torture of animals that I could wish away, for instance——"

"Yes, you do hate people!" Mrs. Elles insisted, unconsciously cutting short his little dissertation on his idol, Turner, far too impersonal in its application to interest her. "You have all the instincts of a recluse, although you force yourself to be civil to bores when they come your way. Tell me, didn't you hate me when I first came?"

'You took me by storm rather," he admitted. "You were so rapid in your tactics that you didn't even give me time to harden my heart against you. Of course I am speaking of you as a mere tourist, as I thought you were the first time I saw you. And I was rather rude to you at first?"

"Very," she said. "You did your best to put me off the inn, but you are not sorry now that you failed, are you?"

"Of course I am not!" he replied, cordially, and it was quite the nicest and most encouraging thing he had ever said to her.

"It seems to me that I have frightened away your other bore—the Vicar," she said, carelessly. "He never comes here, and she has never called on me, as you said she would. Not that I think you mind not seeing anyone! Yes, you are an arrant hermit at heart—Shelley must have meant you when he wrote Alastor—the Spirit of Solitude. I was reading that the other day in your Shelley; I am studying Shelley, now.''

''I admit that my instincts are unsociable,'' he said, with his brush between his teeth. ''I don't see how I am to help it. The conditions of a landscape painter's life make it necessarily a very solitary and inhuman one. You see I am in the country for the greater part of the year, and I never tell anyone where I go. I call my pictures by fanciful titles, so as not to have to put the name of the place in the catalogues. It is absurd, but then it happens to be the only way I can work. I generally don't open my lips from June to November, at least not to talk to persons of culture! The other sort doesn't matter.''

''Don't you care to study people?'' she said.

''It is my business to study the physiognomy of clouds, the character of tree trunks, not faces!''

''Don't speak so ferociously!'' she said laughingly. ''You mean that your only books are—not women's looks. It is Nature who is—your mistress——''

''Yes, and a nice capricious mistress she is, and very hard her service!''

''But she never did betray the heart that loved her —we have that on good authority!''

''Betray—no, but she does lead him a dance!'' the artist exclaimed passionately. ''She rains her tears on him, she blows hurricanes on him, she plagues him with flies, and, what is worse, wasps—she lets him break his back, and contract his chest with stooping, the better to deal with her. She is never the same

for two minutes together. She is exacting and
exclusive. 'Thou shalt have no other mistress but
me!' she says. 'You shall dance attendance on all
my moods, and submit to all my caprices, and you
shall go on trying to paint the unpaintable all your
life, and die before you have succeeded in doing it!'"

The painter, having grown a little serious and
excited over his own tirade, ended it with a little laugh
at himself, and she murmured with apparent inconsequence, "Oh, I think it such a pity—such a waste!"

"What do you mean?" he asked her, negligently,
and stayed not for an answer—it was a little way he
had. She would have been ashamed to admit to him
what her meaning had been; that he was still young,
that he was handsome, that, in her opinion, such a
man was thrown away on the service of Nature. She
changed the conversation by offering to read him some
passages from the Newcastle paper.

He nodded in assent. She first gathered and
fastened two large fern fronds behind each ear, as a
clerk his pen, to keep away the flies which Rivers'
mistress Nature continued to send him. She felt
herself already so hideously travestied, that an
added touch of grotesqueness or so did not matter.
Then she began to read aloud in her quick, impulsive
way. She had not read more than a few sentences,
when she stopped suddenly. The painter might, or
might not, have been attending to her, but the sudden cessation of her voice inevitably excited his
attention.

"Well?" he asked her sharply.

"I stopped.   It was getting so dull in that part of the paper," she said, confusedly, bent on herself getting the gist of a certain paragraph that had caught her eye.

It was an account of an archæological meeting that had recently been held in Newcastle, where Mr. Mortimer Elles had seconded the motion of somebody or other, and had "given an exceedingly humorous turn" to the debate.

She pored over it with a certain sense of bitterness, mingled with relief.

"So he is cheerful enough to make bad jokes! He is getting on all right.   I need not have troubled to be anxious!   He will have told all my friends and his that his gadding fool of a wife is away amusing herself on a visit.   He is quite clever enough to invent some excuse like that!   Men don't care to admit that they have been run away from!"

Mr. Rivers had meanwhile idly taken up the few letters she had brought and laid down beside him as usual, ready to his hand.   He was quite capable of leaving them for hours unopened, to her continual surprise and somewhat to her annoyance.   She could not understand dilatoriness in such matters.   But he was reading one now, of which the immense signature inevitably caught her eye.   It was Egidia's real name —Alice Giles—which she happened to know.

"I—had a few letters this morning," she remarked, pointedly, "but they were all very dull."

"This one of mine is rather amusing," returned the guileless artist. "It is from my cousin—I daresay you know her by the name she writes under—'Egidia.' "

"Why, I told you I did when I first came here!" she exclaimed. "Don't you remember? It is through Egidia that we know each other. And is that from her? Oh, do, if you can, read me some of it."

Rivers tossed the letter into her lap.

"Read it all, if you like. It is a lively account of her Northern experiences. There seem to be some odd types in Newcastle, to judge by what she says!"

Thus empowered, Phœbe Elles devoured the letter. A great many of her friends were mentioned in it—the poet, Miss Drummond, and Mrs. Poynder, while there was a whole page entirely devoted to the muse of Newcastle.

"I met her at a lecture I was giving. Somebody or other on the platform introduced us. I had noticed her big eyes fixed on me, and her lips parted, following every word I said. It was flattering. She implored me to call. It was because I wrote books. I went because I liked her. She was an audience in herself! And her home! She has, I could see, a hard fight of it, poor little thing, to cultivate culture there. It was quite pathetic to see her straining every nerve to be modern and morbid and blasée, as she thinks we are in London. But give me the provinces for morbidity and unconscious Ibsenism! In spite of her amusing little affectations and preciousnesses, she is a dear little woman, and I think I shall ask her to come and stay with me in town—there is no one who would enjoy it more. If I do, you must come and meet her, you would like her. Pretty, too, though I don't think you care much about that. But so intensely interested in everything, so eager, too nervous, perhaps, to be soothing, a woman with more brain than temperament, and perhaps not so very much of that. Incapable, I should think, of a grande passion, but so anxious to have one! She is really to be pitied, I think, for the milieu she lives in is naturally abhorrent to one of her way of thinking. It is unfortunately that of nine-tenths of her class, the provincial women whose wits outrun their opportunities, and their aspirations their social possibilities. The type is so sadly common. English Madame Bovarys!

"She has a husband, but I did not see him. I was going to dine there to meet him, but she put me off. Perhaps he explains her. At any rate, from what she told me, and allowing for her very strong bias, he furnishes a very good excuse for any vagaries she may choose to commit. I believe he drinks, though she did not say so, and I respected her for not giving him away. An ordinary, middle-class brute, my dear Edmund, incapable of making even a goose happy, far less a woman who has educated herself into some of the subtleties of refinement.

"I don't know why I write all this about a perhaps not specially interesting person, but—her eyes—when she looked at me, and was not posing!—were the eyes of a prisoner. I see them now!"

Interesting as this document was to the subject of it, there were things about it that she did not quite like. She was silent for a little time, quite ten minutes. Then an irresistible impulse prompted her to say, "I happen to know that woman Egidia writes of, very well."

"Do you really? Then perhaps I ought not to have shown you the letter. One never knows."

"Oh, it doesn't matter. Phœbe Elles is one of my greatest friends—poor thing!"

"Why poor thing?"

"Oh, don't you know—she is one of the unhappy ones. She made the usual mistake, ten years ago, and has been repenting it ever since."

"What was that?"

"She married, that's all. They all do it. But Phœbe—my friend—complicated matters by marrying a man who was unworthy of her, though I am bound to say she was in love with him at the time she married him—or thought she was."

"If she thought so, she probably was," came from behind the easel.

"You think that proves it? Well, 'there is nothing either good or bad but thinking makes it so,' as Hamlet says. However, poor Phœbe Elles never knew what it was to be happy with the man she had chosen, though she had a vague idea that there was happiness somewhere in the world for her, as all we poor deluded fools of women have. There was nothing to make her happy, her life was starved, maimed, stunted—no colour in it at all. He had been married before, and the house was full of—what shall I call them?—obstacles to sentiment, in the shape of stepsons, and awful aunts——"

"How many aunts?"

"Only one, perhaps, but a horror, a perfectly awful woman! I shall never forget what I——"

She recovered herself and went on. "He—her husband was not unkind to her—not cruel, oh no, he took good care of that! but he contrived to make himself generally odious to her, and was antagonistic in every possible way——"

"Poor man!" ejaculated Rivers, in rather an incomprehensible manner.

"Then," Mrs. Elles went on, complacently, warming to her subject, "there came a final scene—such a sordid affair too, but it brought matters to a head. He sent away all her servants at an hour's notice, on the very flimsiest of pretexts, and when she ventured, very naturally, to expostulate, he turned round on her and insulted her grossly. He told her that he had never loved her, but had only married her out of pity, because she had so obviously set her affections on him; and that now, when she had entirely lost her looks and her youth——"

"The man must have been an utter cad."

"Yes, wasn't he!" exclaimed Mrs. Elles, delighted with his concurrence. "I was sure you would say

so. And then he abused her and called her names—
I am sure you could never bring yourself to use such
words as he used to Phœbe, to your wife!" She
snatched a fearful joy in the use of this phrase.

"No, I suppose not," said Rivers, who, for some
reason or other, did not seem inclined to treat this
story very seriously. "No, I suppose not, unless she
aggravated me beyond endurance. Then there is no
knowing what I might not say."

"Oh, yes, I quite understand, if she was a nagging
woman—but poor Phœbe—I know her so well—is
incapable of anything of the sort. She is too gentle
ever to make a fuss—and too dignified, besides. She
behaved simply like an angel all through—a perfect
martyr—she hardly said a word, but——"

"But what?"

"She did the only thing that was left her to do.
She left him."

"I call that rather a strong measure!"

"Oh, but alone! She did not leave him to go to
another man!"

Here the narrator of Phœbe Elles' fortunes stopped
and hesitated, a little overcome by a reflection that
necessarily occurred to her. Presently she resumed.
"Tell me, do you disapprove of poor Phœbe?"

"I can hardly form an opinion, can I, without
knowing the rights and wrongs of the case. But as
a general thing—Was he unfaithful to her?"

"No indeed, she only wishes he were!" Mrs. Elles
broke out, in an uncontrollable burst of candour.

"Now, I've shocked you," she said, looking up into his face and bitterly repenting her flippant outspokenness.

She went on, nervously, "You think she ought to have stuck to her post—ought not to have thrown up her cards like that."

She was translating the thoughts that she thought she could read on his face, and expostulating with them. "But still, you know, I had—a woman has surely a right to live her own life?"

"Only another phrase for selfishness," he retorted vehemently. "I hate it. Nobody has a right. Our lives are far too inextricably bound up with other lives for us to be able to assume complete freedom. We can't live our own lives—anything like it—for the very sufficient reason that it isn't to be done without spoiling other people's."

"But you seem to be able to manage to do it—live your own life—in the way I mean?" Mrs. Elles retorted, in the heat of argument, carrying the war into the enemy's country.

"I am a selfish beggar, I daresay, and don't practice what I preach."

He spoke sharply, bending down over his drawing, and she felt that she had been tactless to force the personal application.

She fancied that it was a touch of remorse at his curtness that made him say presently, in a benignant manner, "And what is your friend doing now?"

"Oh, Phœbe is all right for the present. She is

comparatively free; she does not have to sit opposite that man at breakfast every morning and listen to his coarse jokes and shiver at his impossible manners all day long. Now, she is in the society of—persons— congenial to her, at least. . . . I really must write to Phœbe.''

"Don't bring her here, for heaven's sake!" exclaimed Rivers, in real or affected alarm. "I should have to pack up my traps and bolt at once.''

"Oh, don't be afraid of poor Phœbe!" pleaded Mrs. Elles, not without some appreciation of the humour of the situation.

"You really wouldn't mind her if you knew her, I do assure you. Anyhow she wouldn't be any worse than I.''

"Oh, by Jove, though, but she would! A woman with a grievance is worse than anything else in the world.''

"Of course," Mrs. Elles replied, with some dignity —she did not like being snubbed, even in the person of her pseudo-self,—"I am not thinking of asking Phœbe here. I shall not even put an address when I write. I will send the letter to a friend to forward. You know I have my own reasons for not wishing the world to know where I am—at present.''

She made this statement for about the hundredth time, and the artist, as usual, completely ignored the allusion to her ambiguous position at Greta Bridge. And yet—he was obviously Bohemian, but of the world where such social rules are used to be enforced.

Another instance of the anomalousness of the artist nature!

She was not without tact, though she was so impulsive, and she now fancied, with the morbid and strained apprehension of one whose feelings are deeply engaged, that he was colder to her as they walked home together. She felt, in some indefinable way, that she had lost ground with him, and that her relation of and flippant comments on the story of Phœbe Elles had been the cause of it.

Her brain was working furiously as she walked on, treading rough and smooth at his side, her head bowed, and her eyes fixed on the enormous dried-up hoof marks that the cows had made on their way down the bank to drink at the ford, and into which she sedulously and mechanically made a point of fitting her little foot. Higher up, in the upland field, the footpath was so narrow that she was obliged to walk, not beside, but in front of Rivers, who was universally beloved of farmers because of his fixed principle never heedlessly to widen a footpath, though he would fight tooth and nail for the right of way. He and she were thus perforce more or less silent, but nothing would have surprised the modest artist more than to think that he himself was the subject of the cogitations that were agitating the brain behind the little knot of brown curls which was presented to his gaze, as they walked along about a yard apart from each other.

"I have vexed him—I have shocked him! He is a

gentleman, and he isn't modern, thank God!—and I have talked flippantly of things that a gentleman — and an old-fashioned gentleman—takes seriously. He has a higher moral standard than I have, and I have been fool enough to let him see that mine is lower. How tiresome!''

Then she consoled herself a little. ''He is sweet, but he is not quite human. It is very easy to talk about duties and self-effacement and all that, but what can a bachelor—he is not married, I am sure—what can a hermit, a recluse, know of the stress of life? How can a bachelor possibly enter into the agonies of the married? How can Alastor sympathize with the miseries of Incompatibles?''

''You must think me a very odd kind of woman,'' she said to him that night, adding hastily: ''That is, if you think about me at all.''

It was a habit of hers to put leading questions of this kind to the artist, but generally, like Pilate, she stayed not for an answer, and nervously hastened to fill up the pause by a further remark of her own. The result was a somewhat one-sided conversation.

''Yes, I am mysterious, I suppose,'' she went on, leaning her elbows on the table in front of her and looking fixedly at him through her glasses. She had drunk nothing but water at dinner, yet her cheeks burned with an unaccountable flush, and her eyes were bright with excitement.

''How strange it is!'' she went on. ''You cannot have the remotest idea of what I am really like—as if it mattered!" She laughed apologetically. "It is strange, though, to think that though we are such friends, you have never seen my face."

"You mean because you wear those glasses?" he replied, in the blunt, matter-of-fact way in which he generally did receive her personal allusions, and which disconcerted her and drove her to utter desperation sometimes. "I suppose you have some good reason for wearing them?"

"I have a reason, but I don't know if it is a good one," she replied in tones sharp from nervousness.

"You wear them under advice, I imagine?"

"No, really my own idea," she said, airily. "Shall I take them off? Tell me to, and I will!"

Her voice was trembling, her hands were twitching with the overmastering desire to do away, once for all, with this absurd barrier between them. A woman, shorn of her powers, mulcted of her charm, handicapped, at the very moment when she needed the full arsenal of her feminine armoury! That was what she was, and his imperturbability irritated her vanity, and made it, for the moment, paramount.

She realized the full gravity of the situation, she felt it a turning point, she had attached an almost fetish-like importance to the insignia of her virtuous resolutions, but in the wild desire to assert her womanhood that mastered her now, she was prepared to abandon anything and everything that stood in the way of its accomplishment.

"Shall I take them off? Shall I?" was her irresponsible cry. "You have advised me to. Remember that."

There was a pause—a century of vital emotion for her, the mere opportunity for an added touch of the brush on to a ticklish corner of his foreground for the painter.

"Did I?" he asked, carelessly, as she deliberately laid aside the spectacles, and looked him full in the face.

But the heavens did not fall or the solid earth fail, and with the single unconcerned remark: "I should not have said that your eyes were at all weak!" the painter continued tranquilly to deposit brushes full of diluted sepia and water on to his drawing. There were tears in her eyes next time she raised them.

CHAPTER VI

Mrs. Elles never put the spectacles on again. They had made no difference—except to herself. And further intimacy with Rivers convinced her that any such artificial safeguards against flirtation were quite unnecessary.

She realized his want of sympathy and humanity, his elaborate attitude of standing aside from the problems of life in favour of a closer contemplation of those of Nature. It was Nature he loved, and Nature only, with his full heart. The human interest was a purely secondary consideration with him. Not "in many mortal forms" did he seek "the shadow of that idol." He was Alastor and she was the Lady. She must remember that. Alastor could doubtless have done quite well without the Lady. She represented the ever-restless Spirit of Humanity which Alastor had come into the wilderness to avoid. And, for his sake, for the sake of her valued privileges, she must learn to keep it in abeyance and suppress it as far as she could. She must love Nature too. It was difficult, for though, in her quality of romanticist, she had always talked a good deal about it, Nature, to her, was merely a background for people, just as flowers were an adornment for her bodice or her parlour.

But the very conditions of her tenure here demanded that she should accommodate herself to the mood of her companion. Since, by happy chance, she was admitted to be an inmate with him of the terrestrial Paradise of which he was the tutelary God, she must contrive, as animals do, to adapt herself to her new habitat. She thought of herself as a tremulous, storm-tossed soul, newly entered into bliss, and afraid to compromise her precarious happiness by any assumption of right or too marked a signalizing of her presence there.

With this end in view, she began to cultivate a capacity for silence, an art of self-effacement, a spirit-like vagueness of outline. Her wish was to dissimulate her personality as far as was possible, and merely to form, as it were, part of the silent, unobtrusive world of Nature that he loved. It was a stiff novitiate to a complete education.

Her plan was successful, on the whole. The painter began to take her as a matter of course, to treat her as if she had always been there, as a busy man might treat a sister, or a college companion, without ceremony, but with much protective kindness and camaraderie. She was sure that the notion of her being in any way compromised by her stay with him in this lonely inn never so much as entered his mind. It was not that he was ignorant of conventions; he was simply too preoccupied to think of them.

But, indeed, the new brightness of her eyes, bred of her happiness, the lovely, natural colour in her cheeks, the conscious curve of her red lips, inevitably suggested the world's cry for a chaperon. She had been an interesting woman when she came to Rokeby; she was now almost a beautiful one. The little hollows in her cheeks had filled up; her figure had improved; she was like a blue serge wood nymph darting about the broken pathways and shelving banks of this embowered painter's paradise.

She knew, with a woman's intuition, that he was not entirely blind to her beauty. His eye rested on her with the same searching and affectionate gaze with which it might linger on a "beautiful bit," as the technical phrase runs; and the light in her eyes and the changes in her expression, as the varying moods flitted over her face, were to him as the cloud shadows chasing each other over Barningham Moor, or the sunlight glinting in the brown pools of the Greta where it was deepest. It was something, but not enough. A woman does not care to be looked at as if she were a landscape by the man whom she passionately loves. She longed to draw from him some personal expression of admiration; but, beyond an occasional "Well done!" upon the performance of some unusually agile feat of climbing, she was always disappointed.

Others noticed the improvement in her looks and health and told her of it.

"On my word, Miss," remarked the landlady of the "Heather Bell" to her, one afternoon, when she was "learning her," by a course of practical demonstration, to make the cake of the country, "ye're fair credit to the 'Heather Bell!' Ye look twice the woman ye did when ye first comed here, not near so peaked and piny like! I'll be bound the gentleman thinks so, too! Eh, we shall see what we shall see!"

"What shall we see, Mrs. Watson?" asked Mrs. Elles, complaisantly, leaning her elbows on the floury table. She was always most susceptible to any kind of compliment, and to do her justice, she had no idea of the woman's meaning.

"You and he will be setting up together, one of these fine days! Eh, I see what I see! I'm none blind, honey."

"Nonsense, Mrs. Watson!"

"Nae nonsense at all! He tak's a good deal o' notish on ye, I consider. I was just a-saying sae to oor Jane Anne later than yesterday. Sorrow befaa' my tongue—she's fair upset aboot it, I can tell ye!"

"Jane Anne! Upset?"

"Ay, sure, who but Jane Anne Cawthorne? She's got a bit fancy for Mr. Rivers hersel', ye mun knaw. She sends a' the ither lads away on his account, he that's never thinkin' of her! I whiles say to her, 'Hout, lass, he'll never tak' that much notice on ye, beyond lending ye some beuk ye's a deal better without.' I don't hold wi' readin', mysel', he knaw. But the fond lass shakes her head and says nowt, and throws away the bonny flowers ye put in his glass, and sets some on her own pickin' there."

"Yes, I have noticed that," said Mrs. Elles sharply.

"And I'll wager. he's niver so much as gien her a chuck on the chin, for all she's walk barefoot to Barney Cassel and back for him. Eh, it's you that's got him. Mistress Popham was axing me, only the other day, when ye was going to get the vicar to call ye?"

"Call us! What's that?"

"Ask ye; call the banns in church. Eh, that'll be a grand day for us all. Noo, there's a bonny cake," she ended, clapping it on to the "girdle," "and you and he can have it cold to your teas."

"Did you ever lend or give Jane Anne books?" she asked Rivers, at dinner, that night.

"I ordered her a set of George Eliot's novels once," he said, "and all Scott's. She's clever enough to get something out of them. I see that from what she says to me about them. She is quite a superior girl."

"I don't like her, and she doesn't like me. And novels—that she only half understands—put things into her head that are better out of it. Now, suppose this girl, Jane Anne, were to write to my people and betray me," she said, with a slightly simulated expression of apprehension.

"Why should she betray you?" he said, showing by his slight accent on the betray that he thought it somewhat too forcible. "She would have no object."

"Oh no!" said Mrs. Elles. "I am not a criminal. And besides, there is no one for her to betray me to. I owe nobody any allegiance. I am perfectly independent. There is not a soul in the world who cares what becomes of me!"

She sighed appropriately as she uttered this fiction, but if she had expected Mr. Rivers to openly commiserate her, she was disappointed. It was by no means the first time. Alastor always refused to take any interest in the fortunes of the Lady before she came to him.

She wondered if he even took in the idea of the lonely and friendless condition. Did he really swallow the legend of herself that she had been at such pains to concoct and serve up to him when she first came?

The lies she had told him, in the light of the new morality that her intercourse with his blameless rectitude had flashed upon her, began to weigh heavily upon her regenerate soul. He was so straight, so sincere, so guileless, so simple, she might tell him what she chose and he would credit her story as that of one holding the same rigid code of honour as himself. She was beginning to realize, as she had never realized before, what that code of honour—what every gentleman's code of honour—was.

It was not so much that it was wrong to lie, but it was a mark of ill-breeding, and her cheeks burned at the recollection of the imposition she had practised— was still practising—on this gentleman.

He had asked her no questions, and she had told him lies!

The only little point of comfort which she could wrest for herself from circumstances was the possibility that he had not chosen to burden his mind—full of tree and cloud forms, and such artistic lumber—with her story as she had related it to him. Was it likely that a man, with his strange and disconcerting capacity for the ignoring of details and all the minor facts of life, should have permitted anything so human and unimportant to make an impression on his mind? No, it had probably glided off him, while every mutation of the sunset they had watched together yesterday was indelibly fixed in his memory. Of what consequence were she and her trifling affairs in comparison? So she thought and hoped, in the new humility which her love for him had engendered in her.

Still, in spite of these halcyon days, it was impossible that she could entirely shut out the thought of the future. Things could not stay as they were. The stack of canvas umbrella covers, and packing cases, piled out of the way in all the four corners of the sitting-room, reminded the poor young woman only too painfully of the dies iræ, dies illa—when the autumn tints, beloved of amateurs, would begin to show and bear their indubitable message. The leaves would turn brown and fall, and the lover of Nature would pack up his colour box, and strap his easels together, and look out a train in Bradshaw, and order the trap over-night to take him to the station at Barnard Castle.

What should she say then? What should she do? He was everything to her, and she was nothing to him. She was the wife of Mortimer Elles, and her home was in Newcastle!

But it was borne in upon her that, come what might, she could never go back to Mortimer. The mere contemplation of a renewed term of life with him was terrible and impossible to her, now that she had known the greatest good, the highest development of which human nature was capable, in the person of this man in whose intimacy she was living.

There were times when she could not bear her own thoughts, when she would jump up and leave the room where Rivers sat composedly working, and, hatless and cloakless, run out into the moonlit road and even into the Park itself. The painter, in his absorption, would never even look up or seem to hear the panting breaths that betrayed her emotion.

Bitterly did she con this and other signs of his indifference, as she wandered deviously about the glades and alleys of the great demesne, now under the staring moonlight, now where the over-arching trees shut it hopelessly out and made walking a mere matter of outstretched hands and groping steps. Even the darksome yew grove—the haunt of the Lady of Mortham—had no terrors for her now. Love casts out fear; a woman in her state of mind has no horror of the supernatural.

One night, the most beautiful moonlight night of the whole year, she wandered far into the Park and along to the banks of the Greta, where it runs under the shadow of the cliffs crowned with fir trees, and the desolate tower of Mortham stands out against the sky behind them. She scrambled down the bank, on the hither side, to one of the little stretches of pebbly shore that line the stream here and there and stood wistfully gazing into its flow, her hands crossed at the back of her neck, a white lady, "mystic, wonderful."

The further shore lay all in mysterious shadow, but at her feet was a sheet of rippling silver, with dark oily rocks, like islands or sleeping seals, breaking through its course here and there. She saw, in imagination, a drowned woman lying there in mid-stream, face upwards, caught among the snags and snares that clogged the shallows, and irradiated by the same moon rays that turned the brown water white.

"Look there!" she said, wildly, turning sharply round to Rivers, who was standing behind her. "Look! I see myself there!"

She was so wrought up that she felt and showed no surprise at his presence. It was so picturesquely natural that she should be standing there in the moonlight, on the bank of the most romantic river in the whole world, with the only man she had ever loved. Time and chance had combined to bring about this hour. Rivers had never thought of following her before.

But he completely ignored her morbid speech. She was hurt, though, indeed, it was what she might have expected. She said no more, but stood looking tragically down into the flood.

"By Jove, but it is fine!" the artist presently murmured to himself, in tones of deep conviction.

Nature—mere non-sentient, abstract Nature again —and a woman, eager, passionate and romantic, standing by him!

"Don't you wish you had your sketch book here?" that woman asked him, bitterly.

"Oh, I can remember it!" he replied, simply. "But I am very glad I came out. How did you happen to know there was a moon, and that she would be shining over this reach of the river?"

"I didn't know," she said. "I just came out—I don't know why—I suppose, because I was restless."

She sighed, and fingered her sash, and sighed again.

"How did you know where I had gone? I have been" — reproachfully — "an hour away, and you never even looked up when I left the room!"

"I missed you, though," he said. "I feel things, sometimes, when I am very busy, without seeing them."

"Perhaps, then, it occurred to you that I might have got into mischief," she went on lightly. "You didn't know that I come here nearly every night?"

"Why not?"

"And yet this is the first time you have followed me!" she said, regretfully. "Yes, I come here, night after night, and I look down into this pool, and I imagine myself lying in it with my face turned up to the moon, drowned and dead, and at an end of all my troubles, and you hearing of it, and being a little—a very little—sorry for me!"

"But you are surely not thinking of committing

suicide, are you?" he asked her, quite calmly, "for, really, no one would have the slightest excuse for falling in off this miniature beach?"

She made a gesture of impatience — then she laughed, in tragic impotence.

"One can drown oneself in a teacup, if one has a mind. But I think I will go up the bank, now, and put myself out of the reach of temptation."

"Do you want to go indoors? If not, let us walk a little way to the Junction, if you don't mind? I want to see the Greta meet the Tees under this strong moonlight. It must be magnificent. It is a shame to stay in the house when the moon is out like this. Browning speaks of her 'unhandsome thrift of silver.' There's plenty of her now, isn't there? Glorious! It is a night of nights!"

Mrs. Elles agreed with him—but from a different point of view.

"Are you frightened?" he asked her, as they left the river bank and began gropingly to follow a track between two darknesses of tangled brushwood.

"Not with you!" she said, manfully; and he did not offer his arm.

She walked along, a little in front of him, in the narrow path they had chosen, a short cut to the place where the two rivers meet. She was wearing her thin, clinging white gown, and, without the unromantic adjuncts of hat, parasol, or gloves, she looked as ghostly, as unreal, as far removed from the commonplace, as even she herself could have wished.

They reached the Junction, just outside the Park confines, where the brown moorland flood of the Greta, hasty, capricious, passionate, like herself, merged into the broad, calm flood of the Tees—flowing quietly, in its great volume and depth, over its granite-bouldered bed under Wycliffe. Rivers, for some reason or other, took off his hat, stood—his hair looking quite white in the moonshine — silent, his artist soul, presumably, stirred to the very depths by the mysterious harmonies of tone and magnificent lines of composition which the sight afforded him.

"How well that comes!" he murmured, passionately, while the woman beside him stood breathless, affected, too, by the vision, but in her own way; weaving her fanciful, personal allegories of him, and her, and the two rivers, and longing for some signs in him of the more human enthusiasm that she could have shared.

She shivered, but not from cold. "We must go back!" he said, in response to her unspoken complaint.

They turned and walked up the glen—the moon had gone behind a cloud, and the Greta lay dull and sullen under the hanging terraces of trees. But in the yew grove was darkness unspeakable.

"Oh, I can't see you," she murmured, involuntarily; "I shall lose you!"

He silently held out his hand to her, and she took it.

When they came out into the Broad Walk where it

was lighter, she dutifully made a little movement to withdraw her hand—a very slight movement—but he did not accept it.

He had forgotten! Was there another man in the world who could thus hold and retain a woman's hand without knowing it?

In all her life, such pure, unalloyed happiness had not been hers, as they walked up to the gates of the Park together. It was just ten o'clock.

In the hall of the inn, he lit her candle, as usual, and gave it to her. She held it just under her chin, and it lighted up her face, blanched and spiritualized by the emotions she had gone through. He looked at her, for once, very closely.

"You look, to-night," he said, in the dreamy voice he only used sometimes, "like the Spirit of the Greta that peered through the window at me the other night. I told you about it at the time, did I not? It was a strange hallucination! Quite white and pale, and its eyes fixed meaningly on me. The lines of the face, as I remember it now, were curiously like yours, or is it that you have identified yourself with that spirit in my thoughts? I have never got it quite out of my head, do you know!"

"Why should you try?" was all that Phœbe Elles could find to say. A mist seemed to have come over her eyes, and she bade him "good-night," and stumbled helplessly over her gown as she went upstairs.

She lay awake all night. She cried quietly to her-

self.   This was what she had wanted.   This was life.
She was very happy and yet most miserable.

Did this man care for her? Yes? No? A little?
There was no knowing.   His ways were not as the
ways of other men—at least, not the men she had
known—and the ordinary canons of flirtation, as she
knew them, had no correspondence with his conduct
towards her.

She thought he liked her; she knew she loved him;
that was what it all came to.

She was an honourable woman, with a newly super-
added canon of honour, and she did not dream of
being false to her husband.   If Rivers loved her as
she loved him, she ought to go away.   That was her
clear duty to herself, to him and to Mortimer.

Mortimer would take her back—of that she had not
the slightest doubt.   There was no reason why he
should ever hear of this, her vagary, among the green
shades of Brignal.   She might take the train back to
Newcastle, refuse to give any further account of herself than that she had been away for a holiday or any
reason for that holiday except the usual "nerves" of
society, and resume her end of the matrimonial chain
without let or hindrance.

But since she was uncertain as to Rivers' feelings
with regard to her, hardly that, indeed, since he gave
her, literally, no reason to suppose that he looked
upon her in any other light than the light of a friend,
might she not—oh, might she not!—take the benefit
of the doubt and stay there till he went away, and be

as happy as she could for as long as she could? She
felt that she must not quarrel with Rivers' reserve,
since it gave her the title to his company. She
decided not to do so.

She was beginning to find him less obscure, for she
had learned to seek for the expression of him in his
art: the art by which he chose to reveal himself to
those who had the will and the skill to read. Where
other men spoke or wrote, he painted. She had only
to look at the beautifully stained bits of paper that
issued from his hand, to watch the wonderful combi-
nations of colour—subtle, passionate, striking, tender
—that were evolved by this man of few words, to see
that he was no stranger to the whole gamut of human
emotions, full of delightful, undisciplined moods, and
mutabilities, and pleasant perversions of character.
There were strength and force in certain abrupt combi-
nations that stirred like the sound of a trumpet;
there were tenderness and the fancifulness that women
love in certain harmonies that moved almost to tears.
She read sentiment and sweetness in the delicacy of
his sunsets, and character and passion in the gloom of
deep cloud-shadows, and sullen mist-wreaths lurking
in clefts and hollows of the hills, and mystery in the
tangled undergrowth whose complication and variety
he rendered so well.

There was one drawing of his that she specially
cared for, and whose progress she surveyed as she
might that of a beloved child of his brain and hers.
"Oh, Brignal Banks are wild and fair!" says the lady

in Scott's ballad, and here they were, caught and immortalized forever on one piece of Whatman's paper, three feet by two. There was hardly any sky in it. The leafy, heavily-berried coverts hung tossing from the cliff, streaming down to the water's edge, that lay, in brown pools, deep and immutable, like a true man's heart, at its base. In the immediate foreground was the broken mass of stones that formed the bed of the wayward river that had so many moods, both of grave and gay. There the painter sat, on one of these stones, with the water parted and rippling all round him, in the most precarious of positions, his drawing propped on his knee, uncomfortably, his feet nearly in the stream. The burning sun shone straight down on his head, for there was no foothold for his umbrella in the spot which he had chosen. He never spared himself, or complained of the terrible constriction of the chest, which the constrained attitude of stooping necessarily engendered. Perhaps he did not notice it in the excitement of his work. She sat under his umbrella, on the bank, and watched him.

Morning after morning she sat there, as it were in a bay of opalescent colours; the horizon of her landscape bounded by the pink cliffs and overhanging belts of trees, the foreground quivering with refraction, and golden with the flowering ragwort. She was drunk, but not blind with light, and lulled continually by the hum of the bees at their task and the self-satisfied purl of the stream at her feet, she sat peacefully noting and enjoying the dreamy transitions of a painter's day.

To herself, she seemed to be fast becoming a "green thought in a green shade"—the fanciful title of Rivers' picture, adopted from his favourite poet, Marvel—her favourite, too, now. Rivers was for ever associated in her mind with green, the colour of hope; she had banished grey—the colour of despair and Newcastle—from her mind, as it certainly existed not in the landscape before her eyes. Newcastle, under its smoky pall, and Rokeby, in its gorgeous vestiture of many colours, could not surely form a part of the same hemisphere. And the extraordinary thing was, that she had run away to find adventure, and had found peace! She had thought she had need of a world full of men, and now the society of one summed up all interest, all excitement, all hope, all that she had ever dreamed. She had longed for the fuller life of cities; now a lonely grove by the side of the river sufficed her.

Her eyes—she never read, or cared to read—were continually fixed on the stooping figure, in its neutral garb of brown, perched so precariously on a rock in mid-stream. In front of his post was the dell of Brignal, where the river wound round abruptly, and seemed to issue from a darksome hollow, formed by the meeting trees on either bank. Suddenly, her eyes grew eager and then startled—she fancied all was not right. Something was different. The hollow was filled up. A brown wall of water was gathering from that hollow, was advancing, rushing, with a dull, murmurous roar as of distant thunder, straight down between the two banks towards the painter.

She sprang to her feet.

Rivers had told her of the Bore of the Greta—she knew how, after a very slight rainfall such as they had had, the river was used to come down without warning. This was it! And his life was in danger! She screamed frantically to the artist, whose head had for an unconscionable time been bent over his drawing. She screamed as loudly as she could, but her voice came thinly and hoarsely, so he did not hear her.

Then she began to leap from rock to rock to go to him, when she saw him suddenly spring to his feet, take in the whole situation at a glance, and, his drawing held high in the air in one hand, begin to make for the shore.

Then he caught sight of Phœbe Elles, and his course deviated. She had not got very far from the bank, but she was in danger, and he was coming to her. The flood was very nearly on them both. Even in her agony, she noticed his slight pause of hesitation before he tossed the drawing he held recklessly on to the bank without looking after it, and the next moment his protecting arm was round her, and the flood swept partially over them. His other arm was round the bough of a tree that hung over the stream near where she was standing when he reached her. They were both overthrown by the rush of water, which passed over them, and then seemed to subside somewhat. She fainted, for the first time in her life,

She was lying on her bed at the "Heather Bell," with only a very confused recollection of what had happened, and a bandaged foot that hurt dreadfully. A doctor had been sent for from Barnard Castle, so she was told, who had pronounced it only a slight sprain, but the skin of her leg was abraded from knee to instep, and that was the cause of the pain. She could not remember how it had happened—there was a jagged bough, or a snag, she supposed, of the tree that Rivers had held on to, as the flood rushed past them, and which had caught her, somehow, as she slid down in his arms. She was a little light-headed still, and she kept calling out for the artist like a fretful child, and upbraiding him for refusing to come to her. Jane Anne, who was in and out of her room a great deal, treated these appeals sternly, and ministered to her with stony, condemnatory eyes, but Mrs. Watson's motherly heart was melted by her distress.

"Just ye get yerself well, ma honey, and then ye'll see him! He's sore put out about ye, sure and that he is, and he's alway axing me how you's getting on. But ye must just keep yerself quiet!"

Realizing that her only chance of seeing Rivers depended on her recovery, the restless woman put great constraint upon herself, and in a couple of days, was well enough to be carried downstairs and laid on a horsehair sofa in the sitting-room.

Her first day downstairs happened to be a hopelessly wet day, and the artist was perforce kept indoors, and painted all day at her side. He was busy, of course, but with extreme unselfishness he offered to read aloud to her.

Tears of gratitude came into her eyes as she realised this.

"I couldn't let you," she said, "but if you would let me talk to you a little, and go on painting—the foreground, or some part that doesn't matter—?"

He smiled, and turned so as to face her. "Don't let me get absorbed, then, and stray into the middle distance! I can't promise anything when I have got a brush in my hand."

"Tell me all about the other day," she said. "You saved my life!"

"Which you very foolishly risked to save mine!" She was weak and he unconsciously spoke in the aggressively cheerful, indulgent tone one uses to an invalid. "I was very angry with you indeed for jumping in after me like that. A shout would have done."

"I did call to you, but I could not make you hear."

"Your voice must have been drowned by the rushing of the water. I knew that there was something wrong, though. I looked up from my drawing, and saw the water coming, and you a yard from the bank!"

At the sound of the word drawing she gave a little scream—she had quite forgotten it!

"I know—I know—the drawing! What became of the drawing?"

"Well, you know, I had to have my hands free—" he began, almost apologetically.

"Of course! For me! And now I remember seeing you fling it away on to the bank. Was it"—she spoke with bated breath, as one might speak of the fall of empires—"was it quite spoiled?"

"Pretty bad," he answered, moodily.

"You can't think how I wish you had not saved me at its expense! Why did you? Why did you?" she asked, with absolute sincerity.

Rivers seemed to repent of his lapse into temper, slight as it had been. He said, laughingly, "Well, I must tell you that I thought it over! It was a fearful wrench, of course, but I decided in your favour. Do you blame me?"

She resented his not taking her seriously, and replied, gravely, "Yes, I do. I was not worth the drawing to you, I am sure. You should have considered it first of all. Who was it—was it Cæsar—who swam across the Channel with his Commentaries in his mouth?"

"He did—something of the kind—but I never heard that he had a woman to look after as well."

"And then—you carried me home?" she went on, in a tone of sentimental reminiscence.

"Yes," he replied, briskly. "One couldn't have

got a carriage down there, and I could hardly have
packed you into Farmer Ward's wheelbarrow!"

"Did anyone see you carry me across the fields?"

"Mrs. Popham did," he said, laughing at the recollection. "She even offered to help me! A woman
who could hardly lift a fly!"

"I must have looked awful!" Mrs. Elles pondered;
she had often thought it over. "A wet woman is
such an abject object! . . . And then you carried
me up to bed?"

"Yes. Mrs. Watson was very anxious to get her
son, Jock, to do it—but I thought of Jock and how
he would have knocked your head against the banisters
at every step, so I insisted on doing it myself."

"And then?"

"And then the doctor came, and saw you, and saw
me, and told me it was not much—and then I was
easier in my mind."

"Then you were anxious about me?"

"Very," he said. "Poor thing, you suffered so;
and you were so good about it!"

"Was I? I am glad."

She then returned to the subject that was distressing her. "Are you sure you don't regret the drawing—are not cross with me about it? Isn't it in that
portfolio—what remains of it? Show it me."

"Oh, no, no!" he said, shuddering.

But she had reached out for the portfolio that lay
near her hand, and, with the wilfulness of illness,
insisted on taking out the hopelessly blurred, grey-

streaked sheet of paper stretched on a board.   There
was a hole in the paper, the size of a shilling, just
where the sky-line met the cliff.   It was   utterly
ruined, as the merest tyro in art must have realised.

"Oh, poor, poor thing!   A snag has caught it, too,
like my leg," she moaned.

Rivers dabbled furiously away in the glass of water
with his fat brush.   He was an artist and human.

"I wish you would take it away!" he said, sulkily,
without looking at it or her.

"Where to?" asked Mrs. Elles, almost weeping.

"Oh, anywhere—to the devil, if you like."

"I'll put it in my room, then," she said, calmly.
"I shall like to have it as a memento."

She slyly dropped it behind the sofa until she
could carry it upstairs, and he did not seem even to
notice what she was doing.

.   .   .   .

The next day was very fine, and the artist had perforce to go out and paint as usual.   Mrs. Elles felt
unutterably solitary.   She could not walk as far as
Brignal, but she could not expect Rivers to stop at
home and neglect his picture in order to amuse her.
She virtuously stayed upstairs on one floor, as she was
recommended to do, until evening, but she was too
restless to sit or lie still, and wandered about from one
room of the old inn to another.

There were three bedrooms on the first story, hers
and Rivers' and one unoccupied room whose floor was
on a somewhat higher level than the others, up a tiny

flight of stairs. She "changed the air," as Mrs.
Watson put it, by sitting in there some part of the
morning, and once an irresistible impulse led her
into the artist's room, which was the most ascetic and·
the least comfortable of the three.

She stayed a long while looking out of the window,
gazing fondly at the view which must meet his eyes
every morning as he lay in his bed. It was very
nearly the same as that which met hers, naturally,
since the two rooms adjoined.

She noticed a chair, drawn between the dressing-
table and the window. He sat there, she supposed,
sometimes, and looked out. So would she.

But she found herself looking in, not out. Her
loving eyes gloated on all the details of his room; the
little heap of sketch books on the corner of the dressing-table; the martyred pocket-handkerchief, stained
all the colours of the rainbow, that he had used to
dab his drawing with; and the razors, that he kept
so sharp, wherewith to scrape down its surface, lying
beside those devoted to his own use; the three mother
o' pearl studs placed neatly on the ledge of the look-
ing-glass, beside the heap of pence he had last turned
out of his pockets; the fair white china palettes that
he made a point of washing out carefully with his own
hands, and whereon it was now her adored occupation
to "rub" the delicate proportions of each colour
required during the day. All this curious intermix-
ture of art materials and objects of personal use, so
characteristic of the artist's room, struck her sense of

dramatic incongruity and pleased her. Then she leaned out over the sill in a dream of what never could be, and forgot herself. Half an hour elapsed.

A slight rustle behind her warned her of the presence of Jane Anne, who, aggressively remarking, "I came to see to the blind," established herself there with a needle and cotton and drove Mrs. Elles away, although to uninitiated eyes the blind seemed in very good order.

She went into her own room and spent the afternoon there; she fell asleep, or she would have heard voices in the room below—the sitting-room she shared with Rivers.

A little, thin, consumptive-looking woman of fifty, in a homely utilitarian suit of tweeds which made her look like a schoolgirl, was interviewing Jane Anne on the subject of the harmonium's programme for next Sunday. She was the Vicar's wife, and, that subject concluded, the pair had moved across the hall and over the threshold of Rivers' sitting-room, the door of which stood carelessly open.

"Out?" said Mrs. Popham, with an interrogatory gesture. "Both of them?"

"He's out," answered Jane Anne. "She's upstairs!"

"Now, who and what is she?" asked the other, in the tone of decent curiosity. "I asked your aunt, but she says she knows nothing, and doesn't care."

"Aunt's fulish!"

"I told her she'd care fast enough if her inn were

to lose its character, as it's in a very fine way to do with all this. Mr. Popham and I have been talking about it only to-day. Everybody is talking about it!" Mrs. Popham spoke as if Rokeby were a centre of civilization. "Several people saw Mr. Rivers carrying her back across the fields, the day of her accident, and we all wonder what her relationship .to him can be! Frick is a foreign name. Is she a foreigner?"

"Nay, she's right English?" Jane Anne replied, with conviction, forgetting, in her excitement, to mince her words as usual. "And Frick is not her name, neither!"

"How do you know that? Then I am right and my husband is wrong. He is for taking the most charitable view of her, as indeed he does of everyone—but I told him that I was perfectly convinced, in my own mind, that the woman is an adventuress of the most disreputable kind! Everything proves it!"

"Can you tell me what is meant precisely by an adventuress, Ma'am?" her favourite Sunday-school teacher enquired, pedantically.

"People mean by an adventuress," Mrs. Popham replied, "an unclassed creature, a person with no visible means of subsistence or regular occupation. They go about the country seeing whom they can make fools of. There are plenty of them about, I am told. Russian spies, some of them, who worm themselves into families as governesses, and so on, in

order to surprise secrets.   What this one can possibly
want with Mr. Rivers, I can't tell, but no good, I am
sure!''

"Him to marry her!" said Jane Anne sombrely, as
one who had thought out thoroughly all the tragic
issues of the case.

"It is possible," said Mrs. Popham, "and he is so
good, so trusting, that anybody could take him in
who set herself to do it, as this creature is probably
doing.   I can't tell you how it distresses me that
such a nice man should be made a prey of!   It must
really be put a stop to, Jane Anne!"

"Yes, Ma'am," eagerly agreed Jane, forgetting to
be dignified.   Whether Mrs. Elles should prove to be
a Russian spy or not, the important thing was to
separate her from Mr. Rivers.   "She isn't fit for
him.   I can't abide her myself.   I mistrusted her
from the very first time I set eyes on her.   Nasty
painted thing!   She's only got two dresses to her
back, and yet she wears rings worth I don't know
how much!   Great big stones.   She sings foreign
songs to him, of an evening, in all sorts of queer lan-
guages—on my piano!   He niver speaks a word to me
now that she's come!   He used to say a kind word
now and then.   She was out with him in the Park,
one night lately, till I don't know what hour.   It's
not decent!   I was waiting at my window and I saw
through a chink in the trees—I can see all down the
Broad Walk, if I have a mind.   I waited long enough,
and I saw them come back down the walk together,

and the moon was shining full on them, and I
saw—" She hesitated.

"Was he?—Was she—?" Mrs. Popham asked, with
timid, scared eagerness.

"They were walking hand in hand," said Jane
Anne, shyly, "and if that's not being lovers, I
don't know what is!"

Her face relaxed, and she burst into tears.

"Don't, Jane Anne, don't go on like that! Perhaps they are engaged. My husband says so," said
Mrs. Popham, assuming that the staid girl's tears
proceeded from her sense of outraged morality.
"But still, it is a very odd way to behave. They
ought to get married, that's all I can say!"

"Oh, ma'am, Mr. Rivers and a woman like that,
with her painted cheeks and her hair — well, I
shouldn't like to have to swear that it is even her
own! She's not respectable, even if she is engaged
to him. I could tell you things — and so could
Dorothy, who waits on them!"

"Sh-h!" said the Vicar's wife. "But we must get
her away from him, somehow, Jane Anne."

"Oh, Ma'am, if we only could! Dear Mr. Rivers!
I'd do anything I could. Only, she can't walk now."

"If she is what we think her, that sprain of hers
may be just a ruse. It probably is. I can bring
myself to believe anything of a woman who masquer-
ades under an assumed name. How do you know, by
the way, that it is so?"

Jane Anne went into Rivers' room with the air of

one performing a religious rite, and fetched an umbrella out of the corner and handed it solemnly to the Vicar's wife.

"That is hers!" she said.

Mrs. Popham held it up to the light and read—in characters half effaced by time, not by prudence—the letters "P. E." on its battered, silver handle, and, furthermore, the address, 59 Saville Place, Newcastle.

"E. doesn't spell Frick!" said the Board School girl, proudly.

"I don't quite like doing it," murmured the Vicar's wife. "But—really—I can't let this go on! It can do her no harm if she is respectable, and if she isn't—? One must think of Mr. Rivers! Read out that address again, Jane Anne."

Jane Anne looked quite animated as she did so, and Mrs. Popham wrote it down in a note-book.

"Now, put the umbrella back!" that lady added, in rather a shame-faced way, "and leave it all to me. And, Jane Anne, mind you practise up that thing of Arcadelt's in time for Divine service; you seemed rather weak in it last Sunday, or perhaps you were not attending? I saw her in church. She probably gets Mr. Rivers to take her there to throw a little dust in all our eyes. I notice she never kneels or sings. It is evidently the first time she has ever been regularly to church in her life!"

CHAPTER VIII

Two days after this incident, of which she naturally remained unaware, Mrs. Elles was well enough to walk across three fields to meet the artist on his way back from his work. She exulted in the fact that she had become so countrified as to disdain to put on a hat even, and her red-golden hair, less elaborately arranged than it used to be, shone beautifully in the slanting light of the setting sun.

She waved her hand to him as he came in sight, crying, in accents of frank camaraderie: "Have you had a good day?"

"Not at all!"

"He's cross," she thought, and as he answered her so curtly, and moreover stared at her in an oddly unconscious way, as if he were taking her in for the first time, she felt all her joyous welcome frozen on her lips and at once jumped to the conclusion that somebody had been abusing her to him.

"You look at me as if you didn't know me or like me!" she said, undiplomatically, because she felt it so acutely.

"And as I happen to do both——" He spoke quite roughly between his teeth the justification she forced upon him. He re-adjusted the sketching bag

148

on his shoulders with a hasty impatient movement. The bag was heavy, and it had been a very hot day.

"Did any tiresome tourists come and overlook you?" she asked presently. She knew how he hated being overlooked, and even here in these wilds, periodical intrusions of the outer barbarian were possible. An encounter with an 'Arry of Leeds or Scarborough would account for any amount of ill-temper.

"The Vicar came and spoke to me," he answered her grudgingly.

"Ah! Like old times," she said. "It was I who frightened him away. Ever since the Vicaress saw you carry me home, I think she has disapproved of us both. She never came to call on me, as you said she would. I don't want her to, I am sure, I could not return a formal call in a sailor hat, and that is all I have got. . . . Do you mind not walking quite so fast? It hurts my foot."

"I beg your pardon!" he said. "I keep forgetting you are an invalid still. It is most unfortunate!"

Again she noticed the accents of irritation and wondered at them. He had always been so nice about her accident till now.

"It will be all right if we go on gently like this," she said with intent to soothe. "In a few days I shan't mind what I do. We can go one of our nice long Sunday walks again." He made a movement. "They are the greatest pleasure I have in the world— even when it thunders and lightens. . . . By the way, I have some news for you—bad news. There is a

new arrival at the hotel.   I heard the noise of instal-
lation.''

"The deuce there is!'' he said, the current of his
thoughts, whatever they were, entirely changed in a
moment by news so stirring.   "A man or a woman?''

"A man, I think.   His boots made such a noise,
stamping over my head.''

"One of those wretched touring bicyclists probably.
He will perhaps only stop the night.   Any luggage?''

"I saw none.   That rather helps the bicyclist
theory.   But then, I saw no bicycle.   Oh! I do
hope, though, that it is all right.   We don't want
anyone else here, do we?''

She came a little nearer to him, unconsciously, as
she spoke.   "We''—she enjoyed using the pronoun.
Together they walked down the espalier-bordered path
of the inn garden; and, as they turned in under the
porch, she raised her arm and broke off a rose and put
it, somewhat obtrusively, and a little against his will
perhaps, into the artist's button-hole.

It was all done in the sight of Jane Anne, who
came rushing downstairs from the upper rooms as
they entered, looking, somehow, very busy and
excited.   It was Jane Anne, not Dorothy, who for
some reason or other brought in the lamp to them
that evening, setting it down heavily, so heavily that
Mrs. Elles, looking up, saw that the girl's hands
were trembling with nervousness.

But through some unaccountable swing of the
mental pendulum Phœbe Elles was to-night so nearly

absolutely happy that she did not waste a thought on the causes of the young woman's excitement, or that other problem, the possible duration of the mysterious visitor's stay.   Tourists might—and would—come and go, she and Rivers were there it might be for ever. For ever!   Yes, she felt to-night as if that might really be, and life remain for ever a fairy tale.   The prince was here, in the enchanted castle, in willing bonds to the enchanted princess, and so far, no dragons—or other princesses contested him with her.

She sat in the low window seat and leaned back against the sill, her hands idly clasped behind her head, and closed her eyes now and then, and felt so happy that she smiled without knowing it.   She had bidden truce to her eternal self-consciousness for once.

Rivers looked up now and then, but there was no apprehension in his eyes.   He did not see her—he was in another world—a world where neither Phœbe Elles, nor any other woman, could follow him.   That could not be helped, but meantime his physical presence sufficed the woman who adored him.   Her tense nerve fibres were momentarily relaxed, she was soothed and lulled into a state of happy acquiescence in the present order of things.   It had been very hot all this August day, but now the cool airs of evening were just beginning to qualify the dry heat that had been so intense as to blister the window shutters, and make the air seem to dance on the distant skyline of the moors.   Mrs. Elles was very lightly dressed, her thin muslin shirt showed the rosy skin of her shoulder that rested against the jamb of the window frame, half in, half out. She deliberately inhaled the sweet aromatic smell of the jessamine and the phloxes that grew under the window, and the mild breath of the cows that leaned over the fence. There were people in the garden, she could hear their whispering voices.

"Lovers probably," she thought—"the landlady's sons courting their lasses. How sweet it all is!"

After half an hour's steady work, the painter became restless. Perhaps he remembered the advent of the presumed cyclist, and if he did, it worried him. He seemed to be listening once or twice to vague sounds heard in the passage outside, then he began to walk about. Once he brought up sharply in his walk in front of the stack of umbrellas and travelling gear in the corner of the room, and stood there. She happened to be looking out into the garden just then, or she would have thought this terribly ominous, and all her peace of mind would have been destroyed. When he came back to the table, he looked at the drawing and shook his head. That gesture escaped her too. Then he left the room and she saw him stroll deviously up the garden and look over the gate into the fields. When he came back, she had not moved or in any way modified the picture of restful contentment she presented. He looked at her—a puzzled look—then he said:

"I have seen the new lodger!" he said. "At least I think it was she!"

"You have? A woman?"

"Yes, a tall, handsome personage, dressed all in forbidding and ponderous black. She was sitting in the arbour out there, talking to Jane Anne in a very friendly way."

"It was the girl's own mother, probably. Every girl of her class has got a bombazine mother that she produces on occasion."

"Jane Anne is an orphan. Besides this was more than bombazine — it was — it was something very handsome, if I know anything about it—which I don't!"

"No, there's no black in nature!" said Mrs. Elles, smiling fondly at him. "And I should not expect you to know much about women's dress. My—er—father knows there are such things as ruches and pipings, and that is all."

"I do happen to know that there is such a thing as jet, and that it is very expensive. A sort of glittering coat of mail, you know, that women wear."

"Egidia does!" cried Mrs. Elles, with a sudden little pang of jealousy. "She wore one in Newcastle, I remember, when I went to see her. Sequins!"

"Yes, the 'bombazine mother' wore little shining things like hers," he replied, with a disconcerting apprehension of the intricacies of feminine apparel in Miss Giles's case which disclosed to the woman at his side the parlous state of her own heart, if indeed she had been under any doubt about it.

He went on, "As for this wretched woman, I do

hope we shall not come across her! Her voice was enough for me. I wonder how a woman with a strident unsympathetic voice like that can find anyone to live with her. I could not be in her company an hour."

"I daresay she is somebody's mother-in-law," remarked Mrs. Elles, with pathos.

"And eyes like gimlets! She had a good look at me!"

"And now she is most probably pumping them about you, and me, and who and what we are!"

"Probably," he replied rather grimly, and sat down in front of his drawing, and began to work at it with all the signs of intense concentration.

She stayed where she was, in the window seat, and watched him, with an ardent, timidly devouring gaze. This time, he was too much absorbed to look up, so it was quite safe.

She found herself wondering how a man could live in such an atmosphere of passionate regard, and not know it. It seemed to her that the cloud, as it were, of devotion and admiration with which she enwrapped him, was so intensely actual—a positive physical fact, —it seemed to her that she could see the halo with which she crowned him.

For literally half-an-hour she heard nothing but the intermittent plip-plop of the brush in the glass of water, fast growing muddy coloured. He seemed to her to dash the brush into it with more energy—nay virulence—than usual.

She presently observed aloud, with the sweet impertinence permitted by intimacy: "How you are dashing it in! I call that the splash and carry one of art, but I suppose it will all come out right in the end."

"Or all wrong," he said—and his voice was so changed that she looked up in surprise. "The chances are that I shall never finish it. I am thinking of leaving this place to-morrow!"

"What?" she screamed, rather than said; and her voice from excess of emotion was shrill and strident enough to apprise even one so absorbed as Rivers that his intelligence was of no ordinary degree of importance to his listener.

She had known all along that this must come and she had made up her mind how she would behave when it came—but not so suddenly, good God! Her resolution deserted her and her voice betrayed her.

The painter deliberately laid down his brush, and came to where she was sitting in the window-seat, and taking her two unresisting hands, led her a few paces into the room.

"There are people in the garden," he said quietly. He screwed up his eyes, and looked at her exactly as if she were a "subject,"—and a difficult one, as she thought afterwards.

"Now, please listen to me," he went on, with a little gentle pressure of the hands pushing her into a seat. "I have been thinking——"

"Oh, dear!" she murmured, like a spoilt child. She was so acutely conscious that any reflection on his part was likely to mean a conclusion inimical to her peace. The moment he thought about it, he would be sure to see how wrong and impossible the whole situation was.

"I am a careless fellow," Rivers proceeded to say, "and my head is generally full of my own work, to the exclusion of everything else. . . . I can't say I ever thought about it, but I have heard something to-day—Mr. Popham made an absurd suggestion to me—which shows me that I am very stupidly compromising you by my presence here."

Mrs. Elles interrupted him with vehemence, stung by his generosity in putting it so.

"Indeed no, it is I who am the interloper! I is I who ought to go—and I will!" She drew herself up proudly. "You to go! Why, your picture isn't anything like finished."

"The picture is a minor matter, compared with——"

"It is quite the most important thing in the world," she rejoined, with a little touch of irony, bitterly aware that to him it was so, indeed. Then her spirit oozed away, and she said, weakly, "No, no, it is for me to go, of course—but, oh, we were so happy! Why must you make me——"

"I don't make you go—of course not!" he said irritably. "I intend to go myself. Did I not say so?"

"Nonsense," she answered, quite rudely, in her extreme anguish. "That would be no good at all. Besides, do you suppose I should care to be here at all—unless you were?"

She uttered the crude fact recklessly, imperiously, contemptuously almost. Surely he must see; she had nothing to conceal from him now! She hid her face in her hands a moment after, and tried to leave the room, but Rivers caught her to him as she passed.

"Then, for God's sake, don't go!" he said, tearing her hands down from her face. With one quick look at him as he sat across the chair holding her body, she flung her arms round his neck, and returned his embrace with all the passion and abandonment of one doomed. Married to one man and beloved of another, she felt herself to be so. A look in Rivers' eyes had warned her that Alastor's asceticism was only skin deep; a mysterious, material rapport was established between them. She felt as if she had known him all her life.

"It is all right, then, if you care for me," he said, in a matter-of-fact voice. "What do you suppose it was that Mr. Popham wanted to-day? He wanted to marry us, by way of looking after the morals of his parish!"

He laughed; he was gay. Even she had never dreamed that he could be so charming! She removed herself a few paces away from him, and stood, sobbing convulsively.

"Oh, forgive me, forgive me!" she repeated.

He became grave and stern in a moment, struck by the utter conviction in her tone.

"What for? Because you don't care for me? Why should you? I have made a mistake, that's all!"

He turned away impatiently, possessed for the moment by the mere surface irritation of the man who has been refused.

"No, no, not that! Oh, I adore you!"

She laid frantic hold on the lapel of his coat. He covered her hand with his.

"What then? How nervous you are! What can it be?"

He laughed.

"You are not going to tell me that you are married already, I suppose?"

"Yes, yes, that's just it. I am!"

There was a pause. Then—

"I said it in joke. Do you mean to say that you are not joking?"

"No, no, I wish I were. I have deceived you shamefully."

He stared at her, then he sat down heavily on the chair by the table in front of his work. He looked a little bewildered and very angry.

"Shall I tell you all?"

"Oh, yes, if you care to—not that it concerns me now."

He idly picked up his brush, charged with colour as it was, and let it fall full on the drawing in front of him.

She caught his hands.

'Oh, don't, don't spoil your drawing because of me! And listen to me, for it does concern you, since I love you, and you say that you love me. I must tell you, I must explain what I have done. Oh, don't look at me so! You were my lover a moment ago, and now you are my judge.''

"A woman has no right to let a man——''

"No, I know she hasn't. I ought not to have let you tell me that you cared for me. But I am so glad you did! It will be something to remember afterwards. I must tell you my story—my true story! I told you once, you remember, the story of Phœbe Elles—the woman who left her husband, because he was so unkind to her——''

"Oh, so that is your story, is it? And the one you told me about yourself—your pretended self——''

"That I invented. I had to tell you something ——'' He rose from his chair. She went on—"Oh, forgive me, forgive me! I have not told you the truth——''

"So it seems!'' he replied, coldly, opening the door, and going out. "Good-night.''

.   .   .   .

She was left alone, with the worst of all scourges that a woman may have to suffer, that of reading in the eyes of the man she loves the expression of the scorn, deserved or undeserved, that he bears her.

.   .   .   .

For a long time she sat there, in this little narrow room that had framed all her brief happiness, half stunned by the judgment that had been passed on her, and also by the shock of self-revelation that went with it. She felt mean, as well as miserable.

The noises about the house ceased gradually—there was no sound of footsteps overhead, yet she had heard Rivers go to his room and close the door. He was probably sitting brooding by the window in that chair she had sat in. He had omitted to put his drawing away,—presently she rose and tenderly put a sheet of tissue paper over it, as she had seen him do sometimes, when called away even for a moment. Then she sat down again. Her eyes fell on a Bradshaw on the mantelpiece; she thought of getting it and looking out a train to go home by to-morrow. She had no longer any thought of committing suicide, the idea of expiation of which she was now possessed did not admit of any selfish solution of that sort. But she had never yet been able to find out anything in Bradshaw for herself; she would have to ask Mr. Rivers.

That she must not do; on the contrary, she must never see him again! She must arrange to breakfast in her own room to-morrow, wait till he went out to his work, and leave Greta Bridge without even attempting to bid him good-bye!

The lamp began to gurgle, and she realised that the oil in it was getting so low that it would be out in a few minutes. She would be left alone in the dark! She was afraid of the dark like a child. The window was still wide open to the night, she could tell by the cool wind blowing in on her and chilling her through her thin blouse. Suppose, too, that the Spirit of the Greta, evolved in happier days by Rivers' imagination,

should suddenly appear, framed in the black square!
She was indeed haunted by the vision of a face seen
there during her recent interview with him; it had
impressed itself somehow on her consciousness, though
she was too much excited to take cognizance of it at
the time, but now the impression returned to her
with extraordinary vividness, as of a real person who
had been there!.

She started to her feet in terror, and made for the
door.

She ran upstairs all in one breath, as it were, and
then paused, by the door of his room, panting a little.
She gently proceeded to run her fingers down its
uncommunicable surface. Behind those boards was
the man she loved, and who despised her.

But he had said he loved her, before he had found
out that she was a liar. Nothing could take that
away.

She crouched down by the door, forgetful of every
consideration of prudence. She was a chidden child,
that longed to sue childishly for pardon.

Yes, she was a liar, a criminal!

She had almost tamely accepted his view in the first
instance, because it was his view, it was his contempt
that had made her feel contemptible. But now her
eyes—the eyes of her spirit—were opened, and she even
exaggerated the heinousness of her crime, the black-
ness of her own soul, till she felt herself absolutely
shrink from her own carefully cherished and pampered personality. She saw herself morally naked and

unpicturesque. All her little ingeniously disposed veils of sophistry and plausibility she tore rudely away. She took a quite savage joy in shattering her own elaborate life-system of pose. The truth, she sadly, tragically perceived, was not in her—it never had been, and again she blamed her mother's training,—and Truth was everything.

No sound came from the room within. Had she but known it, the artist had flung himself on the bed in his clothes as he was, and had fallen asleep, the heavy complete sleep of a man whose lungs have been breathing in the fresh outside air all day, under circumstances of intense creative excitement. Even now, Art came first.

The door of room number three, a few steps along the passage, opened and closed again. It was the room necessarily occupied by the unknown lodger. Mrs. Elles was too much absorbed either to hear or notice. Her thought, like the thought of a hypnotic subject, was concentrated on the yellow brass handle of the door against which she crouched, which mesmerized her, in its shining immutability. In about half an hour, she made an effort to shake off the lethargy which had taken possession of her, and walking away, like a somnambulist, her hand to her head, and stumbling over her gown, regained her own room.

CHAPTER IX

She cried a great deal—and she slept a little. She would have died sooner than own it, but luckily for her newly developed sense of veracity, there was no one to question her on this point. About eight o'clock in the morning she rose and dressed, resolved to go downstairs to breakfast as usual. She found it practically impossible not to see Rivers again. If he wished to avoid her, he easily could do so.

So at the usual hour, she drifted into the little sitting-room, her face composed to a certain extent, but her eyelids swelled, and her cheeks bleached and seared by a sufficient percentage of the hours of the night devoted to weeping.

The man of her thoughts was sitting at the breakfast table, bending studiously over a Bradshaw. He hardly looked up, but he muttered something civil. Mrs. Elles was woman of the world enough to be able to murmur her conventional "Good morning" in return, for the benefit of Dorothy, who was in attendance, and who watched them both so intently as to justify Mrs. Elles' peevish remark, "I do wish Dorothy would not stare so."

"Does she? I have not noticed," he replied, listlessly. "Would you mind pouring out the tea?"

163

This commonplace suggestion brought her back from the verge of hysterics, as it was perhaps intended to do.

"Oh, I forgot," she exclaimed, taking her hands out of her lap, and becoming suddenly and inefficiently active. Rivers never got a worse cup of tea in his life, probably, than the one Mrs. Elles gave him that morning, and he took it without sugar, comment, or complaint.

They ate and drank in silence. Mrs. Elles could bear anything but that.

"Will you look out a train for me—a train home?" she asked, in tones as nearly devoid of all emotion as she could compass.

"I will, if you will tell me where you live!" he replied, with equal coldness.

"Newcastle," she murmured, in a voice choked with incipient sobs.

"He opened the Guide with cruelly assured hands. "There is a train at 12:45," he said, looking up.

But the strain had been too much for her, she had flung down her napkin, and had risen from the table, and hurrying across the room to the sofa, had flung herself down there in a heap, with her face to the wall. He caught the white gleam of a pocket handkerchief, which alone told him she was weeping.

There was a silence. Rivers groaned—the nervous groan of a man who is too well bred to swear at a woman.

She tried to refrain from sobbing aloud. She lay quite still. Her eyes, half open in the dim penumbra of the sofa corner, saw only, as in a nightmare, its rough horse-hair surface, like a dreary hill, studded with briars of incommensurate proportions, and over which she somehow imagined herself climbing. Her ears, preposterously sharpened by her excitement, next heard the faint click of a teacup, hastily pushed aside. A panic fear overcame her, lest this should be the signal of his rising, and that the clash of the door closing behind him, as she had heard it last night, and remembered it, would be the next sound that would come to her ears. But as in some stages of the mesmeric trance, she was powerless to stop him; she would not be able to raise a finger even to save her life, and her life it would be that she would lose. He would go out of the room—out of her world for ever! She listened . . . her ears were tingling . . . it was positive pain. . . .

He did rise—and she presently felt his hand on her shoulder, and heard strange, unexpected words of tenderness from his lips.

"Dear—I love you—but what can I do? You are another man's wife."

She turned her whole body round, and caught his arm to her, and hid her face on his sleeve.

"Yes, I know, but can you ever forgive me—for the lies I have told you? That is what I want to know."

"I have said that I loved you," he said, simply.

"I can't say more than that. Women are different, I suppose."

She never remembered anything sadder than the sigh with which he said this. She realized that in order to exonerate the woman he said he cared for, and to condone her fault, he had been obliged to involve the whole of her sex in her disgrace, and to set all womankind a few degrees lower.

"What am I to do then?" she asked like a child, sitting up, and pushing the disordered hair off her brows without regard to order or becomingness.

"Obviously," he said, and his tone was almost brutal, "go, unless you will let me? Only, as you have a home and a husband to go to——"

"You might have spared me that!" she said, with a flash of her old spirit, rising, and wandering deviously towards the door, like one in a sad and hopeless dream. "Of course I must go!" she said meekly, fumbling with the door handle. "Will you please open it? I have things to do . . . give up my room . . . pay my bill. . . ."

"Have you—are you sure you have enough money?"

"No, I daresay not," she answered with dreary inconsequence. "But it doesn't matter!"

"What nonsense! Of course it matters. You must let me lend you some."

She shuddered. "Oh, I couldn't borrow of you."

"Why not? You don't know what you are saying, poor thing!"

At that word she began to cry.

"Look here——" His words were rough, but his voice was gentle. "For Heaven's sake, don't go and expose yourself—expose us"—for she had made a gesture expressive of entire disregard of all malign inferences with regard to herself—"to the whole household! It is bad enough already!"

He took her hand, and she ceased to weep, and looked up into the face of her supreme arbiter with a dull submission.

"You must take these three notes that I am going to give you," he said authoritatively, "and go quietly up to your room and ring for the servant and ask for your bill and pay it—I can't do all this for you, or I would—but I will order the trap to take you to the station in time for the 12:45!"

"Drive to the station with me," she murmured.

"No, I must not do that, but I will tell you what I will do. As soon as you have made all your arrangements, we will take a little walk in the Park, shall we?"

He spoke like an ascetic, dealing himself out many penances, and but one indulgence. His tone throughout was businesslike and decided, he was no longer the quiet indifferent dreamer of dreams, but the efficient man of the world, the man of action; and the fanciful hysterical woman at his side was completely dominated by his decision, and stilled for the moment into something like acquiescence with her fate.

She carried out all his directions faithfully and

accurately, and in less than half an hour, joined him in the road outside the inn, veiled and spectacled, and demure as a nun about to take the vow!

"I have told them," he said, "to bring the trap round to the Park Gates to meet you. So you will not need to go back to the inn at all. We have just half an hour."

"But you are wasting your whole morning's work," she said as they turned in at the Park Gates. It was the first thing that occurred to her to say.

"Oh, just for once!" he replied. "My work will have no cause to complain of me—after to-day."

She shuddered at the grimness of his accent—she apprehended his meaning only too well. She seemed to see him in her mind's eye, as he would be henceforth, stooping, brooding, gloating over his work in the dell of Brignal, alone, as he was before she came there, and mildly, dully happy perhaps, as he may have been, before the Human Interest came to trouble him.

And yet—"He does not want to let me see how he feels it," was the secret consolation that lay all the while at the back of her thought, explaining his brusqueness, his taciturnity, his hardness, which her surface mind could not help resenting and deprecating. Her soul's life, which was then at its lowest ebb, lived on that thought, and her body took courage from it.

She walked into the Park almost briskly by his side, and when they had travelled a certain distance

along the broad path, he made a significant movement of his hand towards her spectacles.

"Can you take those things off?" he asked her,
imperiously.

She obediently doffed the symbol of her martyrdom
and return to the paths of virtue, and handed them
to him. He folded the spectacles and put them in
his coat pocket.

"The bill was only thirteen pounds," she next
remarked, holding out the notes he had lent her.
"I had plenty of money of my own, so I return
these."

The notes, too, he put into his pocket without comment. Then she said reproachfully:—

"Don't you want to know my name?"

He started. "Your name? That does not matter,
does it?"

"But you surely must know my name to write to
me by?"

"I am not going to write to you."

"Why not?" There was a sharp note of prescient
anguish in her voice.

"I am not good at writing letters."

"Ah, no, it isn't that," she answered sadly. "You
mean of course that you want to go quite out of my
life."

"What can I do?"

"Do!" she repeated after him vaguely. Then—
"Must you?"

"Yes—I must."

"But it isn't possible,—no, it isn't possible!" she cried.

"Quite possible," he answered her doggedly. "I did not know you a month ago—I shall not know you a month hence, that's all!"

She wailed out gently, like a child. "But what am I to do? What are you going to do?"

"I am going to do my work," he answered her severely and coldly. "My work, that I have been letting go to the dogs lately. I shall paint and paint—like the very devil—as I did before you came. You must do that too. Work is the only thing, I find."

"Work, work, honest work!" she repeated mechanically. "But will you tell me what work I have to do? It is all very well for you—you speak as if you quite looked forward to your life without me—but I shall eat my heart out."

"Oh, people say that, but there is a certain savage pleasure in renunciation, as you will find."

His tone was so extraordinarily bitter, that she cried out joyfully, "Oh, then you do care a little? You speak of renunciation! Then I can speak. I was afraid to. I was beginning to think—that you had only—oh, how difficult it is to say these things!—that you had only—proposed—to me, because I had compromised myself by staying here with you so long. Out of pity, you know!"

They had left the Broad Walk, and were wandering down a track in the undergrowth. He turned round to her, and his voice was quite different from the one he had been hitherto using.

"You are quite wrong if you think that. On the contrary——" He stopped, and seemed embarrassed for the first time. "It was what I wanted—I said that I loved you—and I did. I do—only——"

"Then — then — if you can say that —— " She seized his hand, raised it to her lips, and kissed it. "Then let him—let my husband divorce me! I must say it! I can't let myself drown without a word! Mortimer will have every excuse to divorce me, don't you see? I have been living practically alone with you for a whole month! It looks bad enough— even old Mr. Popham saw it. I could not defend it —and I won't! Mortimer will have to divorce me, and we will marry each other and be happy. . . . Why do you shake your head like that? No! But why not? You think my proposal dreadful! So it is, but I would do anything—anything in the world to come to you."

"And so would I for you—you must not doubt that!" he replied, and his slow deliberate tones in no wise expressed the emotion that, for her comfort, she could see in his eyes. He gave her back her hands, as it were.

"Anything," — he repeated gravely, "but a dishonourable thing! No, not even for you! . . . Look here! it is now half past eleven—you can only just do it! The trap will be there already! You shall leave me here. . . . Please—don't make difficulties, my dear. It has to be. We have decided it, haven't we? Good-bye . . . good-bye!"

She did not cry. She stood still and leant her head against the trunk of a huge beech tree, and felt her hair catch in its rough bark, and half closed her eyes in anticipation of a parting that would be worse to bear than a blow. Would he kiss her? He must, and yet she would not ask him.

He did; he took her in his arms, and gratified her great love with a kiss more perfunctory than passion-ate, perhaps, and which yet awakened the woman's heart in her body once and for all. Then he turned sharply on his heel and raised his hat—she smiled even in her misery at the irony of it, but she under-stood him now—and left her.

She dared not watch him go, lest she fall into the crime of calling him back to her. He might hate her for that. She looked up into the branches of the tree overhead, till a sudden rush of tears mercifully blinded her!

Ten minutes later, she made her way down the Broad Walk to the Gate, turning a foolish unintelli-gent stare on the porter who opened it for her as he had done for Rivers ten minutes before—she felt a wild desire to ask him how her lover had looked as he passed through. Still in a merciful dream she mounted the steps of the dog-cart that was waiting in the road for her, and was whirled away in the direc-tion of Barnard Castle.

She was wrong in her supposition—Rivers had not

left the Park, but had turned down a little side path to the right.   He stayed in the Park till he heard the sound of the wheels of the dog-cart going past the high boundary wall.   Then he walked with his quick elastic step to the gate, and back to the "Heather Bell."

"I wonder if I shall ever paint another decent picture?" was the purely technical remark that he made to himself.   He was very pale, and he lifted his hat off, once or twice, and breathed deeply as the cold morning air met his forehead.

"A lady to see you, Mr. Rivers," said Jane Anne to him, as he crossed the porch.

"Where?"

"She asked to be shown into your sitting-room, Sir," answered Jane Anne, with great suavity of manner.

"You should not have done that!" the painter said wearily, and passed in.

The first thing that caught his eyes on entering the little parlour that he had shared with Mrs. Elles was her tear-stained handkerchief lying like a white blot on the black horsehair sofa, and her long tan-coloured gloves spread at length upon the table.   If he had thought about it, he would have recollected that the gloves had not lain there when he left the room, or at any rate, were not in the same position.   In the very middle of the room stood a tall commanding presence, the "Bombazine Mother"—as Mrs. Elles had insisted on calling her—the lady he had seen talking to Jane Anne in the garden last night!

One bony hand was firmly planted on the table in the neighbourhood of the gloves, the other flourished a letter in an aggressively judicial manner. The artist bowed, and waited for her to speak.

"I daresay you know my name, Sir!" she said.

"I have not the pleasure," he answered, curtly. Her voice had a most painful effect on him.

"Poynder—Mrs. George Poynder—I am the aunt —by marriage—of the lady who has been living with you here for one calendar month! Don't attempt to deny it, man——"

She spoke so preposterously fast that he had no opportunity of doing so. Pointing to Jane Anne, who had slunk into the room during her speech, she continued:

"This young lady will bear out what I have said, and the good people of the inn. There are plenty of Phœbe's things about; for instance, that object on the sofa—you will hardly say it is yours, I presume? I saw besides, with my own eyes last night, an unparallelled scene of——"

Here the painter interrupted her by almost roaring out:

"Please to leave the room, Jane Anne!"

The girl, cowed, crept out. The painter continued:

"If this lady is your niece, Madam, you will hardly wish to discuss her reputation in public. Now, all I have to say to you is this, that this is the parlour of the inn, common to all, and the only available sitting-room. Your niece, Miss——," he hesitated, he did not remember to have ever called Mrs. Elles by any name—"has been good enough to consent to share it with me during the time you name——"

"Nonsense! Now look here! it is no earthly use your beginning to tell me a pack of cock-and-bull stories like that!" struck in the old woman, and her overpowering emphasis actually silenced the man with the mere physical oppression of volume of sound and harsh quality of tone. The genius was no match for the virago.

"I have stayed here, in this very inn, from last night. I meant to see for myself—and I have seen! The Vicar's wife—if there is such a thing as a vicar in this God-forgotten place!—who was scandalized by the goings on here, wrote to me and apprised me that Mrs. Elles — my niece—by marriage — perhaps you will have the brass to say that you did not know that she was a married lady?"

"I certainly did not know"—began the artist, almost mildly—for the sake of another woman, grown suddenly dearer to him than she had been, he thought to exercise diplomacy in dealing with the coarse virago who held that woman's fate in her hands—but it was of no avail, since she interrupted him again, stridently, volubly, overwhelmingly, so that his forehead contracted, and he turned pale under the mere shock of the impact of the words she flung at him.

"Yes, my niece Phœbe ran away from her husband —my nephew—and came straight here to you, and has

been living here with you for a clear month under an
assumed name.   That looks pretty bad, doesn't it?
So bad that Mortimer—my nephew—will have no
difficulty in getting his divorce?"

"Divorce!" muttered Rivers, taken by surprise,
and foolishly allowing her to see the shock her words
had given him.

"Yes indeed, divorce, what else would you have?
He will be perfectly justified.   The woman has
always been a constant source of trouble and disgrace
to him.   She has never known how to behave herself, and God knows what might have happened, and
I, for one, am rare and glad to be shot of the little
baggage!   And now——"

Mrs. Poynder was not without a certain kind of
penetration, and seeing herself in imminent danger
of being ordered out of the room, adroitly concluded
to be beforehand with the man whom she had goaded
into fury.

"And now, Sir, I will wish you a very good day!"
she said, quite quietly, moving towards the door.
"And since you are so very careful of Phœbe's reputation—there isn't much of it—but the landlady here
tells me she was under the impression that you and
she were courting.   Well, perhaps now that you
have ruined her, you will be gentleman enough to
marry her.   It is the very least you can do, when
you have got her kicked out of her husband's
house!"

"And by God, I will, if it comes to that!" Rivers

said, with sudden and determined emphasis. He strode to the door.

"Now, Madam, have the goodness to leave my room."

He held the door open for her as she passed out. He was white with rage.

"I am sure I thought I heard you say it was the common parlour?" the terrible woman remarked to him, over her shoulder.

.   .   .   .

A moment later, he seized his hat and went out. Jane Anne was waiting for him in the passage, her comely face marred with tears. She caught his hand and held it.

"Oh, Mr. Rivers, do please forgive me! Mrs. Topham wrote the letter, she did indeed, and the other lady stayed here all night—and saw you——"

He shook her hand off his sleeve, and passed out into the road, without even looking at her.

Jane Anne looked at her hand—the hand he had disdained—as if she would like to cut it off. Her heavy brows contracted—met together in a dull frown of rage and disappointment.

"Then I'll just swear anything they like!" she muttered to herself.

CHAPTER X

Mrs. Elles, on arriving at Newcastle, took a fly and drove straight up to her own door.

This detail was significant of the course she had undertaken to pursue, and the attitude she meant to assume with regard to her own life—what was left of it.

She was only thirty, she had presumably as many years again to live, and she had no intention of committing suicide. On the contrary, she meant to go through the process known as picking up the pieces.

Her policy of life was optimism—pessimism was her pose. But her unconscious tendency was to look forward—very much forward. The past she ignored, the present she disdained, the future she brooded over. It had always been so with her, even in the old days before this cyclone of emotion had swept over her, and the trivial round of things pleasant and unpleasant had been all her care and preoccupation. It would be so again.

She had the peculiar shrewdness of the feather-brained, the perspicacity of the trivial-minded; and the practical basis of her nature, which had been overlaid and smothered for a time by her spasmodic access of passion for the artist, began to reassert

itself.   As the train passed easily through stations
and scenes familiar, the domestic campaign of the
immediate future took form and shape in her mind.

All that was now possible!   She arranged it hopelessly, drearily, but as satisfactorily as might be under
the gods' dispensation.   The door of Paradise was
closed to her, she would make purgatory endurable.
She had known the poetry of life, now for its prose.
But dramatic and artistic fitness demanded that there
should be no loose ends, no rough edges, no interfus-
ing and overlapping of incompatible and discordant
periods of existence.   Her month of soul-fruition was
to be a thing apart, a memory, complete, perfect,
enshrined in her heart for ever and kept entirely clear
of entanglement with the squalid phase of life that
she was going to take up again.   She was a reluctant
but resolved Eurydice returning to the grey neutrali-
ties of the Hades from which Orpheus had so nearly
rescued her.

Ché farò!—   She knew the song.   What would
Orpheus do without Eurydice?

Alas!—in her shrewd heart of hearts she knew that
Orpheus would do very well.   Orpheus loved his
Eurydice, but even the legend is compelled to admit
that he went harping about the world; and Rivers
would go on painting noble pictures and would soon
forget her in his work, which even in the heyday of
her influence had been paramount with him.

She did not allow herself to lose sight of that fact.
She knew in her humility and consequent clearness of

perception that the idyllic month in the Brignal woods had been her epoch—his episode. Propinquity and a vague sense of responsibility had led him to propose to her.

She wished he had given her a ring—a sketch—anything, as a memorial of their sojourn together. She had literally nothing of his but a stump of pencil which he had lent her the day before, and which she had forgotten to return. It was only a stump—she must never permit herself to use it; it must last her her life. She laughed at herself for thinking of this.

Rivers would certainly approve of her plan. He had not allowed himself to preach at her, but he would of course wish her to make the best of Mortimer and be a good wife to him henceforward. She would try—but the very thought of Mortimer brought one of her headaches!

Driving up Grey Street from the station, she caught sight of various members of her little society. Miss Drummond was picking her way through the perennial mud of this unromantic city, and the poet was holding an umbrella over her. This looked like love—like an engagement! Had they got it settled during her absence? She was disposed to be kind to all lovers, but preferred them of the distressed variety! She would have liked something left to her to do! But there were other lovers and other people in the world. She would begin her Friday "At Homes" again and her friends would muster and she would give them tea, and they would wonder why she looked "different." There would be a look in her eyes which no one would remember having seen there before, a kind of "Love among the ruins" look, and she would not be able to smile quite so freely.

The thought awakened her own ready sympathy for herself and there were tears in her eyes and a flush on her cheek when she stood on her own door-step and rang the bell of her own house.

A new parlour-maid—she could not help starting—though she must have known on reflection that this would be the case—opened the door and stood looking politely receptive.

Mrs. Elles saw the comedy of the situation and laughed gently. Then she put a florin into the girl's hand, and, bidding her pay the cabman, brushed past her into the house and into the dining-room.

The room was empty, unchanged, a little untidier than it used to be in her day. A sour look came over her face as the accustomed horrors smote her sense, fresh and undulled by previous contact with them.

"If he has dared to touch my drawing-room!" she muttered and, opening the door of that apartment, surveyed it.

It was just as she had left it, a passably pretty and tasteful room. She went up to the wall and instinct-ively set the frame of a picture straight.

"Bring tea at once," she ordered peremptorily of the astonished maid, sitting down in her own especial place at the corner of the sofa. "Where is Mrs. Poynder?"

"Oh, Miss, did you want Mrs. Poynder?" said the servant, with obvious relief. "Mrs. Poynder is away. She went into Yorkshire yesterday. Mrs. Elles is away too."

"I am Mrs. Elles," said that lady calmly, judging that the comedy in the maid's case had lasted long enough. "You are the new parlour-maid, I suppose. What is your name? When do you expect Mrs. Poynder back?"

"Mrs. Poynder only went for the night, Miss— Ma'am. She expects to be home for dinner."

"What an extraordinary thing for Aunt Poynder to do!" said Mrs. Elles, speaking aloud. "Now go and get tea. I am dying for it."

The girl went. Then her mistress gave one despairing look around the room and hid her face in the sofa cushion. Sorrow's crown of sorrow had come upon her suddenly—the contrast between her own drawing-room and the little ascetic room at Rokeby, that spoke so clearly of its inmate, had come across her mind with cruel poignancy.

"Oh, God, if it is going to be like this!" she murmured, choking with sobs. Only a few hours ago, in the plain bald room that was Paradise to her, and now here among all these pictures, photographs, books, symbols of the tedious domesticity she had been prepared to take up, but which struck her now as horrible, so much more horrible than she had anticipated!

"I hate you!" she said to the grandfather over the

mantelpiece. She kicked the early Victorian embroidered footstool at her feet savagely away.

The door opened a little and she wearily raised her eyes. Her little cat came wandering deviously in, having pushed the door open for itself, and, purring for joy of seeing her again, rubbed its head against the footstool and the foot. She looked down with a sudden fiendish instinct—then seized the creature and kissed it and buried her face in its soft fur and let it lick away the tears that coursed down her cheeks uncontrollably.

There was a crash of sticks in the hall—how well she knew that sound! Mortimer! In spite of the comedy of the situation Mrs. Elles turned pale. It was the first time in her life that her husband had had that effect upon her. Through the chink in the door that the cat had made for itself, she saw a vertical slice of her husband. In a moment he would enter the room and the comedy would have to begin. She put down the·cat and dried her eyes on the muslin chair-cover.

Very rarely did Mortimer enter the drawing-room. If she had only thought of that! He did not enter it now. He walked into his study and closed the door.

Now he had made her feel foolish—another rare occurrence. The only thing for her to do now was to go and "dig him out," in pursuance of her plan of making things go smoothly. She would do it, for once. And if she could only bring herself to put her arms round his neck and kiss him, also for once, domestic peace would be fully ensured, for a season at any rate.

The memory of Rivers' farewell kiss that morning assailed her and she sat heavily down again, struggling, striving, gathering up her resolution. No, she could not kiss Mortimer, but she could be nice to him, and she would.

She presently rose and with an assured step went to the study door and opened it.

Mortimer was standing with his back to her, in front of a case of liqueurs that he kept there, and was in the act of pouring himself out a glass of brandy. Kiss him, indeed! Under these conditions she could hardly be expected to go up to him and say "Peep-bo!" or "Guess who this is!" as she believed was done in the best bourgeois circles.

She merely said "Mortimer!" as jauntily as she could.

He turned. His face expressed no emotion but surprise, and he took a gulp of brandy from the glass he held before answering.

She shuddered with disgust, but remarked in a lively tone: "Well, Mortimer, here I am—and so much better for my little change. I simply had to go, and quickly too, or you would have had me break down on your hands. I hope you realize that—but men never do!"

Mortimer said nothing and she began to get a little nervous.

"You don't seem to take much interest in my

travels, so I won't enter into particulars; but you can imagine the sort of thing for yourself—perfect rest and quiet, and away from Aunt Poynder. By the way, where is Aunt Poynder?"

"Haven't you seen her?" the man asked, with grim intention.

"No. How should I?" she replied innocently. "Jane—Mary—whatever you call the new one—said she had gone into Yorkshire for the night. What a funny thing for Aunt Poynder to do! What possessed her? Perhaps she has gone away for a cure, like me."

Mortimer here made an inarticulate sound and his wife was quick to interrupt him.

"Oh, please don't begin to question me! Don't you see I am still rather nervous? Take me when you have got me, and be thankful. Are you not one little bit glad to see me?"

"God, Phœbe, what a liar you are!" he exclaimed, making a step forward.

"Really, Mortimer!"

"Read this!" he said violently, taking a crumpled sheet of notepaper out of his breast coat pocket. "Read it, and then perhaps you'll know where your aunt is—if you don't know already, which of course you do!"

Mrs. Elles took the note out of his hands. "Don't, Mortimer, look at me as if you hated me!" she added deprecatingly.

The address of the letter—The Rectory, Greta

Bridge—was the first crowbar levelled at the fabric of the pose she had been keeping up so valiantly. Her knees shook under her.

"Dear Sir," (the letter ran)

"Will you excuse a perfect stranger for writing to you, but I fancy you will perhaps care to hear what I have to tell you. A young lady, who bears the address to which I write engraved on her umbrella, is staying here at the inn of this village under circumstances which impel me, as the wife of the Vicar of this parish, to give you at least a hint of her whereabouts, so that you may exercise the powers of a guardian over her. The only other inmate of the 'Heather Bell' is a single gentleman of the name of Rivers. The young lady calls herself Frick, a name which is not borne out by the initials on her objects of personal use. I may mention that she and Mr. Rivers share the same sitting-room.

"Yours faithfully,
"Florence Popham."

Mrs. Elles raised her eyes, full of angry fire. The fighting instinct was aroused in her.

"Silly meddlesome creature!" she said scornfully. "Why may I not stay where I like, and call myself what I like, and what is it to me or to you either who happens to be staying in the same inn?"

"That's all bluff! We'll hear what your aunt has to say about that!"

"My aunt! What on earth has she to do with

it?" And again her accent was truly surprised and therefore convincing.

"You're a damn good actress, Phœbe! . . . By Jove! Here is your aunt! . . . Stay where you are!"

He seized her wrist with some violence just as Mrs. Poynder flung open the door of the room and stood aghast at the sight of Mrs. Elles. Then she banged her reticule, a strong, black, noticeably shabby one, down on the table, and Mrs. Elles's eyes fastened on it.

"You got a bit start of me, Fibby!" she said grimly, "but no matter. The old woman will be a match for you before she's done!"

Mrs. Elles slid her wrist out of Mortimer's grasp, which tightened disagreeably when he gathered her intention of escape.

"No violence, please, Mortimer," she said stagily. "I almost think I will leave you to discuss me with Aunt Poynder!"

She left the room with no signs of unseemly haste, delighted to feel the grasp of her husband's fingers literally smarting on her arm. Cruelty! She had heard of that.

She went straight upstairs to her own room and locked herself in. It had been a sudden and brilliant inspiration of hers to leave them. She wanted very much to hear what it was that her aunt had to say to her husband, but still more she did want time to think. The ground had been cut beneath her feet.

She felt like Alnaschar when his basket of eggs was rudely kicked away from him. A completely new plan of action was imperative, and how could she act when she was so dreadfully in the dark and so puzzled by her husband's constant allusions to Mrs. Poynder, whom she had not seen since she left Newcastle?

But stay! In her hurried glimpse of Mrs. Poynder she had realized that that lady was wearing a black dress, trimmed with little shining things, as Rivers had called them, and that the black bag that she had slammed down on the table was the one that Rivers had described as belonging to the unknown visitor at the Heather Bell on that summer night that seemed so long ago and was only last night. And the face seen at the window at the very moment when she had fallen into her lover's arms, for the first and only time! All these things came crowding into her mind; a bewildering vision of what had been rose before her eyes, with the damning significance in ears inimical of all the little foolish foolhardy things she had done in the innocent audacity of her unreturned love—and she realized how she and Rivers had been betrayed!

She must find out how much and what Aunt Poynder had seen before she committed herself by a single word. She must be clever and diplomatic to the full extent of her powers. Her excitement grew as she sat there on the edge of the bed thinking out a plan —many plans, and she bounded to her feet when there came a very ordinary knock at the door.

"Come in!" she cried, forgetting that she had locked it.

There was a furious rattling and "How can I?" came in Mrs. Poynder's angry voice.

Mrs. Elles had taken her line.

"Oh, I forgot," she said, insolently. "Well, you can say what you want to through the keyhole. I shall hear you well enough."

"Do you want all the servants to hear what I have to say?"

"I haven't the slightest objection, if you haven't," said Mrs. Elles, airily.

"You're quite shameless, then?"

"Perhaps, Aunt, you had better take care what you say, for your own sake."

"For my own sake, says she! Jane Poynder has nought to be ashamed of. But I should have thought, after what I saw last night with my own eyes——"

"Through the keyhole?" interrupted her niece impertinently.

"Through the window, woman!—the window of the hotel where you were living with——"

"Hush, Aunt," Mrs. Elles interrupted again—this time really for the sake of the servants and common decency. And then there was nothing fine, dramatic or romantic about this discussion; it sickened her. Not so should a husband accuse his wife of infidelity: through the mouth of a vulgar, foul-mouthed beldam. How different from Hero's "Let me but know of what man I am accused"! Still it behooved her to listen and learn, if she could, from Aunt Poynder the precise terms of the indictment against her.

"And I saw you in his arms," continued the old lady, "and the girl Jane Anne saw you walking hand in hand out in the public street! Don't attempt to deny it!"

In point of fact Mrs. Elles said nothing, but Mrs. Poynder thought she did, and her fury rose.

"You have the face——! Well, it's more than your man has. He turned as white as a leaf when I was giving him a piece of my mind this morning. He'd nothing to say for himself except that your room was the common room."

"So it was!"

"Tell that to me! I know what's what. It's I that made him promise to marry you, when all's said and done. But, Lord!—trust him! He'll not touch you with a pair of tongs! Men aren't so fond of marrying the women they have disgraced. Mercy, what's that?" she added in extreme perturbation.

"Only the dinner gong, Aunt," said Mrs. Elles, spitefully smiling on the other side of the door. She had learned what she wanted. "I can't come down," she said decidedly. "Tell Mortimer to come up here and speak to me after he has dined."

"You give your orders, my lady!" grumbled the older woman. "What's to say that Mortimer's going to condescend to even speak to you?"

"Give him my message," said Mrs. Elles peremptorily.

Mrs. Poynder's footsteps creaked on the stairs as she withdrew, and her angry mutterings were like a heavy ground swell at sea as she went downstairs. How her niece loathed her! And the man whose comfort and well-being she placed before every other earthly consideration had been exposed for at least half an hour to that malign influence. She realized the full horrors of the scene at the Heather Bell which her aunt had only faintly adumbrated, and most of her thought was for him.

"I must get him out of this," she said to herself, "at all costs! I used to think myself clever—I shall be clever if I manage this. I don't care a pin for myself, but for him! If I only knew something about it all—how they set about these things. What can be done? What is possible? If only I could look it up somewhere."

A vain glance at the little bookcase stocked with Ibsens and Merediths did not help her.

"What is the good of you?" she said, apostrophising them violently. "You are no good when it comes to the serious crises of life. Even a common old 'Enquire Within' would be better. I don't know what it is I am in for—what it all means. Can Mortimer divorce me straight away? What is the formula?" She wrung her hands. "If only I could keep his name out of it?"

She unlocked the door of her room and went out

upon the landing and looked down over the banisters. Mortimer was dining! "Though empires crumble," she murmured to herself. She heard the clatter of knives and forks; through the long well-like slip between the banisters she could see the parlour-maid carrying dishes. Mortimer was dining well, and intending to divorce his wife!

She was too frightened to properly enjoy the antithesis. She went back into her own room and lay down upon the bed, shaking in every limb. She had eaten hardly anything that day.

She must have dozed a little. She woke with a start, to see a broad shaft of light coming in from the doorway, and her husband, a stout undignified sort of avenging angel, standing on the threshold. She sprang into a sitting posture.

"Make some light!" he said impatiently.

"Why bother?" she said languidly. "You can see to scold me quite well enough in the dark!"

"Scold!" he said, in an accent of contemptuous reproach, coming nearer. He was flushed, but quite sober. She wondered if he really had had the heart to dine.

He enlightened her. "You don't seem to realize," he said, "the position of affairs. I have been quite unable to eat any dinner."

"What about me? But, however, that is neither here nor there. The point is"—assuming as viragoish an air as she could—"will you please tell me what you can have meant by allowing Aunt Poynder to come up here as your emissary and abuse me, your wife, and say awful things out loud for all the house to hear?"

"You are begging the question, Phœbe," her husband said, and in his earnestness and sincerity he was almost dignified. "You must know how serious all this is! What have you to say in explanation of the charges which Aunt Poynder brings against you, and that woman's letter to me which I showed you?"

"What are the charges?" she asked valiantly and without the flippancy with which she had thought fit to characterize all her previous remarks.

"Wait!" he said, and she gave a little frightened cry, and clutched his arm.

"What are you going to do, Mortimer?"

"I am going to look at your face while you sit there and lie to me!" he said, striking a match, and lighting the gas. It showed her countenance frightened and pale, his reddish and set. Even in her agitation she was struck by the expression he had used.. It was the second time she had been taxed with the mendacious habit. She began to think there was something in it. It was, however, the first time Mortimer had permitted himself to allude to it so roundly. She was nonplussed by his attitude; she had expected him to bluster and be ridiculous. He was dignified even to a tragedy. The thought crossed her mind that he still loved her, which would make it difficult for him to adopt the point of view she was intending to put before him.

"Mortimer," she said, raising her eyes to his
with an intentional effect of extreme and busi-
ness-like candour, "what Aunt Poynder tells you
she saw she did see, but the inferences she draws are
false."

"Explain yourself more clearly."

"I mean"—she strictly persevered in her steadfast
gaze—"that it is not true that I have been unfaithful
to you."

"Not——!"

"I swear it," she said simply, "but I do not expect
you to believe me. Are you going to divorce me?"

"What—and leave you free to run off and join
your lover!" roared Mortimer in a spasm of jealous
rage. "I'm——"

"I have no lover—I wish I had!" she interrupted.
Her sad sincerity had a convincingness her husband
was too angry to apprehend.

"Mortimer," she went on, clasping her hands,
"could you possibly divorce me—I know nothing of
these things—without having a co-respondent at all?
I do so hate having him dragged in!"

The solicitor stared at her.

"Mortimer, isn't it possible? You are a man of
business, you ought to know about these things. We
do get on so badly together, don't we? It is quite
hopeless our trying to get on. Isn't there—there
must be—some sort of arrangement by which husband and wife can agree to live apart because they are
unsuited to each other, without dragging in a third

person?   There isn't a third person, I do assure you, and I know how he would hate it.   This poor man Aunt Poynder saw is a painter—a hater of women.   I bored him really, only I laid myself out to please him and plagued his life out!   I interfered terribly with his work.   You would not understand how.   He wanted to be left alone.   Artists are like that.   He did not know I was married, and when he found I had compromised myself against him—that's the only honest way to put it—he proposed to me because he was a gentleman and thought he ought.   It is I who am to blame, for trying to make him like me.   I kissed him, not he me! . . .   I am a wretch, I know, but if only you knew how miserable my life is here with you!   We ought never to have married.   Let me go!   I am sure you will be happier without me, believe me!   Let me go quietly—let it be between you and me!   Don't let all the world in!   Don't ruin an innocent man's life over it—for it would!   He is a Royal Academician and might be President some day, and if he is forced to marry me he will lose that and his position in the world, and it is such a good one.   Besides, he is engaged to be married to another woman—he really is!"

She paused breathless, and caught hold of his hand.   He shook her off.

"Lies!   Lies!   Lies!" he said.   "I don't believe a single word you have been saying, Phœbe.   And as for a judicial separation between us, which is what you seem to want, I say 'No, thank you.'   The laws are made to enable a man to get completely rid of such a woman as you!''

He left her and she heard him leave the house. It was exactly nine o'clock.

CHAPTER XI

She knew what she had to do. She composed her features and covered them with powder, and rang the bell.

It was the cook who answered it, not the new parlour maid. The cook, whom Mrs. Poynder worked hard and bullied, was in consequence a firm ally of the young and far niente mistress of the house, who preferred pleasant and flattering looks even to good service.

"Mary," Mrs. Elles said urbanely, "come and help me! I want to catch the night mail for the south."

They pulled open drawers and dragged in trunks. Mrs. Elles was not sure that she was not leaving her husband's house for ever, and she did not mean to go without her things. The two women worked hard, carrying on a fragmentary conversation the while.

"How has your master been while I was away?" she asked of the cook, proud of being able to show that amount of good feeling.

"He's not been to say sae well. The doctor's been in once or twice, to please the missis—Mrs. Poynder, I mean. But the master doesn't seem to hold with doctors much."

"No, I know he hates them," said his wife, carefully controlling her surprise. It was natural that Mortimer should have given way a little during her absence, partly through temper, and partly for want of her supervision, but still a little fit of excess did not seem to indicate so important a step as the calling in of doctors. "But I wonder why I have not heard anything of all this except through you?" she added, forgetting to be prudent. "What was it?"

"Oh, just a fainting fit like. Missis Poynder found him in his study a day or two back, and it took a fair half hour to bring him round."

"Why wasn't I telegraphed for?"

"Eh, ma'am, ye were away for your health, and so Missis Poynder thought she wouldn't go for to agitate ye. It's all passed off, but the doctor he says as Master behoved to be car'ful."

"Heart?" murmured Mrs. Elles, with the interrogative inflexion, not liking to ask a direct question. She was really a little anxious. She did not positively hate her husband.

"Yes, that's what doctor said. Avoid excitement—sperrits the worst thing!"

Everyone in the house knew that this prohibition was by no means unnecessary.

"Well, Mary, you must look after him while I am away. I am going up to London on business. See that he has what he likes." She pressed five shillings into the cook's hand, feeling the glow of accomplishment of the whole duty of a married woman and picturesque forgiveness of insult and injuries.

Her packing was done. It was half-past eleven. She had a whole hour before her.

Of the laws of her country she had about as much practical knowledge as most women—that is to say none at all! She was full of the proposition she had made to Mortimer, of a bloodless duel, an amicable separation, a social catastrophe which should affect herself only, leaving Rivers untouched. The engagement between Rivers and Egidia, which she was going to London to suggest, would surely tell very much in favour of her plan, but she must neglect nothing, leave no stone unturned for the accomplishment of his salvation. She had made up her mind to work this thing for Rivers, to be his diplomatic angel, and that her heroic plan involved the surrendering of him to another woman only added to the sublimity of the act.

She went down to her husband's study; she knew he was out; she hoped she would not have the ill luck to meet Mrs. Poynder.

The house was perfectly still. There stood the row of collected legal wisdom, dusty, dull, abstruse, but full of vital truths for her at this moment. In a few minutes she was deep in law, and covered and daubed with its dust.

She found no hint of a previous engagement of the co-respondent being considered as a circumstance invalidating the divorce, but she saw that she and her husband must on no account sleep under the same roof to-night. That was why he had gone out.

He probably did not intend to return. It was a pity he did not know that she was going to take the initiative and leave him, and could not see her boxes at that very moment standing in the hall, strapped and corded and mountainous.

She stood there, taking down one volume after another, feeling the thief of knowledge, since it was from her husband's own books that she was gleaning the wherewithal to discomfit him when the time came. At any rate they would start fair! About on a level with her hand, she noticed a Blue Book on the Laws of Divorce. She eagerly took it down from the shelf. It seemed clearly written and fairly explanatory.

"There is no divorce by mutual consent of husband and wife."

She saw that she had been talking nonsense to Mortimer upstairs. How he must have laughed at her absurd proposition!

"The Causes of Divorce." This seemed a useful heading! She read on eagerly.

"Attempt by one of the parties on the life of the other, either personally, or by an accomplice."

But she had not attempted Mortimer's life, nor had Rivers attempted that of Mortimer, and though she had heard of cruelty, she had not thought of this definition of it.

"I had no idea the laws of my country were so absurd!" she exclaimed, laying down the blue book in a pet. Then a glance at its cover showed her that the volume she held referred to the Laws of Foreign

Countries, and this was the procedure of the Argentine Republic that she was looking at!

She gave that up, and reached down Stephen's Commentaries, and tried to find some hint there that would be useful to her.

She read on it for a good quarter of an hour, but the legal phrases puzzled her, the scantiness of details left her uncertain, the heavy volumes tired her hands to hold. She was no wiser, and a good deal wearier.

The door opened behind her. Instinctively she turned round.

"Oh, Mortimer, what is a femme sole?"

.   .   .   .

She laughed to herself, as the train sped southwards through the night, when she thought of her last sight of her husband as he stood in the doorway, apparently transfixed by her extraordinarily indiscreet question. His abrupt volte face and retreat reminded her that an injured husband is not to be used as an Encyclopædia Britannica. Henceforth she was as a noxious animal, to be got rid of, not argued with. She laughed, and then she cried, but finally her offended dignity won the day, and the train deposited a heroine, rugless, hopeless, comfortless, but still a heroine, every inch of her, on the platform at King's Cross in the early dawn.

She took a room at the Great Northern Hotel and waited in all the day till the calling hour, except for a little excursion to a jeweller's shop near the station, where she sold her one magnificent diamond ring for

about a third of its value. At four o'clock she
dressed herself beautifully and took a hansom to
Queen Anne's Mansions, where Egidia lived. She
made sure of finding the novelist at home; she had
heard her say she was at home on Fridays; if she was
not alone she would outstay the other callers. As she
drove along she looked at herself critically in the
little glass in the corner of the cab.

"Talk of the empire of the mind over the body, it
is nothing to that of the mind over the complexion!"
she said to herself, but was pleased to see that two
sleepless nights had only made her eyes larger and
her face more interesting. Looks are the sinews of a
woman's war and, though she was not going to
quarrel with Egidia but merely give up her lover to
her, her prettiness would serve to mark and accentu-
ate her heroism.

It was five o'clock when her cab drove under the
archway and pulled up at the big door which is the
portal to so many homes. Egidia lived very near the
top, but she preferred to walk up, she was afraid of
the lift. On the threshold of the door which was the
novelist's, as the boy who rang the bell for her
informed her, she caught her dress in the mat and
stumbled as the maid opened the door.

"It means something!" she said to herself.

It meant that she was nervous. She was going to
do an absurd thing; make a most curiously intimate
proposition to a woman she hardly knew! It was like
a scene in a novel. If only Egidia would not be too

matter-of-fact,—would consent to stay in the picture, as it were! As a novelist she would be apt for irregular situations, and able to enjoy and employ them.

The parlour-maid mumbled her name, which she had mumbled to her. Egidia, in a red teagown, like a handsome velvet moth, rose from a low seat to receive her, and Mrs. Elles felt like a frivolous butterfly in the somewhat freakish, bizarre habiliments in which she elected to express her personality.

"Oh, it is you!" exclaimed the novelist, her lips breaking into a kind smile and her eyes diffusing cordiality, as she held out both hands.

A tall figure rose from his seat on the other side of the fireplace, and Mrs. Elles's eyes were fixed on him while Egidia was speaking.

"So you have found your way here at last! Where are you staying? Let me introduce Mr. Edmund Rivers—Mrs. Mortimer Elles!"

Why should he not be calling on Egidia? It was the most natural thing. Mrs. Elles had never thought of this contingency, and yet she would not have had it not happen for the world. She was not a woman who would go out of her way to avoid situations. She bowed—he bowed; and then Egidia seeming by her manner to prescribe a greater intimacy, they shook hands. Oh! why was it so dark? She could not see his face.

"Will you ring the bell, Edmund, please, for another cup. Mrs. Elles, you must have some tea!"

"Thank you, no. I think I won't——" began

Mrs. Elles. To calmly sit down and drink a cup of tea at a juncture like this! It was not to be thought of.

"Oh, but you must. North country people can't do without their tea, I know that. Only in London we don't have sweet little cakes like yours. What do you call them—girdle cakes?"

So Egidia ran on, putting her visitor into a chair and pouring out a cup of tea and looking after her comfort in the most solicitous manner. Mrs. Elles felt that, considering "everything," this made her look ridiculous—but then Egidia could not be expected to know about "everything"! Rivers would surely not have told her about what had happened in the woods of Brignal. That was their affair —hers and his. Egidia would never have received her like this had she known. She felt a warm glow of pleasure on recognising the bond between her and him of a common secret.

But he was very cleverly neutral in manner. As he handed her the cake his eyes met hers with a curious look, searching but impenetrable. It disconcerted her. It seemed to take her all in, but it gave nothing out. But she was at least positive that there was no love in it, no pleasurable excitement in a loved mistress refound. Under the oppression of this idea she took a draught of hot tea that scalded her and in the access of pain that ensued persuaded herself that she was glad of the counter-irritant.

"Look, Mrs. Elles, at this little sketch Mr. Rivers

has just given me for my birthday," Egidia was saying, as she held up a framed water-colour drawing
lovingly.

Mrs. Elles looked at it. The rush of recollection
was not so blinding as she expected, but poignant
enough.

"Where is it?" she asked, for form's sake. She
knew well enough.

"May I tell her, Edmund?"

He made a little nod in the affirmative.

"Well, he could scarcely try to keep that knowledge from me," Mrs. Elles thought to herself.

"It is Rokeby," Egidia went on, "Scott's Rokeby
—that place where Mr. Rivers works so much.
Rather near your part of the world, I believe."

"I know it well," Mrs. Elles said.

Rivers was standing abstractedly a few yards away
from the two women. Mrs. Elles resented his lack
of emotional interest.

"It is quite charming!" she said, raising her voice.
"And is that a little figure I see—on the edge of the
stream? Some village girl you got to stand for you, I
suppose?"

It was no village girl, and she knew it. It was
herself, done by her own desire. She had begged
him to put in some human interest for once, and he
had indulgently agreed to do so, on condition she
supplied it herself. She had posed for twenty minutes under a broiling sun, and had refused the gift of
the sketch when it was done. She had somehow

wished that the memento of her should be retained by him, not her.

No, he could never have cared for her, or he could never have borne to give away that sketch to another woman! Her lips stiffened and then quivered. Had she known what was actually the fact, that the circumstance of her posing for that particular sketch had completely lapsed from the painter's memory, would she have been less distressed?

"That is the very reason I chose it," Egidia said, taking the drawing out of her hands. "Mr. Rivers gave me my choice of the Rokeby sketches, and out of a whole quantity of them in his studio I chose this one because it had a little human interest in it. I like people, you know. I should feel the world so cold, so dull, without them. I can't think how you, Cousin Edmund, manage to do without them so nicely!"

The painter actually laughed—from an excess of nervousness, Phœbe Elles hoped.

"Do say that I may bring Mrs. Elles to see your studio one day? I am sure she would like to see it!"

"I should be delighted," he said, "only you know a landscape painter's studio is not much to look at. Now Tadema's——"

"Ah! but then Mrs. Elles is not blasée on the subject of studios as yet, are you, Mrs. Elles? She wants to see a little bit of everything now that she is here, don't you? You remember our conversation in Newcastle? We must go about a little together and see the sights. I don't mean the Tower and the Monument—you are of course far above those. You might ask us to tea in your studio," she ended, turning, suddenly appealing, to Rivers.

"She wants to show off her intimacy with him," Mrs. Elles thought bitterly.

"I will," said Rivers gravely. "You must write and name your own day. It will have to be when I come back from Paris."

"Oh, are you going to Paris?" Egidia exclaimed, obviously surprised and completely uninstructed in his movements.

"I think I shall have to, on business; but I will let you know when I come back, and I will try to get a few interesting people to meet you — and your friend!"

Mrs. Elles had to make what she could out of the slight hesitation. He smiled, forcedly—she was sure it was forcedly.

Egidia's face was wreathed in kindly natural smiles as he bade good-bye—so was hers. It was pathetic. Mrs. Elles, with her superior knowledge of "fearful consequences, yet hanging in the stars," felt as if they were all dancing on a grave—treading a volcano. She knew well enough that she would never go to tea with him, never touch his hand again perhaps, as she gave hers, and dreamt of the accustomed thrill of pleasure that the mere contact used to give her. It did not now. Was it that she was too nervous, too frightened to be receptive, or was it that his magnetism had ceased to flow for her, as a consequence of his indifference?

He raised the heavy portière, and the light seemed to go out of two women's lives as it fell to behind him.

"Well," said Egidia, complacently, "that will be the first tea party my cousin has ever given in his studio in his life, to my knowledge! I do hope it will come off, for I want you two to be great friends. You will—you are the veritable antithesis of each other."

Mrs. Elles interrupted her with a sudden burst of hysterical laughter.

"Friends!" she said. "Friends! And my husband is going to make a co-respondent of him!"

CHAPTER XII

Egidia laid her head on her hands. The tale of Brignal Banks had been told. "Good God!" she said passionately. "And it is to Edmund Rivers that this thing has happened!"

She thought of the poignant tale of love and disaster only as it affected the man. It was natural; Mrs. Elles had expected that she would do so, and yet she was a little aggrieved at not being treated as the central figure of any romance that happened to be forward. She valiantly stifled her feelings on this occasion, however, and rising from the low prie-dieu chair from which she had delivered her confession, knelt at Egidia's feet, and gently pulled her hands down from her face. The gesture was pretty and appealing, but at this juncture it irritated the other woman almost beyond endurance by its dash of theatricality. Thus behave erring heroines of melodrama when they reveal "all" to their mentors. Egidia sat and stared at the little flushed face opposite her with an almost unfriendly gaze, and listened but coldly to the trickle of her excitable speech.

"But it must not happen!" Mrs. Elles was saying. "It must not! It must not! You can save him, if you will, and that is why I have come to you. I

209

have travelled all night, and I have not slept for two. If I tell my story badly, that's why. There's an iron band across my forehead. And I have had nothing to eat for ages. But I knew that you and he had always been great friends, to say the very least, and that it would be so easy for you—— You must forgive me, and understand that I did what I could. I acted for the best—on the spur of the moment. I thought it was the only way to save the situation—"

"What, in the name of Heaven, have you done?" exclaimed the other. "Do, please, tell me exactly."

"I used your name——" began Mrs. Elles, hesitatingly.

"Please go on!"

"I am afraid I told my husband straight out, when he pressed me, that Mr. Rivers was engaged to you!"

"To me! Mr. Rivers! What possible authority——"

Egidia rose to her feet, and Mrs. Elles perforce rose too.

"Have I done such a mischief?" she asked supplicatingly. "Stay! the lace of my dress has got caught in yours!"

She disentangled it, while Egidia stood, a prisoner, shivering with impatience, and some disgust.

"Surely," Phœbe Elles went on, "you are very fond of each other? I always thought so, from the way he spoke—or rather did not speak of you. With some men reticence about a woman is the sure sign of their feeling keenly about her. Indeed, I was quite jealous of you sometimes!" she added ingenuously.

Egidia's face had stiffened into the very haughtiest expression a proud face can assume. She was a woman who could curl her lip, and she did it now, but Mrs. Elles was too tactless and too much excited to notice.

"So you see that I am doing this entirely for his sake—quite against the grain, I assure you, but it seemed the only way—and I thought you would want to do anything to keep him out of it!"

"Keep him out of it!" exclaimed the other, pointing down towards the basement of her own house, as to the depths of an imaginary Divorce Court. "I should think I did! But how could you suppose that such an absurd lie as that could do him any good?"

"Couldn't it? I thought it could. And I seem to be always being scolded for telling lies now!" sighed Mrs. Elles, "but I really thought I was splendide mendax this time! And though it was a lie, of course, you can make it true to save him, don't you see?"

Egidia recovered herself. What was the use of being angry?

"But supposing Mr. Rivers did care for—was engaged to me—I don't see what possible difference it could make?"

She succeeded in smiling almost indulgently on this sweet simpleton, who was to be suffered gladly, for the sake of Rivers.

"Well, of course, I don't know much about these things," Mrs. Elles said, plaintively, "but I thought if the co-respondent——"

"Please don't use that word," said Egidia, shivering.

"It is the word, I know that much. Well, if the man is already engaged to someone else at the time that the accusation is made—it surely makes it less— likely that he would—wouldn't a jury think better of him? He would have to marry her at once, of course, and send the slip of the Times containing the announcement to my husband——"

She looked so serious, so innocent, so like the fair Ophelia, "incapable of her own grief," so utterly woe-begone, that Egidia's mood changed. She laughed, and sat down, and took her visitor's little soft, incompetent, feverish hand in her own cool firm one, and held it.

"My dear Mrs. Elles, have you been all these years married to a solicitor, and know so little of it all as to suppose that a jury would be affected by such a detail as the one you have mentioned! No, no, we must get your husband to stay proceedings altogether. I hope it isn't so bad as you think—in fact, I am sure it isn't! Your husband could not, I think, possibly divorce you merely on what you have told me—and perhaps you have even exaggerated that a little? You are very tired——"

"I am not hysterical!" exclaimed Mrs. Elles angrily.

"Forgive me, but your voice and your eyes belie you. Besides, you said yourself you were ill. Of course you are, naturally, after what you have undergone!"

"It was pretty dreadful!" Mrs. Elles owned, mollified.

"To-morrow," Egidia continued, with a little imperceptible shudder, "you must go over it all again to me. After you have had a night's rest, you will be able to think and marshall your facts more clearly. I ought to know exactly where we stand. Meantime, will you send for your things from the Great Northern Hotel and pay your bill?"

"But I must live somewhere!" exclaimed the other in a sick fright. "You surely don't want me to go back to Mortimer, when I have just run away from him?"

"No, but you must write to him, and tell him you are staying here with me. Though literary, I am supposed to be respectable." She smiled. She had taken her line. "And, by the way, I have a dinner party here to-night, and I want you to enjoy it and look nice."

"I have an evening dress in my box at the Hotel," said Mrs. Elles, eagerly.

"Well, then, we will get it here in time for you. I will send at once."

She rang the bell, gave her orders, and then turning, stopped and kissed the little bit of thistledown who stood there, grateful and apprehensive. It was an effort, the whole scene had been one long effort, but she flattered herself she had come out of it well, and had not betrayed herself. In the exercise of her profession she had studied the feelings of others and their development and outward manifestations so closely that she had grown almost morbidly desirous of not showing her own.

"Please call me Phœbe!" her visitor had murmured as she led her to her room and left her there.

Yes, she, a simple, honest, unsophisticated woman, would do anything, dare, contrive, and practise anything that might deliver Edmund Rivers from the consequences of his accidental connection with this miracle of indiscretion, this butterfly, who, unfortunately for others, took herself so seriously.

He should not, if she could help it, have to rue the day when he had allowed the human interest to come into his life, and occupy even a portion of his mental foreground. That was all he had done; he had never flirted with her, Egidia felt sure. "Love plays the deuce with landscape!" he had once laughingly proclaimed, to excuse himself from marrying. No, he should not be forced, by the stain of the courts, the horrors of imputation, to take on himself the shackles of the marriage tie, with which the little woman who had played the part of his evil genius, would so carelessly invest him!

.   .   .   .

"She kissed me, but all the while, she would like to scratch my eyes out," Mrs. Elles in the silence of the spare room was saying to herself. She was not

spiteful—oh no, that was not her character at all—
but she had studied and could not help knowing
human nature! There was no misprision of motive
in her mind; she was perfectly aware of Egidia's
reasons for being kind to her. That lady had taken
her rival to stay with her because, as the saying is,
she preferred to see mischief in front of her—she
would keep her safe under her own roof the better to
control her. It was all for the man's sake, not for
the woman's at all!

The welfare of Edmund Rivers was the object of
Phœbe Elles too, she must not forget that, and she
must consent, for his sake, to be the creature of his
cousin's bounty. It must be so, but it was very
hard. Egidia, perhaps unconsciously, assumed
proprietary airs. Her visitor stamped a little modest
stamp of the foot at the thought, and was assailed by
a wild desire to prove to Egidia and the world the
genuineness of Rivers' love, by purposely losing her
case, and letting him marry her!

But would that prove it?

.   .   .   .

"Les hommes sont la cause que les femmes ne
s'aiment pas!" Mrs. Elles murmured to herself, as
arrayed in her prettiest dress, and conscious that she
became it, she went to dinner, in the big public
room of the Mansions, where Egidia mustered all her
famous little parties of twelve.

This was Mrs. Elles's first taste of London
society. She had thought of it, dreamed of it,

yearned for it for years. Now it had come to her, like a draught of heady champagne, vivifying after the two nights of waking misery and anxiety she had undergone. Only two nights ago, she had stood, a shaking, quaking figure in the dark passage of the inn at Rokeby, hearing the clock tick, and the rustle of the heavy leaf screen against the pane outside the door of her lover's room, whence no sound came—no voice of pardon. Here in the successful novelist's pretty electric-lighted rooms all was gaiety, easy, social merriment, facile smiles and light-hearted repartee. She was made for this. She held her own. She smiled and retorted with all but the last touch of up-to-dateness, and her hostess put her forward, and gave her every opportunity of shining. Mrs. Elles thoroughly appreciated her generosity, and, woman-like, was far more deeply touched by Egidia's kindness in this instance, than by her greater charity in so ardently espousing her cause in the matter of the divorce.

She for a time forgot the Damocles sword that hung over her head. In a few months, perhaps, nobody would care to speak to her; now they were at any rate glad enough to do so. She went in to dinner with Mr. St. Jerome, the popular novelist, and he seemed to think her interesting. She had intended at first to try to sink her disqualification of country cousin, but by the time they had got to the first entrée, decided otherwise, since the assumption of mundaneity prevented her asking questions, and she did so want to know so many things. She would make conversational capital out of it instead.

"Is every one here a celebrity?" she asked.

"So much so, that they are all trying to hide it," St. Jerome answered. "Did you ever see a more modest looking set of people, calmly eating their fish, and saving their good things for their books?"

"Are you doing that too?" she asked with the sweetest of smiles. She knew he wrote novels. She allowed a little time to elapse before she removed the sting, then—"Because, if so, you succeed very badly. You have said several things I shall feel obliged to use again in the provinces. But—forgive me, I am like Pope's definition of a mark of interrogation——"

"You want to know who that is?" he said briskly, indicating a dark, bearded man, with impressive eyes, who sat next Egidia.

"How quick you are!"

"Not at all. Everybody wants to know who Dr. André is!"

She felt snubbed; he went on.

"He is the celebrated occultist and oculist. The first is his business, the second his pleasure. But he works the two together with great success. I don't know if he quite succeeds in taking in our dear Egidia; she is very shrewd, for a woman novelist. André's theory of ocular practice consists largely of the due relation of the state of the eyesight to general health, and thence to hypnotism, do you see? People are unkind enough to call him a quack, but I think that very unfair, for he is quite amusing!"

Mrs. Elles did not know if St. Jerome was amusing or not; she was sure he was spiteful. She felt that his flighty and casual manner suggested some disrespect towards the Lady from the Provinces, but perhaps that was London's way? She meant that London's way should not by any means astonish or perturb her, so she went on calmly.

"If I were not afraid of your thinking me conceited, I should say that I think the hypnotist is looking at me!"

"Of course he is. He is trying to mesmerize you. That is his little game. He boasts that he can make anyone in the world cross the whole length of the room to him if he has a mind—and yet he lives only three floors down, in these very Mansions."

Mrs. Elles again suspected Mr. St. Jerome of making fun of her.

"I hope he won't care to thoroughly exercise his powers just now," she said, "for I am a very impressionable subject. I might get up, and go to him this very minute, and that would be awkward. Introduce me after dinner, and I will tell him that I once wore blue spectacles for a month without stopping."

"That is why your eyes look so bright!" said St. Jerome, lightly. As a matter of fact he suspected her of taking morphia.

"Oh, I had a better reason than that!" she said,

impatiently. "Tell me, do you know an artist called Rivers?"

"Was he your reason? And a very nice reason too!"

"Mr. St. Jerome, you are chaffing me, and it is not fair, as I come from the provinces! Besides," she explained, beginning to be terrified at the possible consequences of her imprudence, "I hardly know Mr. Rivers. I met him here for the first time at tea."

"Of course you did!"

Mrs. Elles inferred from this speech that Rivers was a constant visitor at Egidia's tea-table, which is perhaps what St. Jerome intended her to do. She was piqued. "I—that is we—are going to tea with him in his studio, one of these days," she remarked.

"I congratulate you! Rivers is not a quiet tea-party man at all, and enjoys the reputation of being a misogynist. I have long tried to acquire it in vain. Naturally all your sex are devoted to him. He takes it very well, I must say, and shows no signs of being unduly puffed up. A lady's man sans le savior!"

"There are a good many people like that!" remarked Mrs. Elles, though in her heart of hearts she thought there was but one. But she wanted to draw the polite and analytical novelist, and lead him on to discuss the man she loved.

"Yes, and all the women adore them, confound it! They mistake; they see the man full of energy and spirit, making for a given point in life, and allowing

nothing to distract his attention from it, like a horse
with blinkers on.   They naturally want to remove the
blinkers, and divert a little of that force and energy
into a more useful channel, i. e., love-making.   They
take no account of the correlation of forces; they
don't see that what a man gives to one thing he cannot give to another, that dominated as he is by an
abstraction, charming concrete objects''—he looked
at Mrs. Elles—"have no chance at all!"

"You are making Mr. Rivers out a mild kind of
Robespierre!"

"Oh, well, I don't go so far as to suppose that he
would wade through seas of blood to his ambition—
let us say the painting of the most perfect landscape
in the world; his easel is not a guillotine, and besides,
he has more or less realized his ambition, he has
everything he wants, name, and fame, and money,
and the right to be as misogynistical as he pleases.
He is no curmudgeon, but he is eminently unsociable.
I have never even been in his studio myself, for he
doesn't go in for the vulgarity of a Show Sunday,
and he is away in the country half the year, propitiating the deities of woods and streams.   I meet
him now and then at the Athenæum—young women,
you know, are not admitted there, only bishops and
so on!"

"Isn't it a great honour to belong to the Athenæum?"

"Yes, especially if you are elected under Rule II.
Rivers is a great swell.   I shouldn't be surprised if

they made him President some day—that is, if they
ever make a landscape painter President of the R. A.,
which they have a natural prejudice against doing."

Rule II. of the Athenæum Club—the limitations of
landscape painters as Possible Presidents of the Royal
Academy—it was all Greek to Mrs. Elles, but still
she managed very well. Her eyes sparkled, she was
gay and sympathetic; the two things that London
wants. There was no denying it, she was happy here,
happier than she had ever been, dining in the lonely
inn with the man of her heart, though she would not
for worlds have admitted such a truth had she been
taxed with it. She would have liked Rivers with her
here; she would have been friends with God and
Mammon. Love, and the World! Rivers and she
were true incompatibles; but that again she would
not have owned.

Looking down the table, she sometimes caught
Egidia's deep-set, serious eyes fixed on her, and
immediately composed her own face to a decent
semblance of mental distress, subdued and controlled
by the dictates of social standards of gaiety.

Egidia smiled sweetly at her now and then, as a
mother might at a promising débutante daughter.
She herself was feeling it an effort to sustain her own
reputation for brilliancy and repartee. Her spirits
were so leaden; she had received such a shock. She
could think of nothing but the painter's affairs, and
the crushing blow that was so soon to fall on him.
Edmund Rivers, a very Galahad of stainless life, a

knight sans peur and sans reproche! The social fall
of such is always the severer, since the eager hounds
of envy are so glad of an excuse to worry a name that
has heretofore stood high. What though the asper-
sion was so utterly false, it would be cast all the
same; the mud would be flung, and some of it would
stick. And she who would lay down her life to save
him a moment's annoyance must endure to look on
the little enemy of his peace, sitting opposite her,
careless, irresponsible, drinking in flattery and
champagne, flashing her bright eyes about, and wav-
ing the little fluttering hands that held the future of
a man worth twenty such as she, in the might of his
art and intellect!

However, that Phœbe Elles should thoroughly
enjoy her dinner party was necessary for the further-
ance of a plan of action that Egidia had conceived—
one of the many plans that she had conceived. The
better pleased Mrs. Elles was, the better would the
particular plan work, but though Egidia was an
authoress, she was human, and presently found herself actually avoiding her guest's laughing eyes.

Looking round at her own neighbour, she noticed
the mesmeric eyes of Dr. André fixed on her guest,
and knew that he had singled her out for his particular line of experiment. Egidia was "apt now at all
sorts of treasons and stratagems," and a new idea shot
through her brain. She was no believer in hypnotism, except in its extraordinary power over a certain
kind of silly woman, in the way of suggestion.

She turned round to Dr. André.

"I see you are considering the little lady who was the occasion of my wild appeal to you to come and dine in a hurry. Do you think she would be a good subject for hypnotic suggestion?"

"No."

"Too clever?"

"She could never succeed in making her mind a blank, I fancy. She thinks all the time—nothing particularly worth thinking, I daresay. Still, she is so pretty, I should like to try. She is not a London woman?"

"How do you know that?"

"Oh, she is beautifully dressed. It isn't that," he said smiling. "The dress may be Paris, but the soul is Newcastle."

Egidia started. "You are really a wonderful man, Dr. André, or else you have the luck of coincidences!"

He smiled, with the fatuity of the occultist.

"You are right, she does come from Newcastle, but let me tell you that when I introduce you, you will find her quite au fait of all the latest London fads. She makes it her business to be. These illustrated papers do a great deal to prepare the provincial mind for the more startling developments of our civilization. Mrs. Elles has looked on the Medusa head of certain aspects of society through the medium of 'Black and White,' and the 'Ladies' Field.'"

"How you hate her!" said Dr. André.

Egidia wore mental sackcloth and ashes for the

rest of the evening, conscious that she had for once allowed herself to be drawn to the very verge of the fathomless gulf of feminine spite.

.   .   .   .

"Did I look nice?   Did I seem too dreadfully provincial?" was what Mrs. Elles said to her hostess when the door had closed on the last guest.

Egidia had sunk into a chair, and sat staring at vacancy.   Mrs. Elles's voice recalled her from her reverie.

"Not at all—I mean provincial.   You and the Doctor seemed to get on?   Did he propose to mesmerize you?"

"Oh, yes!" Mrs. Elles answered eagerly.   "Soon. May he?   Here in your flat?"

"Certainly!" Egidia replied, feeling now a little apprehension of the consequences.   "But you must not believe in him too much.   You must not let him get an influence over you!"

"I shouldn't mind.   I am sure he would not use his power for harm against me—or any woman!"

"Oh, no, he is a good old thing!" Egidia said condescendingly.   "And this little social trick of his amuses people, and makes him a personage, and asked out a great deal!"

"I believe very much in hypnotism as a serious force in life," said the other sturdily.   "I can't laugh at it.   And I think Dr. André is a most interesting man who could give one a real glimpse into one's self and into futurity, if he chose, and one turned out to be a good subject."

"And he thinks you a very pretty woman—he told me so."

"Oh—pretty!" said Mrs. Elles, as much as to imply that she did not wish to stand on anything so trivial as good looks in the seër's good opinion.

"At any rate, you enjoyed yourself?"

"Enormously! I mean, that I did not want to be a blot on your party, so I screwed myself up, and was gay!"

"You mean you were acting a part?" Egidia answered, coldly.

"Well, partly," Mrs. Elles replied; then she added with the pretty smile that leavened so many of her little insincerities, "but I confess—I forgot every now and then, and let myself feel as if nothing had happened, and I was a girl again, beginning life—the life I always wanted, the life I was made for, I think. Oh, don't you see how hard it all is for me, this course I have to take—that I must take for his sake?"

With a comical little twist of the mouth, she went on: "Some are born virtuous, some are—something or other—what is it?—and some have virtue thrust upon them! I know that I must defend this wretched case for the sake of other people, but I can't help thinking that if Mortimer did win it and get his divorce, it would be the very thing for me!"

"I confess I don't understand——"

"Mr. Rivers would marry me," she said, wistfully, "and then I should live in London!"

Egidia laughed—she could not help it! This, then, was the net result of her carefully arranged plan for indoctrinating her guest with the pleasures of respectability and the advantages of a defined social position.

"My dear woman, forgive me!" she exclaimed. "Have you the very remotest notion of what you are saying? You cannot have the most elementary knowledge of social laws if you imagine that a man having married a divorced woman—divorced on his account—could take her out, and expect his friends to call on her! On the contrary, you and he—God help you both—would have to forego all society. You would have to live abroad in some shady place, and be thankful for the company of blacklegs and second-rate women, or else make up your minds to live entirely apart from the world. He would not mind that; he is used to it; but you! What would you do without life, movement, and, above all, consideration? That is what I was asking myself when I looked down the table to-night, and saw you happy and gay——"

Mrs. Elles demurred.

"Well, pretending to be happy and gay—though I really and truly believe you were. As you have just been saying yourself, you were in your element. And I thought what a volcano it was that you were standing on, and how, if the worst came to pass, how

different a life yours would be from this you covet—
and all the time you were thinking that the very fact
of your divorce would entitle you to it all! Good
Heavens! Instead of sitting there, gay and important, admired and attended to, with people taking the
trouble to mesmerize you and analyze you and take
your soul to pieces for you, you would be hidden
away in some little foreign town—Boulogne, say?—
cut, snubbed, and penned up for life with no other
society but that of the man you have dragged down
along with you, and involved in your ruin, and who
would end by hating you in consequence."

Mrs. Elles cried out, outraged. "You forget—you
forget that he proposed to me—when he thought I
was free!"

"I beg your pardon——" Egidia said, vaguely.

"No, don't beg my pardon, you meant to be kind
—but——" She stopped, and her whole manner
altered as the humiliating suggestion took root in her
mind. "Tell me—you must mean—tell me in so
many words—you must mean to say that he never
really cared for me? For God's sake, speak out!"

"If you ask me to speak out honestly, then I don't
think he really did! He is not what is called a
marrying man. . . . Now you will of course
never be able to forgive me. . . . Let us both
go to bed now at any rate—I am quite worn out!"

She turned aside wearily, and passed through the
portière, letting her hand drag after her, as she went.
Mrs. Elles's vexation at her plain speaking died

before a more generous instinct of gratitude to the
woman who had befriended her in her need. She
caught hold of the fugitive hand——

"Oh, don't leave me like this; indeed, you are my
best friend. Thank you, thank you—for telling me
the truth. I ought to know it."

"It is only my opinion!" said the other, suffering
herself, however, to be drawn into the room again, by
the insistent tenderness of her rival, which touched
her, and made her feel a brute.

"Yes," Mrs. Elles went on sadly. "Only your
opinion, but you have known him so very much
longer than I have." She would have been equal to
the mental sacrifice of adding, "and so much more
intimately," but hardly dared, lest it was taken, not
as a compliment but as an impertinence. "I only
saw him for a month, and even in that time I could
not help loving him—adoring him. . . . How
could anyone help it? Could you?"

"No," Egidia murmured under her breath, too
much moved to resent the question.

"It is just those very silent men whom every one
adores," the other went on. "But he always preferred his art to me. I knew it at the time, only I
was so blinded. Then when he realized that he was
compromising me, he did the honourable thing, and
proposed. Of course I don't suppose he thought me
quite impossible, he felt it would be just bearable to
be married to me, if he had to be married, but he
had never meant to be married, as you say. But you

must see, that if I come to think that, how very much more humiliating it makes it for me—how painful to have to think that one was only proposed to out of pity and a sense of duty!"

She turned her face away, sobbing.

Egidia put her arm round her. She could unfeignedly sympathise with the very real sorrows of wounded vanity. She felt she had spoken plainly—with full conviction and honest intent, it was true, but still plainly and perhaps brutally. She was conscious that her care had been all along for the man, and not the woman.

"My dear, my dear," she said, drawing Mrs. Elles close to her, "there is another thing I see—that saves it a little—a good deal, I think!"

"What?" asked Phœbe Elles.

"You don't really love him either!"

"What, not love him?"

"No, you think you do, you would die for him, of course, but you don't love him. You happen to have chosen him for an emotional centre, every woman, if she is a woman, has to find an emotional centre, but she does not always choose well. Edmund, like all geniuses, is self-centred without being selfish; you understand me; he is to be regarded as exempt from the ordinary responsibilities of humanity, morally and otherwise. He is quite willing to be worshipped—what man is not? but he has no time to worship, or be anx petits soins with anybody. He could not, if he liked, make any woman happy, certainly not a

passionate woman.   She could never exist long in the
rarefied spiritual atmosphere into which dear Edmund
would want to lift her, where he lives—and flourishes.
He can feel, of course, the big things, but he has, as
it were, no small change of emotion at any one's service.   And he doesn't, on his side, ask for anything.
He is sufficient unto himself.   Did you not observe,
when you were with him, how he accepted your devotion, but made no demands on it!''

"He let me rub his colours for him!" Mrs. Elles
said, laughing.

"Do you mean to say you did not feel the curious
sense of aloofness, of want of sympathy with poor
humanity, that the consciousness of a mission—even
an art mission—seems to bring with it?   Not for
humanity's woes;   no one can be kinder than
Edmund, if you are in real trouble, but he is the
kind of man who would never notice if you had cut
your finger, or had got a new frock on.   Now woman
wants more than that here below—at least I think
so!''

She laughed, Mrs. Elles was wondering how she
could talk like this about the man she cared for.

"I am being very didactic, I fear," Egidia said
suddenly.   "And boring you."

"No, no," said the other vehemently.   "I love
discussing people.   I have noticed all you say in Mr.
Rivers, but still——   And do you know," she went
on eagerly, "all the men who speak of him seem very
fond of him, so is it only women he snubs?''

"Oh, men like him and respect him, but they don't slap him on the back, and confide their pleasant weaknesses to him! He is manly enough, but I don't know how it is, he is quite out of it in the smoking-room."

"He is very much at home in a woman's boudoir, at all events!" said Mrs. Elles, a little bitterly.

"You mean mine," the other replied with her usual directness. "Well, he is my cousin, and he knows I like to hear him discuss the only subject he cares to discuss—art. He tells me his ideas for new mediums and the experiments he is making. He laments the volatility of the prettiest colours, such as aureoline, and the impracticability of Nature as a model. We never talk of anything more personal than that, and all he condescends to look at here is a sunset over Westminster as we see it from my windows."

"Do you like that sort of subject best yourself?" Mrs. Elles said wistfully, going out of herself for once, into the other woman's mind, and realizing the bitterness of renunciation that informed the words so laughingly spoken.

"Oh, I—well, I am a woman, and no wiser than the rest. That is why I have been telling you all this, because if you once realize that I—have been there myself, in short—you will more readily let me help you and him. You see, though I am hopeless —absolutely hopeless"— Mrs. Elles stared; this strange woman might have been talking about cooks, for all the emotion she showed—"I am not even miserable about it. I know so well that if Edmund came to me and went down on his knees to me to marry him, I should refuse, he could not make me as happy as he makes me now. If I were a wife, I should not care to be second to anything, not even to Art, nor would you. I have realized the finality of it all, and so must you. But now, you must trust me, please, and not think, when I talk to you of your affairs and Edmund's, that I am fighting for my own hand, and mean to secure him for myself, in the end, as soon as I have helped him to get clear of his entanglement with you. You see—I speak quite plainly."

Mrs. Elles's eager disclaimer of any such interpretation of Egidia's behaviour was not so much the outcome of an emotional confidence in the woman who had so bravely, so wildly, so foolishly committed herself, as of the strong conviction which her words carried. She was secretly a little overcome and puzzled by the spectacle of so much single-mindedness and bonhomie in the unveiling of a soul's tragedy, such as she conceived Egidia's to be. She herself could not have been anything but tortuous in the telling of such a piece of secret history. The novelist's methods were not hers. They went with the whole character of the woman, with the honest eyes, and shrewd, fine, but uncompromising mouth.

CHAPTER XIII

Egidia used her novelist's privilege of supposed social emancipation sometimes, and braved conventionalities. She went once—or twice—to see her cousin in his studio. It was obviously impossible for her to receive him in her own house, while Mrs. Elles was an inmate of it.

Mrs. Elles had now been her guest for some months. She had written at the outset, in obedience to Egidia's instructions, a letter to her husband, long and reasonable, announcing her present whereabouts, and laying the circumstances and facts of her stay in Yorkshire fully before him. His only reply to her had been a curt communication through his lawyers, informing her that he was determined to proceed with the case, and would even consent to defray the cost of her defence by a suitable firm of London solicitors, whose name and address he mentioned.

"He pays to get rid of me!" Mrs. Elles had commented bitterly. She had up to the last moment believed in the existence in Mortimer's heart of a latent love for her. She was a woman before whom every man must necessarily bow the knee, even her husband. She was now a little disillusioned.

"Such a man should be glad to have such a wife as

me, on any terms!" she observed to Egidia. "It is worse than quarrelling with one's bread and butter; it is quarrelling with one's culture, as well!"

But it was painfully obvious that Mortimer Elles did not now set so high a value on the Muse who had for ten years honoured his fireside.

These were the things that amused Egidia, and indemnified her for the trial of housing the delinquent, and being the recipient of her oft repeated confidences. She always thought, and spoke to Rivers, of Phœbe Elles as of a wayward foolish child, whose material interests they both had at heart, and of the impending divorce case as of a mere legal and technical difficulty into which the indiscretion and imprudence of this particular child had plunged herself, and her friends.

"Pooh!" she said to Rivers, in an off-hand manner that was half assumed. "You don't know what Love is, either of you! She talks of it, and you don't, but you are both alike!"

Rivers still used his old habit, the one Mrs. Elles had noticed, and suffered from, that of refusing to take up other persons' speeches unless positively called upon to do so. He was working now against time, standing intent, mahl-stick and palette in hand, under the pale white globe of electric light, which dimly lit the whole vast studio, and concentrated itself upon his head, that was not so dark as it used to be.

"The little fiend! She has managed to turn his

hair grey!'' Egidia said to herself as she stood near him, but not near enough to interfere with the free play of his brush-arm, and talked softly, and in a way calculated to make no direct demand on his attention. Mrs. Elles had learned that art, too, in the glades of Brignal. Rivers never looked round at Egidia, but continued to lay on touch after touch with unerring precision and mastery. He now and then stepped back a few paces, and glanced at her, just enough to avoid jostling her in his backward walk, but that was all.

"Do you like Dr. André?" she asked suddenly.

"Yes, well enough why?"

"Because I think he admires Phœbe!"

"Does he?" was the indifferent reply.

"She is probably with him now—or at her lawyer's."

Egidia spoke tentatively, as if she were consulting him as to her own line in countenancing the intimacy between the two. Perhaps a desire to ascertain Rivers' own personal feelings on the subject of the little flirtation unconsciously influenced her.

"There is no harm in André," said Rivers decidedly. "And, poor little thing, it does her good to be taken out of herself!"

"Nothing ever really does that!" Egidia rejoined. Inwardly she said, "Oh, no, he can't care for her." And her face, unconsciously to herself, took on a joyous expression. She went on, with a manner of detached criticism:

"I never, in all my literary life, met any one who lived in herself so completely. Keats speaks of a woman who would have liked to have been engaged to a poem and married to a novel, but Phœbe goes one better, she is her own poem, her own novel. No spectacle, no literature in the world interests her as much. She is always pulling herself up by the roots, as it were, to account for her moral—or immoral—growth, and telling one all about it."

"And does it bore you?" asked he.

"On the contrary, it interests me deeply. And to do her justice, she is a charming companion, so gay, so lively. No one would imagine what she is suffering. The Merry Martyr, I call her." There was the very slightest touch of mockery in her tone.

He made no remark, and she continued:

"I gave her that drawing you gave me—the one that had a sketch of her in it. She did want it so badly, poor girl, and after all, she sat for it, and had a better right to it than I!"

"I will give you another!" said Rivers.

"Will you really, Edmund? That is nice of you." She flushed with pleasure. "Now I must go back to my young woman of the sea!" She laughed.

"Be kind to her!" said Rivers, "but you are, I know. You are a good woman!"

"Am I? But I get very angry with the lady sometimes, when she talks as if this divorce of hers was a sort of smart tea-party she was going to in the immediate future."

"But that is the right way to look at it," said he, "and a tea party that won't come off either!"

Egidia stared at him; she wondered if this was the flippancy of bitterness or indifference?

"They won't be able to prove what is not true," the artist went on, with some fire, but at the same time carefully laying and mixing burnt umber and madder brown on his palette. "There isn't really the ghost of a case, as I told the old woman, her aunt, when she came and made me a scene. It will be all right. Elles will abandon the charge, or we will get it squared out of court. It isn't worth thinking about."

He applied the mixture he had made with a firm square touch.

"Oh, I see," said Egidia, "that is why you are able to paint away so composedly! I was wondering —I had thought that in the face of such a possible horror you would have not been able to do anything. That is why I have distressed myself so much about it all. Are you sure you are not pretending—that you are not more disturbed than you care to own?"

"I don't let it trouble me," he said, adding with a certain intentional deliberation, "I am an artist before all!"

Egidia said she must go home. Rivers unyoked his palette from his thumb, and laid it down carefully. He led her out of the studio, downstairs, past walls covered with framed diplomas, and medals, and all kinds of memoranda of a life spent in the service and

honor of Art.   His house in Bedford Square was pre-
eminently a bachelor's house; an indurated, deeply
ingrained celibacy was suggested by the presence of
many articles of furniture, and the absence of others.
Rivers was of the orderly description of bachelor, of
all kinds the most inveterate.   Egidia, in her mind's
eye, could not see the little Elles throning it here,
her trivial prettiness overwhelmed by the grandiose
style of decoration appropriate to the mansions of
Bloomsbury, her eyes resting on high wall spaces
hung with old masters, her footsteps treading stair-
cases whose angles were filled with yellow casts of
heroic statues.   There was never a bit of drapery, or
a Tanagra figurine to reduce the scale a little.   It
was all the difference between the atmosphere of the
British Museum, and a Louis Seize Boudoir.   Egidia
felt happier at the definition of this anomaly between
the tastes of Rivers and Phœbe, and went away having absorbed some of the contagion of Rivers' confidence in a renewed term of celibacy for himself.

Mrs. Elles had not yet returned when she got home,
but came fluttering in presently, and touched her
shoulder as she sat over the fire shivering with the
chill depression of thoughts that would rise, in spite
of the consoling visit she had just made.

"Cheer up!" said Mrs. Elles.   "I have brought
you a little present, nothing particular, only to show
that I love you.   A little gold lucky bean.   Will you
wear it to please me?"

She sank down on the hearthrug, and laid her

hand, and for the moment her head, on Egidia's knee. This was one of her "caressing little ways," to which Egidia was ashamed of objecting.

"Where have you been?" she said coldly. "With the Doctor or the Lawyer?"

"Lawyer. Right away down to Holborn. Of course, I got there too soon. I generally do. I am so eager to hear what fresh news they have. A divorce case is so exciting. But then I have to wait, in the lobby, among all that barren brownness of cheap varnish, and trodden oilcloth and japanned tin deed boxes stacked up to the very horizon. There I am on one of an awful row of bulging leather chairs, where the crowd of witnesses sit—I mean the grimy people that keep coming in, wiping their cuffs across their mouths, and sit down apologetically. They are to be examined in this or that disgusting case, as Jane Anne will be in mine. I watch the commissionaire adding up figures inside his queer hutch of a desk, and read up all about Salmon-Fishery Laws on the walls and see the little bow-legged clerks hop off their stools, and run about with sheaves of papers. Why can't they make lawyers' offices prettier?"

"Divorce," said Egidia, "would really become too attractive if it were run in connection with a restaurant or a manicure establishment."

"And then," Mrs. Elles went on, "when I do see Mr. Lawler, I cannot help thinking that he is laughing at me. He treats me like a child——"

"Instead of an erring woman!" said Egidia.

"Well, you should not wear your hats so terribly on one side. The dignity of crime——"

"Yes, I must really get something plainer!" Mrs. Elles returned, taking her literally. "I nearly cried to-day, and it did not go with my hat at all."

"Why did you cry?"

"Because—I can stand a good deal—but when he repeated all the awful things that woman was prepared to swear against me, I nearly gave way. The whole case, they say, stands on her evidence, and it is false, outrageously false. She always hated me, she cared for Mr. Rivers herself. It was notorious that she did."

Egidia sneered a little, almost in spite of herself. "Who next?" she said.

"She was very nearly a lady," Mrs. Elles said apologetically, "and he was kind to her, but he never flirted with her—of that I am convinced. But if the jury believe her, Mortimer will get his case, to a certainty!"

"Did they tell you the details—of what she was going to say?" asked Egidia, shyly and awkwardly.

Mrs. Elles told her, at some length, but without much hesitation.

"Oh, she can't realize!" thought Egidia, brooding. "She can have no imagination!"

Her own conjured up so vividly the horrors of the scene in court—the scene that must come now, in spite of Rivers' pathetically confident assertions.

"She can't love him, or know or care one little bit

what he suffers—or is it that she thinks that she will get him herself in the end? And so she will, for he is a man of honour. Ah, but she shall not, if I can prevent it. It will be the best plot I ever invented, if I can pull it through, and then I suppose I must take the veil, to show the purity of my intentions! ' . . God forgive me, if he loves her! But he does not! . . . He is an artist before all. He said so himself, this very day. And no man loves disgrace, and such disgrace would kill love, if ever it existed!"

"What are you thinking of?" asked the other presently. "You look like the tragic muse, or Althea, before she put the burning brand back into the fire again. You have a very strong face, do you know? It is a pity Mr. Rivers isn't a figure painter, then he could paint you."

"I wish—somehow—you would not talk of Mr. Rivers."

"Why not? I am always thinking of him."

"That you are not."

"You think me very frivolous?" Mrs. Elles sighed out. "But I only laugh that I may not weep—I go about trying to kill thought. If I did not, I should go mad with what is hanging over me! And the worst I have to bear almost is the thought that though I am thinking so constantly of him, he is not thinking of me—except as a disagreeable incident—a burr that has somehow got stuck to him, and that he cannot shake off!" She got up and walked about a little, evidently a prey to real mental perturbation. Then she turned suddenly.

"Egidia, I want you and him if possible to know this, that I shall not marry him, even if I am divorced for him. I could not, after what you said."

She spoke pettishly, like a child or a schoolgirl, but all the strength and sadness of renunciation was in her eyes. She evidently meant what she said. Egidia realised this, but the complication of her feelings about this little Helen kept her silent awhile. She took her hand, however, and held it, in sign of amity.

"I want, Phœbe," she said presently, "to go out of town for two or three days. Do you think, if I did, that you could amuse yourself—and keep out of mischief?"

"You speak to me as if I was ten!" Mrs. Elles said. "I am not sure if I mind? What is mischief?"

"Oh, you know—things that might prejudice you —in your new position. I need not mention them— you know the kind of thing?"

"Can I go to see the Rembrandts with Dr. André?"

"The poor man's in love with you—but there would be no harm in your going to the Rembrandts with him, I think," Egidia answered easily.

By ten o'clock of the next day she was gone.

.   .   .   .

Mrs. Elles felt a really irresistible impulse, to do what she did. "It was as if something called me!" she said afterwards. "I felt that I had to see him."

So two days after the day on which her friend had left London, the dreary gas lamps of Bedford Square fluttered, and the black mud shone prismatically under the feet of a little woman, wandering without judgment or system, round and round the square, enquiring of nodding applewomen, of burly policemen, of scurrying street arabs, and honouring them all with the gracious smile of drawing rooms, the way to No. 99 in that region.

"Why, there, Missie, under yer nose," said the last of the policemen, pointing to the number, written black and jagged over the fanlight of the house near whose very doorstep she was standing. He thought the young lady a little touched in the head; there was indeed a wild look in her eyes, born of the consciousness of her own audacity, and the wild joy of seeing Rivers again.

She rang the bell, and a grim, demure-looking Scotch servant—Rivers' staid old housekeeper, of whom she had often heard—answered it.

"Can I see Mr. Rivers?" she asked.

"Mr. Rivers doesn't paint figures, Miss," said the woman kindly, and with the manner of one delivering an oft repeated statement. "But Mr. Brandard, over the other side of the Square, is always glad for us to send models over to him."

'I am not a model," said Mrs. Elles, vexed and ashamed. "Here is my card. Will you take it to Mr. Rivers, and ask if he will see me?"

The perfectly civil Scotchwoman took it, with a

blank neutral face. She showed the visitor into a half vestibule, half room, on one side of the passage. It was perfectly, ordered and arranged, there were no landscapes on its walls—it was, she knew, a fad of the painter's not to hang his own pictures. There were other people's pictures, etchings, engravings, with flattering inscriptions, "A mon ami—à mon confrère—hommages"—signed with some of the greatest names in the land. A sense of the worldly importance of this man whom she was going to drag through seas of disreputability grew in her mind, and affected her more deeply than Egidia's hints and lectures had done. She was literally a burr hanging on this great name, and she ought to kill herself sooner than let herself be associated with it in men's minds. It was then that the idea of suicide first came to her.

The servant came back.

"Mr. Rivers is very sorry indeed, Ma'am, but he is not able to see any one to-day."

"He——" Her lips trembled; her whole body shook at the blow. She turned, lest the woman saw her face.

"Is there any message I can give, Madam?"

"No, thank you, no message," she answered, with her face still averted, and drifting out into the street.

She leant against the palings of the Square, and sobbed. Was it love, or vanity—or shock?

"How brutal—how brutal!" she repeated to herself.

The policeman on his beat turned his bull's eye on to her.

"Are you going to tell me to move on?" she asked him, plaintively.

"No, Madam," he replied, and she was a little assuaged. At least he saw that she was a lady. She dried her eyes, and crossed back to the pavement, and down a side street. As she passed a little postern-like door in the wall—Rivers' happened to be a corner house—it opened, and the artist came out. He still had her card in his hand.

They stood and faced each other.

"Oh, my God, how ill you look!" she exclaimed, "and it is all my fault. Won't you even give me your hand?"

"Are you mad?" he said, contemporaneously with her speech. "Good God! was there ever a more idiotic thing for a woman in your position to do?"

He seized her arm, almost roughly, and led her away from the door.

"What are you going to do with me?"

"Put you in a cab, of course! You must not be seen here with me, on any account. I could hardly believe my eyes when your card was put into my hands."

So saying, he tore it across with a rancour that pierced her heart.

"You are most unkind!" she complained, following him in his great angry strides down the street, "and unnecessary. It is quite dark, no one could see

me, or recognise me, and I do so want to talk to you.
If you must take a hansom, choose one without a
lamp. Egidia is away, for two days. I don't know
where she has gone. I felt I must see you, do you
hear? It is a month since I have been in London—a
month of agony. . . . Did you hail it?" she
asked nervously, as a cab drew up along the kerb-
stone.

She put her hand appealingly on his arm.

"I won't get in, unless you promise to come with
me, so far. I must—I must talk to you."

"You are behaving like a child."

"I know I am," she said, "only because you are
behaving like a——"

What was she going to say? She did not know
herself, only that a crushing sense of estrangement, of
inevitableness, had come over her; the prop of an
unacknowledged hope that had stayed her for so
many weeks had been rudely withdrawn. The man
she loved was a stranger; she had surely never lived
at his side, day in, day out, through the summer that
was past? A wave of despair overwhelmed her, black
as the mud she looked down on, as she stood, her
foot on the step, prepared to abandon her point, and
go back alone.

But she had gained it.

"Anything sooner than a scene in the street!" she
heard Rivers say wearily to himself, as he got in
beside her.

"How cruel you are—how inconsiderate! Surely

I have the right to a few words with you! I will never perhaps speak to you again in this world!"

He sat, stiff in his closely-buttoned overcoat, like a statue beside her, and spoke no word.

She took his hand, as it lay on his knee.

"Forgive me—do forgive me! I am so sorry—so dreadfully sorry!"

"What for?" he said, gently.

"For bringing this on you—this—this disgrace. And you cannot forgive me, that is just it. I realised it when you refused to see me just now, and sent me a message by a servant."

"I had to. Think, yourself! You must really not be so unreasonable!"

"I am reasonable—quite, quite reasonable; and saying good-bye to you, if you only would let me! Yes, you never cared for me much, and now the little ghost of love is laid forever. This threatened disgrace and exposure has killed it. But it was there— don't take that from me—a little love, and the rest of it pity. Egidia says so, and I believe her. . . . Stop, stop, I am not asking you to say anything—I had rather you did not protest. . . . Oh, look at that great red Bovril sign flaring out! It looks as if the whole street was on fire. It must frighten the horses. . . ."

Her voice broke into a sob of hysterical terror.

"Dear——" began Rivers, clasping her hand more tightly.

"How nice of you! It hardly sounds at all perfunctory! And yet I know it is. Don't try any more. Let me tell you that I don't mind this for myself, but only for you, and I mean to defend myself tooth and nail, only for your sake. I know what it means for you. If Mortimer and his paid accomplices can succeed in lying me away from him, then the world will expect you to marry me."

"Yes," he said, "and I will!"

"Ah, but it takes two!" she replied, in tragic accents. "You can't marry me against my will. Supposing I am not there?"

He allowed the usual empty threat of suicide to pass unheeded.

"I shall ask you to, at any rate," he said, doggedly.

"Oh, yes, you will ask me!" She was playing so well that she almost enjoyed it. "Oh, yes, you will ask me, because you are a man of honour—and I shall refuse, because I am a woman of honour. I will not be behind Egidia, whom you respect, in that. You are right. She is strong and good. And she loves you."

"Please don't."

"Surely you and I have no need to mince words? She loves you, and if you marry any one, it ought to be Egidia. She is devoted, she is an angel, and she would rather see you dead at her feet, than married to me!"

She never looked round, or she would perhaps have realised the exquisite annoyance she was inflicting on her helpless victim, penned up as he was beside her, powerless to prevent or avoid the stream of tactless heroics she was pouring on him. His forehead was contracted, his hands were clenched together over the doors of the cab.

"We are coming to the more crowded streets now," he said suddenly, "and it is really very dangerous for you to be seen with me. Had you not better let me get out, and leave you to go the rest of the way alone?"

She replied, with desperate and intentional incisiveness, "I permit you to leave me, since you wish it."

He put up his arm, and raised the trap door. Mrs. Elles raised her hand to intercept his, but let it fall hopelessly down again, on a glance at his set face. The cab stopped and he got out, and standing half on the pavement, and half on the foot-board of the cab, held out his hand.

"Good-bye!" he said, "for the present!"

The reservation was kind in intention, but she would not accept it.

"Good-bye—forever!" was her answer, as her hand, gloveless, out of her muff, went forth to meet his.

"How cold you are!" he said, as he took it. "I am sorry. But it is better I should leave you now, isn't it? Forgive me for being such a bear, but I have to think for both. I will write if I may?"

"You needn't," she whispered, retreating to the corner of the cab, like a wounded animal. "Tell him to go on!"

"Is there anywhere you can tell him to go—some shop—and then discharge him and take a new one? It would be safer!"

"Tell him to go to the New Gallery!" she said, defiantly, and Rivers accordingly did so, and left her.

CHAPTER XIV

Dr. André was waiting for her in the dim-lighted halls of the New Gallery, where large-eyed solemn-faced women, some of them so like Egidia, as she thought, looked down from the walls on Mrs. Elles in her somewhat elf-like prettiness, as of a picture by Tissot. All she had in common with them, was her large wide-open eyes, eyes without depth or mystery, and with unresting lids that had perhaps never drooped to hide an emotion worth the name, or a secret worth the keeping.

"I was afraid you were not coming after all!" the hypnotist said, in his soft, authoritative voice.

She sank on to a red leather causeuse, and blinked pathetically.

"Don't speak to me for a moment!" she whispered, throwing back her head and turning her profile only towards him.

"You have a headache?" Dr. André asked sympathetically.

She shook her head, and in that nugatory shake strove to indicate the region of her heart, as the seat of her uneasiness. He had the tact to hold his tongue, and presently she remarked, with a little sigh, "What nice pictures!" as a hint that conversation might begin.

"You don't care about pictures to-day," he said, laughing. "You are terribly upset, I can see. Have you had bad news? Have you been fighting with wild beasts at Ephesus?"

She was pleased at his way of putting things. He was alluding to her interviews with lawyers: of the circumstances in which she found herself he was now quite au fait.

"Wild beasts!" she said. "Well, not quite that, but—people are very odd, and never behave exactly as one has a right to expect them to?" Her accent was slightly interrogative.

"Most men will bully a woman if they get a chance!" said he, looking at her keenly.

The butterfly did look a little crushed, a little subdued, as if she had only very recently been brought face to face with some of the crude realities of life of which she was always talking.

"But it is against all my theories," he continued.

"I believe in people too much," she went on. "And the consequence is, I give myself away, and make a fool of myself."

"You don't say so?" said Dr. André, politely, and tenderly.

He was not one who looked for wisdom in women; it was on charm that he insisted. He admired Mrs. Elles extremely. She reminded him of Heine's famous definition of a latter-day Venus—"a cross between a dressmaker and a duchess." The little touch of red on her cheek that was not rouge, but

which gave her the faintly meretricious air beloved of
décadents, pleased him; her large eyes, fuller at this
moment of tears than of expression, were bent on him
sadly and consciously appealing. By what art she
avoided the vulgar catastrophe of falling tear-drops
he did not know, but the brilliant result he could
fully appreciate. He was a poseur himself, and her
assumption of pose on his account flattered him.

"I wish I could help you," he said, wondering if
he would dare to take the little white hand stiff with
rings that lay ungloved on the red-covered ottoman
beside him. "Dare" was not the word—André was
a determined flirt, and would dare most things,—but
would it be advisable? He cared for her enough not
to want to frighten her.

"You know I would do anything for you!" he
confined himself to saying, and in spite of himself
there was the strongest ring of sincerity in his voice.

"I know you would," Mrs. Elles replied with
pretty assurance. She knew that though he imagined
he was only flirting, he was more nearly loving than
he was himself aware. That was the way she liked it
best; if he were to begin to think himself serious, he
would begin to be tiresome, and she would have to
discourage and snub him, and "see less" of him, as
the phrase is. She did not want to lose him. Her
intercourse with the distinguished hypnotist had '
acted as a derivative during this troublous period of
her life. She hardly realized his uses, in that
capacity, but Egidia did, and set no impediments in

the way of their frequent meetings. Phœbe was a fool, but Dr. André was a gentleman.

After having been scolded and bullied, as Mrs. Elles conceived herself to have been, by her ascetic and frigid lover for the last hour, it was sweet to be sympathized with, respectfully petted, and made of much account by Dr. André, who was willing to act as a souffre douleur. And though he was not nearly so handsome as Edmund Rivers, yet his face had a great deal more expression. Though his eyes were not deep like Rivers', they were mesmeric. His soul was willing, nay anxious, to go forth to meet hers; it did not, like that of Rivers, obstinately remain hid in its fastnesses of reserve, to baffle and disappoint her, who was always on the look-out for the evidences of spiritual and intellectual communion.

She rose from the ottoman, giving herself a little shake. She tried to imagine herself in a world that knew not Rivers, or Egidia, or Mortimer. They were not here, what had they to do with her? Did they live? Her senses were not aware of them. Why then should she take them into account? What was this thing that was troubling her? Had she any present evidence of its existence? Did it exist, then?

Trying to solve this intense problem in metaphysics, she went round the Gallery with her accommodating cicerone, who kept up a running commentary of wise, witty, and educational remarks, without, however, in the least expecting her to take in or appreciate them.   He knew exactly the kind of woman with whom he had to deal.

Suddenly they came on a representation of the Parcæ, three dreary, terrible old women sitting huddled up in a cowering circle, weaving, shaping and cutting the thread of the destinies of men.   Mrs. Elles stopped and pondered deeply.   There was a thread, yes, and many destinies were interwoven with the one.   No man or woman stood alone.   She had given a promise that had not been accepted, that day, but still she had made it; she had promised to cut the thread of her own life, so as to leave that of Rivers free.   It was all very well: she stood there ostensibly her own mistress in that room, beside Dr. André, but the thread of her fate was hopelessly entangled with the fates of two other persons, her husband and her lover.   The divorce hung imminent over their heads, the machinery of which they had set in motion, and which now could not be averted.

She turned to Dr. André, and looked mysterious.

"Shall I tell you what had always been one of my nightmares—a suicide manqué!   If a person wishes to commit suicide, he should arrange to do it neatly and completely.   Instead of that, he contrives to make it a hideous and ridiculous fiasco, and generally goes on humbly living after all!"

"Because intending suicides have as a rule got themselves worked up to such a state of nerves before they think of killing themselves, that having decided on it they are not fit to conduct such a ticklish enterprise. They are so agitated, so upset, they are in such a hurry to get out of the world, when once they have screwed themselves up to the point of resolution, that lest that resolution waver, they rush it, and so muff the whole thing!"

"Yes, but what I mean is that if I were perfectly calm and not in the least agitated, I should still 'muff' it, as you say, through not knowing how to set about it—the mere technique of the business would escape me!"

"I shall have to publish a little manual, at your service, 'Suicide Made Easy!' "

"You must not make fun of me. I am serious."

"I deeply regret to hear it!" he said, still laughing.

"No, but don't you know—to a nervous woman like me, it would be an immense consolation to know that I could, at a given moment, get out of it—I mean life—decently and in order."

"If you must go, why stand upon the order of your going?"

"But that's just it. I should hate to do it clumsily, ungracefully, grotesquely. I believe certain poisons make you die—quite hideously!" She shivered.

"Nearly all!" he said, teasing her. "But I might mesmerise you—and never wake you up again!"

"You are just as unkind and unsympathetic as the others!" Mrs. Elles exclaimed, pettishly. "Let us go home."

"Must we?" he said.

"Even if I didn't want to," she said, "they want

to be rid of us.   Look, they are putting out some of
the lights!"

"That is nothing.   You want to punish me!"

"Oh, no, I am not cross with you.   I only am
disappointed in you," she replied, wearily.   "You
can see me home if you like.   I want to walk, it
might drive my headache away."

"I shall be delighted.   Besides, as we live in the
same house—or block—my way is yours, in a literal
sense, at any rate."   He led the way to the door,
and got her her umbrella.   "I live so near," he went
on, as they turned down Regent Street, "that when
the burden of life becomes really too hard to bear, you
can send for me to come in and turn you off neatly."

"I hate that word 'neatly'!" was all she vouch-
safed to reply.   He spoke of other things and she
answered absently and jerkily.   As they drew near
Westminster, she said, looking up at him:

"I do wish you would trust me!"

"Of course I do trust you, in what may I ask?"

"You might trust me not to use anything you might
give me.   I should just keep it by me, the means of
Death, as a man keeps a sleeping draught by his
bedside, and the knowledge that one can put an end
to wakefulness at any moment makes it possible to
stand it, don't you see?   I could bear my awful life
better—oh, so much better—if I knew I could get
out of it at any moment!   But nobody understands
me—no—not even you."

The accent she contrived to throw on the last

words touched him a little. He looked at her keenly but said nothing, and she continued defiantly:

"Well, if I am left to my own devices, there's always the six chemists, and a fourpennyworth of laudanum at each! Oh, I know what one does. I've read novels."

"Too many! They are such a perversion of real life. Well, I will see what I can do," he said slowly.

She turned and caught hold of his hand.

"You can put it in an envelope, and seal it—with black sealing wax! It will be a bottle, won't it? A tiny bottle?"

"I shall put it in one of those little Venetian tear bottles," Dr. André said, smiling. "It will be what Browning calls 'a delicate death.' But"—his tone was as serious now as she could wish, "you must promise me faithfully not to use it ever! I should be your murderer, do you know? Do you want to hang me?"

She promised, smiling at his simplicity. She took his hand more than cordially in the lift that stopped, and deposited him, on a lower floor than hers.

"Is it possible that a magnetical rapport can be established between a man and a woman who loves another man?" she thought. "That would explain. At any rate he is kind to me—far, far kinder than Edmund."

She dined alone and cried. Late that night a tiny little parcel was sent up to her from Dr. André. She shivered when she looked at it, and locked it up under two keys.

CHAPTER XV

Egidia got out of the train at Barnard Castle, as Mrs. Elles had done, months before. She took a fly, and drove four miles to Greta Bridge.

She knew every inch of the ground from the description which Rivers and Phœbe had at different times given her of it.

She was full of purpose. Jane Anne Cawthorne was the worst enemy of the two that she had taken under her protection—Jane Anne Cawthorne was prepared to swear falsely—Jane Anne Cawthorne's mouth must be stopped.

Egidia thought she could do it, fairly and squarely, and without this girl's evidence, so she gathered from the lawyers, the case against Rivers and Phœbe would fall to the ground.

It was Jane Anne Cawthorne herself who came forward civilly when she alighted at the door of "Heather Bell," and asked for rooms. Egidia was as urbane in manner as she could be towards the woman who cared for Rivers, and was yet prepared to testify falsely concerning him.

"A low type!" she thought to herself, "a potential villain, but still susceptible to moral influences. They have bribed her, but all the same, she is doing this thing par dépit amoureux. Therefore an apt subject for diplomacy. How low I feel! But if I can only get him out of this, I don't care what I do."

She secured the very sitting-room that Rivers and Mrs. Elles had shared together, and derived a melancholy pleasure from the idea that it was so. There was the very rose-strewn table-cover, stained and splashed with the dabbling of the artist's brush; there was the piano on which Mrs. Elles had played to him. But outside, in the wintry garden, the dark dank earth lay heavy upon all the flowers and verdure that had gladdened the eyes of the lovers. For in spite of Phœbe's frivolity and Edmund's asceticism, she could read through Phœbe's admissions and falsifications, that for a brief space they had been lovers—the woman in her had been genuinely stirred, the man in him. It had not lasted, but it had been. But now it was winter, "the days dividing lover and lover, the light that loses, the night that wins," the season when no man can paint, and loves that are ephemeral die down and are buried under the wrack of autumn. There was no frost as yet, the December air was mild and subdued, with only a prescience as it were of the snows and disasters of January.

Egidia made a sad little pilgrimage to the scenes of this romance that grieved her so. Brignal Banks under their winter aspect reminded her somehow of a young and pretty woman after a long and devastating illness. It was the same, and not the same, the warm tones had gone out of the green, the ragged

boughs seemed blotted in upon the sky; the moist
sides of the cliff, that no glow of sunset irradiated
now, showed hard and chill behind the streaky lines
of the leafless creepers that still hung on them. The
water still bubbled and splashed over the stones, but
with an empty merriment. So it seemed to the sad
woman who stood by the river bank and looked at the
bridge of stones made by human labour, that was no
longer continuous. There had been a storm or two,
and the rains had flushed the river bed, and the added
flood had washed the stones away. She would never
dare to confess it to Rivers and Phœbe, but she was
at immense pains to gather up a heavy stone and try
to drop it into a place between two remaining ones,
and thus make the bridge passable. She would add
her mite to Rivers' bridge too. Phœbe Elles should
not be the only woman who had helped him.

She came away from there a prey to terrible depression, and resolved to visit no more "mouldering
lodges" of a past in which she had no share.

A fate seemed to be hanging over the whole world;
to the sad Egidia, all the inanimate things that he
had seen and touched seemed instinct with the fore-
boding of the particular disaster that threatened one
man. And Jane Anne, too, who waited on her
entirely now, at this dull season, when the personnel
in the inn was necessarily diminished—was Jane
Anne sad, or was it only the accustomed heaviness of
the lonely, empty-lived, country girl?

Egidia had written her name, Miss Alice Giles,

very clearly in the hotel book, and, in brackets, her nom de guerre, which had a world-wide reputation. She committed this solecism with a distinct purpose. Had her name as a novelist reached Jane Anne's ears? That was the point she meant to work from.

Jane Anne certainly was full of the little civilities and attentions which that name generally evoked among the celebrity hunters of superior rank among whom Egidia's ways were cast. Of taciturn habit though the landlady's niece unmistakably was, she yet beamed on the authoress on every possible occasion, and lost no opportunity of insinuating herself into her good graces as far as was consistent with perfect deference and civility.

At the close of the second day she spoke and asked a question.

"If you please, ma'am," she said, "might I venture to inquire if you are going to make a book about this place? So many do."

"But tell me why you think I am likely to?" asked Egidia, with the elaborate indulgence of the conspirator.

"Because, ma'am, I happen to know that you are a writer. A gentleman that comes here sometimes, he gave me one of your books once, and oh, I do like it so! I got him to write my name in it, and who it was from! So I got his too. May I bring it out and show you?"

With the gracious permission of the authoress Jane Anne fetched the book. It was Egidia's last novel but one, and on the flyleaf was Edmund Rivers' signature. The book had the peculiar sodden appearance of a volume much and carefully read.

"The gentleman gave me lots of books," Jane Anne went on. "And I have read them all over—hundreds of times. But I like none so much as this. I am so fond of novels! And if it was one written about here, why then I should like it all the better."

"But this is such a very quiet place. I should not think that anything ever could happen here?"

"Oh, ma'am, don't be too sure! Last summer now, something happened here, that if you was to put it into a book, no one would believe it! And I am in it too—leastways I shall be!"

"Tell me about it, if you have time," said Egidia, "and then perhaps I could work it into something."

"It is something very serious," said Jane Anne, her heavy brows coming together. "It is a divorce case. I don't know as I ought to tell it."

"A divorce case is known eventually to all the world!" said Egidia sententiously. "Besides, you need not tell me the names!"

"Oh, no, I needn't then," said the girl, relieved, "but they are sure to slip out in the course of conversation. But then that won't be my fault, will it?"

"No," said the other, concealing her amusement at Jane Anne's morality. "It will be mine—I hope. Come and sit down here, if you are not too busy, and tell me about it!"

Jane Anne was a little thrown off her majestic

balance by the distinguished authoress's condescension. She sat down, awkward, handsome, interesting even, as a study, but——

"This creature presumes to love Edmund too!" Egidia thought, and hated the mission she had set herself to accomplish, which involved converse, and an assumption of intimacy with her.

"You see, ma'am, it is like this," began Jane Anne, too humble and modestly conscious of the capacity in which this interview had been granted her, not to begin on it at once. "There is a gentleman, the gentleman who gave me that book, he comes here every year and paints—he always has done—he is not married, leastways we think not!—he is what they call the co-respondent."

She said correspondent, but it was not her mispronunciation that made Egidia wince.

"Well, then," Jane Anne went on, "last summer there comes a lady—leastwise a very funny lady, to be a lady—to call herself one, I mean—she was a foreigner, with painted cheeks, and something she did to her hair, and she nivver let our Mr. Rivers alone! He didn't run after her, he really didn't, but she had made up her mind to have him, and she did. She was married!"

"This is very interesting, and extraordinary!" ejaculated Egidia.

"But she nivver told him so, nor none of us. She called herself Miss Frick, and first of all she wore a pair of blue spectacles, but trust her, she couldn't

stick to that long, because, you see, he couldn't
rightly see her face while she wore them, and so one
fine day, she went and left them off! That's why
Mrs. Popham will have it that she was a spy! A
spy! What for? She didn't want to spy anything.
She just wanted Mr. Rivers, and she got him!
They used to go jaunting into the Park at all sorts of
hours of the night, and loverish things like that!"

"Oh, then it is your opinion they were lovers?"

"Yes, ma'am, I do, and I am going for to say so.
It is me that knows best, the lawyer says so."

"Whose lawyer?"

"Mr. Mortimer Elles's lawyer! He's been down to
see me times out of number. Aunt was dreadfully
fashed; she said it put me out with my work!"

"And this man—the lover—is he a nice man?"

"Oh—ma'am!"

"Very nice?"

"The nicest gentleman I ever saw, or ever shall
see. I would have done anything for him!"

"And she—is she nice?"

"Oh—ma'am!"

"You don't like her so well, I see!"

"Ma'am, I should like to take and run this darn-
ing-needle into her. Brazened painted-up creature,
so rude spoken, too—and great staring eyes, with
black saucers round them——"

"Whatever she is, he will have to marry her now!"
Egidia remarked carelessly.

"Ma'am!"

"Oh, yes, as a man of honour, he is bound to, if she is to be divorced on his account. Did not the lawyer tell you that? How very clever! Perhaps he did not realise how a man of honour would feel under the circumstances. The lover is a man of honour, is he not?"

"He's a real gentleman, ma'am," replied Jane Anne, translating Egidia's description into her own language.

"Well, then, I am sorry for him!"

"But, ma'am, I don't see why? She is a married woman; she carries on with him, her husband doesn't like it—he can't separate them, so he calls in the law to help him."

"Very nicely reasoned, Jane Anne! But the law only helps the husband to get rid of the woman who has betrayed him, he has nothing to do with the other man, who is of course bound to the woman who has lost her position through him. If the man you speak of is a gentleman, he will do what is usual, you may be sure of that!"

The girl was quite speechless with emotion for a moment, then said, solemnly and sadly:

"Shall I be the one to force him to that, ma'am?"

"What do you mean? What have you to do with it?"

"Because the lawyer young gentleman says it is on my evidence they chiefly rely, to prove the case against him!"

"Oh, then, you may consider that you have

married her to him, when the divorce is over! But what is your evidence?"

"I saw them," stammered Jane Anne, "the lawyer says I must tell what I know, and not swear falsely."

"Certainly you must tell what you know to be true."

She looked insistently at the girl, but not too insistently, lest she roused her suspicions.

"But I should make as light of it as I could, if I were you, and wished the man well, as you say you do!"

"Then if nothing is proved against him, he won't have to marry her?" inquired the girl eagerly.

"Obviously not. Her husband will have to take her back!"

"Oh," said Jane Anne, "and Mr. Rivers be just where he was before?"

"Oh, is it Mr. Rivers? I know him slightly."

"Do you? Do you? Ma'am, then if you know him, will you tell him that Jane Anne Cawthorne is his friend, and wishes him well. Why, I would like to die for him, I would indeed!"

"Then you had better lie for him a little!"

She looked keenly at the girl as she spoke, and with ever so slight an accent on the word whose first letter she had altered, and she had the satisfaction of seeing Jane Anne redden.

"Understate rather than overstate, you know!"

She now ventured to say this, seeing by the girl's confusion that the latter course was the one she had intended to take, or had perhaps even been suborned by a lawyer over-zealous in Mortimer Elles's behalf to do.

"Nothing extenuate—but naught set down in malice!" she went on. "Don't deny anything, or hold back anything, but make as light of what you did see as possible!"

"I think I hear my aunt calling me!" Jane Anne exclaimed suddenly. "I will just run and see what she wants, and be back in a moment."

Miss Giles admired Jane Anne's method of gaining time. Did she really go to attend on her aunt, or did she simply stand outside the door for a while? In five minutes she came back, looking somehow quite a different woman, and said simply:

"I want you to tell me how I can help him, ma'am?"

"Say simply what you know, and no more!"

"Then," said Jane Anne, her eyes downcast, "I had better write to Mr. Perkins!"

"Who is he?"

"The lawyer gentleman who came here and saw me. He took down what I said on a piece of paper."

"Perhaps in what you said then you—exaggerated a little—did not you?"

"Yes, ma'am, I did," replied the girl, hiding her eyes in the apron she wore, and bursting into tears. "I was so angry with her and with him, because he would not even speak to me that last day, but shook my hand off his sleeve, that I said the worst I could.

And truly I never saw no worse than him and her
walking up the Broad Walk yonder hand in hand.
It was the old lady saw him kissing her through the
window, and standing by his bedroom door in the
middle of the night. I didn't see that, but I was
there in the garden before,—it was I who took her to
the window of his room, but I didn't look, I couldn't
bear to. But I invented worse, and all I said, I told
the lawyer I would swear to in Court."

"How very awful!" said Egidia. "But if you
write and say that you are not prepared to swear this
then the chances are that the case will fall to the
ground, and you will not have to appear in Court at
all."

"But then I shan't even see him!" exclaimed Jane
Anne.

"See him—no, not then, but if there isn't any
trial, you will have him back here painting as usual
next spring, I should think."

Jane Anne seized Egidia's hand and kissed it.

"Oh, ma'am, ma'am, you know I never wanted
nothing but that. I knew well enough he could
never be anything to such as me, but I didn't want
him to marry anyone else."

.   .   .   .

"I did not expect him to marry me, but oh, I could
not bear him to marry any one else!"

That phrase of the country girl's was in Egidia's
ears all day as the train bore her southwards, her mis-

sion accomplished, and Phœbe Elles and Rivers for ever divided, by her means.

She had done it, and for what motive? Now that it was done, the spirit of self-analysis tormented the woman of letters skilled in the art of heart-searching. The happiness of Rivers was her object, and that she had been convinced lay in his continued celibacy. She herself had nothing to gain by it, wished to gain nothing by it. "I do not, I do not, if I have to go into a convent to prove it!" she said out aloud, in the solitude of the railway carriage. "I am glad we are cousins!" she added, mentally. "All women are dogs in the manger, when the man they love is concerned!" was her reflection with reference to Jane Anne's pathetic speech. The devotion of the servant for the artist revolted while it touched her. "I wonder how many more there are of us?" she wondered bitterly. "And his method—indifference, and innate incapacity to make any woman really happy. Those are the men who are beloved. . . . Phœbe Elles is saved—but she won't think so. So is Edmund—but he won't admit it, perhaps. At any rate, I do not profit. If I did, I would kill myself!"

CHAPTER XVI

She drove up to Queen Anne's Mansions in the dusk, and was whirled up in the lift and deposited in front of her own door. She inserted her little latch-key—gilded, but practical—into the key-hole. The drawing-room, she saw, glancing through the iridescent panes at the side of the door, was lighted up.

"She is at home, then," she thought to herself. "Dear, sweet, tiresome little thing that she is. Entertaining Dr. André with strong tea, and weak philosophy, no doubt. But now that I have got her out of this mess, I intend to wash my hands of her and her amatory affairs. I am sure I hope I may never again see a situation so at first hand. I prefer to invent them myself. It is less wearing in the long run."

But there was no one with Mrs. Elles, the servant said, Mrs. Elles had been at home all day, had eaten hardly any lunch, and had just sent off a telegram.

"Some new folly, I suppose?" thought Egidia. "Luckily, it does not matter now."

She opened the drawing-room door.

"Well, Phœbe," she said in jubilant tones, before she had passed the portière, "congratulate me! I have saved you—at least I think I have."

271

Phœbe Elles was sitting there, staged, as it were, most effectively on a red draped sofa. She was dressed in white, and her face was as white as her dress, except for the famous spot of colour on each cheek. Her eyes were not as bright as usual; they seemed a little glazed, but she smiled sweetly though faintly when she saw Egidia, and raised her hand, in a deprecating way.

"Yes, I have saved you, Phœbe, do you hear?" went on Egidia, full of her subject. "I have completely killed off the Jane Anne Cawthorne you were so afraid of and her evidence, and I venture to predict that your husband will now have nothing better to do than to withdraw his absurd petition in consequence!"

"It matters so little now!" said his wife, closing her eyes.

Egidia was hurt at this little show of gratitude for the three arduous days' work she had done for her.

"Why, what is the matter with you?" she said, coldly.

"Nothing! Everything!" Mrs. Elles flung her arms along the back of the sofa with a despairing gesture, and the lace sleeves of her elaborate tea-gown fell back from them, disclosing a pretty girlish arm.

"That is a ridiculously thin gown to wear if you have got a chill, or a touch of influenza, as I suppose you have," Egidia said testily. "Let me recommend you to go to bed at once, and throw it off."

"Oh, please, Egidia!" came the moan of the wounded pose. "Please! You can't think how it all sounds—now! You tell me to lie down—I shall lie down soon enough!"

"My dear Phœbe, you are rather maddening, are not you?" said the novelist, mildly. "I am sure I do not know what you want to be at, but if you are not ill, and don't want to lie down, then sit up, and give me some tea! I have been travelling since exactly nine o'clock this morning!"

She rang the bell, and ordered tea for herself, while her guest regarded her with lack-lustre eyes, and did not speak, though she held her lips a little helplessly parted.

"Cheer up! You look very pretty!" Egidia said to her soothingly, taking off her hat and flinging it on to a chair. "Rather like Frou-Frou in the death-bed scene. Poor little Frou-Frou!"

She sat down beside Mrs. Elles on the sofa and took her hands.

"Don't you really want to hear what I have done?"

"Yes, dear, I know that you have done something kind, and like you. I want to hear, I do indeed, but I can't somehow, understand properly—my brain seems clouded. . . ."

"Have you been taking things—morphia?" asked Egidia, sternly, as the suspicion crossed her mind.

"Morphia—no," Mrs. Elles answered, with a wan smile. "Surely morphia is no good—it is only temporary in its effects, isn't it?"

"Morphia, only temporary? Do please explain what you mean?"

"Dear Egidia," the other woman said appealingly, "do you mind waiting till Edmund comes? I have sent for him, and then you will know all. He is sure to be here directly."

"Mr. Rivers won't be such a fool as to come to this house, I should hope!" Egidia exclaimed angrily, and her use of the formal prefix alone showed how angry she was. "He knows what a piece of folly that would be, even if you don't!"

"He will come this time, Egidia. Don't be cross with me, or you will perhaps be sorry afterwards. Egidia, I want to thank you—I want you to forgive me for all the trouble I have caused you—the annoyance I have subjected you to. And I know you have done your best for me—about Jane Anne Cawthorne, I mean—but—but I have settled it another and a shorter way, you see. . . . Edmund!——"

She rose from her sofa as Rivers came in, and it was then that the sceptical Egidia noticed for the first time how weak she seemed to be, and realised that it was not all acting, and that the young woman had really gone through some veritable emotion. She looked as if a mighty wind had blown her, tossed her, and had scattered all her energies.

"Edmund!" she was saying, in a faint voice, her fingers clutching the lapel of his coat. "Edmund! You did come! I knew you would. And I don't mind now—Dying is the only way to make you nice to me."

"You should not have come here," said Egidia to Edmund, quite violently, in her anger and bewilderment. Even now, she found it quite impossible to take Phœbe Elles seriously; she had cried "Wolf" so often, that the very accents and circumstance of tragedy. in her connection inevitably suggested farce, or at any rate drawing-room comedy.

"Mrs. Elles sent me an urgent telegram, bidding me come here at once on a matter of life and death," said Rivers simply, "so of course I came."

"It is a matter of death," Mrs. Elles said, tottering back to the sofa. "Listen, both of you. I have done this because I was so miserable, and my life seemed of no use to any one—rather the reverse, in fact. I saw so well, that if I lived, I should live only to disgrace you, Edmund. People have explained to me what it was that I should be doing to you, injuring you, preventing you from ever being President, forcing you to live abroad, and ruining you generally. I saw the thought in your eyes that last time that I was with you, and that you almost hated me—I represented disgrace and shame to you! Oh, don't deny it! I am quite sure that you do not love me, or you would have loved through it all, and been willing to go through it all gladly for the sake of getting me. Men do—some men! So I took the only way—I took poison!"

She allowed herself to fall back exhausted.

"Tchk! Tchk!" came from Edmund or Egidia. The Nemesis of Pose still pursued her votary. They neither of them believed in her.

"Now look here, Phœbe!" said Egidia, speaking to her severely, as to a spoilt child. "Look here! What tricks have you been playing with yourself? I insist on knowing."

"And I want to tell you," Mrs. Elles replied plaintively, "if only you would let me! I never thought people treated—people like me—like this! It isn't even kind."

So speaking, she clearly signified her annoyance at the complete failure of this scene, as a scene, though she knew that she had the trump card of death up her sleeve, and that in less than ten minutes the inherent tragedy of it all would be proved to both these scoffers in the most effectual way.

"Listen," she said to them again, and her voice was very poignant and low. "I will tell you. I asked a man, who had promised me that he would do anything in the world for me, that I might ask him to do, to give me the means of death in an envelope sealed, so that I might use it if the burden of life became too great for me to bear. I told him that the mere knowledge that I could end it at any given time would help me to bear it. I did not tell him that I meant to use what he gave me at once, I perhaps did not—quite—but this morning in the fog—I felt it all so hopeless—so sad—and the future as black as the present, that I drank it off all at once. That was an hour ago—and in another hour I shall be dead."

"Who do you say gave it you?" Rivers asked quickly, when she had finished.

"Dr. André. Now please don't—bother me any more." She sank back—she had literally grown ashen.

"Quick! Go and fetch him! Three floors below!" said Egidia to Rivers, in a frenzied whisper.

"But he can't have been such a devil!" she ejaculated, as the door closed on Rivers. Mrs. Elles's strange and indubitable pallor it was that frightened her.

. . . .

In ten minutes Rivers came back again, followed by Dr. André. The latter was smiling, and his smile did not fade away, when confronted with the serious face of Egidia, and the prostrate form of his victim. Mrs. Elles had not spoken a word during Rivers' absence, she appeared to have sunk into a state of coma. When Dr. André entered she opened her eyes wide, and it was on him, not on Rivers, that her gaze fell.

"Dear lady!" he said, going up to her, and taking one of her little helpless hands. "Forgive me! I have betrayed you!"

"What?" she said, and her voice had sunk to a whisper. "I have taken what you gave me. Tell them. . . ."

"All right!" he said, in his foreign accent, gently stroking the hand which she abandoned to him. "I have given you a mauvais quart d'heure, I admit, but I have not killed you. Could you or any one else seriously imagine that I should be accessory to sending a sweet woman like you out of the world?"

"You have very nearly frightened her out of it!" Egidia, to whom the doctor's flowery language did not appeal, remarked.

"I acted for the best," he said earnestly. "Mr. Rivers will explain it to you. I gave Mrs. Elles something to take when she asked me, knowing that if I were to refuse her, the obstinate lady would have recourse to some other person less scrupulous than I. But what I gave her could not possibly harm her. A little bromide and water. The symptoms exhibited here are actually the result of sheer apprehension. Most curious! But she will not die, but live to be grateful to me."

"Or to hate you for having made her ridiculous," said Egidia, bluntly.

While the doctor had been speaking, he had begun to make mesmeric passes in front of Mrs. Elles, and it was quite certain that she did not hear the conclusion of his speech, or Egidia's answer. Her eyelids closed, she began to breathe regularly, she lay back, but no longer in an attitude of tension. She would have been pleased to know how exquisitely pretty and helpless she looked, and how plainly Dr. André's face showed that he thought so. Even Egidia was touched, in spite of her annoyance at the little trick she had played on them all. But then it had failed so absurdly, so lamentably!

"Poor little thing!" she said thoughtfully to Rivers. "It is curious how comedy dogs her wherever she goes, and whatever she does. It is very hard to seek the sublime always and achieve—the ridiculous. I must be more gentle with her. I am hard."

"No, you are very good!" said Rivers kindly.

As he spoke there was a ring at the outer door, and a pink envelope was put into Egidia's hands.

"For her!" she said, indicating Mrs. Elles.

"Shall I bring her back?" said Dr. André.

"It is only something from her lawyers," said Egidia.

"Why bring her back to worries?"

"But it is a telegram—Immediate. You must take the responsibility of opening it."

"I will," said Egidia. "She empowered me to open all her letters and telegrams once, in a moment of confidence."

She opened it. An expression of intense relief flooded her countenance.

"Thank God!" she cried, almost hysterically, putting the paper into Rivers' hands, "he can't divorce her now, can he?"

"Hardly!" said Rivers, smiling at the clever woman's naïveté. "He died this morning at half-past nine. Poor fellow, though I don't know him!"

Had the widow heard? She opened her eyes at that moment and smiled sweetly at Dr. André, as his hands passed to and fro in front of her face. With characteristic tact, he left her in her happy trance a little longer, dreaming, perchance, of fresh woods and pastures new.

THE END

PRINTED BY R. R. DONNELLEY
AND SONS COMPANY AT THE
LAKESIDE PRESS, CHICAGO, ILL.

www.ingramcontent.com/pod-product-compliance
Lightning Source LLC
Chambersburg PA
CBHW021050030726
47496CB00006B/1768